MARY

TUDOR PRINCESS

TONY RICHES

ALSO BY TONY RICHES

OWEN – BOOK ONE OF THE TUDOR TRILOGY

JASPER – BOOK TWO OF THE TUDOR TRILOGY

HENRY – BOOK THREE OF THE TUDOR TRILOGY

THE SECRET DIARY OF ELEANOR COBHAM

WARWICK: THE MAN BEHIND THE WARS OF THE ROSES

QUEEN SACRIFICE

COPYRIGHT

Copyright © Tony Riches 2018
Published by Preseli Press

ISBN-13: 978-1979919289
ISBN-10: 1979919283
BISAC: Fiction / Historical

Cover Photography by Lisa Lucas LRPS
www.lisalucasphotography.com

ABOUT THE AUTHOR

Tony Riches is a full-time writer and lives with his wife in Pembrokeshire, West Wales, UK. After several successful non-fiction books, Tony turned to novel-writing and wrote *Queen Sacrifice*, set in tenth-century Wales, followed by *The Shell*, a thriller set in present day Kenya.

A specialist in the history of the early Tudors, Tony is best known for his Tudor Trilogy. His other international best-sellers include *Warwick ~ The Man Behind the Wars of the Roses* and *The Secret Diary of Eleanor Cobham*.

For more information please visit Tony's author website www.tonyriches.com and his blog at www.tonyriches.co.uk. He can also be found at Tony Riches Author on Facebook and Twitter: @tonyriches.

La volenté de Dieu me suffit

(The will of God is sufficient for me)

Mary Tudor
Born: 18 March 1496
Sheen Palace, England

For my grandson

Alfie

1

MIDSUMMER'S DAY 1509

She was the daughter of a king, a Tudor princess, yet she sensed her life was about to change forever. Early sunlight streamed through the stained-glass windows of Westminster Abbey as Mary counted twenty-eight bishops leading the coronation procession.

A hint of woodsmoke still drifted in the London air from the bonfires of Midsummer's Eve, and cheering crowds lined every street. She hoped the banquets and jousting would lift the sadness deep in her heart. A new era was beginning.

'Henry and Catherine make quite a couple, Mary. Your father, may the Lord rest his soul, would have been proud to see this day.'

She turned her head to acknowledge her grandmother. Lady Margaret Beaufort, still wearing mourning dress, clutched a small leather-bound prayer book. Although she'd barely recovered from illness her eyes burned with pride.

Mary glanced towards the Lady Chapel at the far end of the abbey, her father's private chantry, now his permanent resting place. It seemed unreal to think her beloved parents now lay there together in a cold stone crypt beneath their grand unfinished tomb.

'This was his wish, although...' She spoke in a hushed tone, as if thinking aloud, painful memories of her father's last days choking her words. 'My brother is poorly prepared to be our new king.'

'He is young – yet he is a Tudor.' Her grandmother nodded in understanding. 'We must pray for your brother,' she lowered her voice almost to a whisper, 'as I fear some adversity will follow.'

Mary frowned at her grandmother's grim prediction. She recalled the avaricious glint in Henry's eye as he took Catherine's hand, two weeks before, at the Church of the Observant Friars in Greenwich. He might be almost eighteen, over six feet tall and engagingly handsome, but he still had the covetous ways of the small boy she remembered.

Despite Henry being five years older than her, they'd been close as children in the rambling nursery at Eltham Palace. He'd always trusted her with his secrets. Before his wedding, after too much wine, he'd admitted doubting Catherine's story about her unconsummated marriage. It suited Henry to believe her, because if the marriage had been consummated he never would have secured the papal dispensation he needed in order to to marry her.

'You must take her at her word, dearest brother,' Mary had reassured him, 'for to lie about such a thing would be a mortal sin.'

In truth, Catherine hinted to her of a great secret, one she'd not dared to confess to her priest. She'd risked God's saving grace to do her duty and become Henry's queen. Mary understood her dilemma and promised to pray for her soul.

Now Catherine wore a crimson royal robe over a gown of the finest white satin. Her auburn hair flowed over her shoulders to her waist, a sign of her declared purity. The crowds cheered for her, proving those long years in obscurity worthwhile after all. She'd never looked more beautiful, more self-assured, more ready to be crowned Queen of England.

Henry had been busy spending his father's fortune on his magnificent royal robe of crimson velvet, trimmed with ermine over cloth of gold. He glittered with sparkling diamonds and rubies like over-ripe cherries. Mary noted the Tudor colours extravagantly represented in green emeralds and gleaming white pearls.

With a jolt, she realised the contents of her father's precious jewel house were now Henry's by right, to do with as he pleased. She would do well to remember that the same applied to everything now, and everyone – including her.

They watched in reverent silence as the dour Archbishop of Canterbury, William Warham, recited a Latin prayer and anointed Henry and Catherine with sacred holy oil. Mary smiled as he finally placed the coronation ring on Catherine's finger.

At last, after eight years of waiting, her friend took her place on the throne next to Henry, a gold coronet on her head, the royal sceptre in her right hand and the queen consort's rod of ivory in her left.

Mary joined the loud chorus of 'Yea, Yea!' when the congregation were asked if they would take this most noble prince as their king and obey him. The sound echoed from the high-vaulted roof of Westminster Abbey. She heard the peal of all the bells in London as crowds waiting outside in the bright Westminster sunshine called out '*Vivat Rex!*' and applauded their new king, Henry VIII.

After the long ceremony Mary sat with her grandmother under a golden canopy of state at the coronation banquet in Westminster Hall. Lady Margaret had offered to act as regent for the first months of Henry's reign. Not one voice challenged her suggestion, a mark of her power and influence.

Henry and Catherine sat on high-backed gilded thrones before the highest nobles and clerics in the land. The men wore scarlet cloaks and the ladies displayed their finest jewels, saved for such special occasions. Mary wore a gold necklace of bright diamonds and pearls, another of her father's treasures, now a gift to her from Henry.

The sense of history being made hung heavy in the warm summer air. Mary swatted at one of the buzzing black flies and frowned as it evaded her. She looked up as it flew high over the guests to join others, circling like carrion crows waiting for the sweet-tasting delicacies to be served.

She regretted the tight lacing of her new damask gown of deepest blue, another gift from Henry. The edges were trimmed with gold lace, despite her grandmother's sharp retort that it was too soon to end her mourning, even to celebrate a coronation. Her long golden hair, plaited and looped under her ornate French cowl, prickled in the heat and she fanned her face with her hand.

Lady Margaret scanned the crowded tables with a critical eye. 'Your brother asked me to select his advisors. I pray he will take heed of their experience and wisdom.'

Mary glanced across at Henry, who was enjoying being the centre of attention. 'It's good to see so many of father's loyal supporters, Grandmother. They will know how to best serve his son.'

Although sure her grandmother had chosen well she guessed many would soon be replaced. Henry couldn't be more different from her father and would appoint his own men, who shared his youthful tastes.

Startled by the sudden blast of a fanfare announcing the first course of the banquet, she turned to see the Duke of Buckingham riding a black charger with richly embroidered trappings. Behind him rode the Lord Steward on a horse caparisoned with cloth of gold, hooves clattering on the flag-stoned floor.

They led a procession of servants in Tudor green-and-white livery carrying heavy gilded platters bearing delicacies for the feast. The servants were all young nobles, proud to represent their families in the service of the new king. The leading server, face impassive as his duty demanded, seemed to struggle with the weight of a whole swan. Others carried silver trays of game birds, spiced larks and cockatrices, made from the front half of cockerels grafted on to the back halves of piglets.

A handsome young servant filled Mary's golden cup with rich red wine. She smiled as she raised her cup in the air and caught her brother's eye.

'To our new king. May God grant you a long and happy reign!' Her clear young voice carried well, turning heads despite the chattering guests.

Henry beamed at her. 'Thank you, my dearest sister.' His voice echoed across the hall and he raised his own goblet. 'To the future!' He drank deep and gestured for the waiting musicians to strike up a lively tune. The music lifted Mary's spirits and she even saw their grandmother manage a smile. The new era had begun.

Bright summer sunshine blessed the celebratory tourney the following day. Mary perched high on the specially constructed grandstand, close to Henry, in her grandmother's place. Lady Margaret was indisposed but Mary doubted she would have enjoyed the spectacle, which was more to her brother's taste.

The staccato beat of a drum accompanied the reedy sound of a crumhorn playing a popular tune. Shouts of vendors selling food and ale mixed with the shrieks of excited children.

The raucous crowd thronging the barriers around the temporary arena cheered and applauded as the competing knights rode into view to present themselves before their new king.

Mary's heart quickened as she spotted the object of her own great secret. She shielded her eyes against the sun glinting off his burnished gilt armour as Charles Brandon trotted towards Henry and Catherine on his powerful black destrier. He didn't glance in her direction as he shared some joke with Henry and complimented Queen Catherine.

Then, with typical bravado, he called out to her. 'Princess Mary, do you have a favour for the king's champion?' His deep, confident voice demanded an answer.

She sensed the eyes of the crowd on her and glanced at her brother. Seeing his broad grin, she pulled a blue silk ribbon from a pocket in her gown and handed it to her servant. Charles tied the ribbon to his harness with exaggerated care. The bond between them was no secret but she prayed no one knew the truth. Brandon was a married man, twice her age, yet she'd fallen deeply in love with him – a dangerous obsession.

She watched as the rest of the competing knights were presented, all on fine horses and heavily armed. Each had one side of their armour-skirts and horse-trappings made of white velvet embroidered with a pattern of gold roses, the other of green velvet and satin embroidered with gold pomegranates, the emblem of Queen Catherine of Aragon.

Behind them, blowing sharp blasts on long hunting horns, came Henry's foresters and gamekeepers in green cloth, with caps and hose to match. With practised ease, they ushered a herd of nervous fallow deer to be pursued by hungry greyhounds.

Henry called out to urge the dogs on and applauded as the first of the deer was dragged to the ground, a greyhound at its throat. Mary put her hand to her mouth in shock at the sight of such savagery.

Bleating does darted in panic around the fenced arena, pursued by the pack of murderous hounds. In no time the bloodied bodies of young deer were heaped before the king like gory sacrificial offerings, their sightless eyes seeming to stare at Mary in silent accusation.

Next came archery contests, skill at arms and swordplay, with purses of gold coins presented by Queen Catherine to the winners. There was a moment of excitement when a stray arrow struck a man in the watching crowd, but Mary was growing bored when at last the main event of the tourney was announced.

Knights on horseback would challenge each other with heavy lances. Charles Brandon was one of the last to ride and an expectant hush fell over the watching crowd. The Master of the Joust made a great play of explaining that a new challenger, a young knight of Anjou, would take on the king's chosen champion.

Mary watched as Brandon's squire handed him his lance and he lowered the visor of his gold-plumed helmet. She remembered seeing knights wounded at her father's jousting tournaments and said a prayer for Charles. Then the order was given and the heavy horses charged towards each other, hooves pounding the hardened earth.

She shouted a warning as the challenger's lance shattered against Brandon's breastplate, sharp splinters flying through the air. Time froze as the hushed crowd watched the champion fight to remain in his saddle, then punch a gauntleted fist in the air to a rousing cheer from his supporters.

Mary breathed again and smiled at his arrogance. He was not beaten yet. She watched as he prepared for the next pass, couching his lance as his squire held back the powerful horse. The Master of the Joust barked a shout and Mary leapt to her feet for a better view as hooves thundered a second time.

The riders clashed and now Brandon's lance struck the

Anjou knight with such force he was lifted from his saddle and fell to the ground with a sickening crunch. Again, Mary stood, this time out of concern for the young challenger. As she watched he managed to raise a hand yet he seemed unable to stand and was soon carried off by his followers.

Charles Brandon showed no concern for the fate of his opponent. He raised his visor and rode back to stand in front of Henry, lowering what remained of his broken lance in salute. Mary's eyes went to her blue ribbon, fluttering in the light summer breeze. He allowed her only the briefest glance yet she saw the flash of a smile.

Brandon's father had been her own father's standard-bearer at the Battle of Bosworth, one of the few men killed by King Richard III. Her father took Charles into his own household, so Mary had known him all her life. He'd become like a brother to Henry, although Mary thought him a bad influence with his drinking and daredevil pranks.

Not for the first time her mind whirled with endless reasons to forget her feelings for Brandon. He'd fathered a child with a young courtier named Anne Browne, daughter of Sir Anthony Browne, the Governor of Calais. Then Brandon caused raised eyebrows at court by marrying Anne's wealthy widowed aunt. Once he had all her lands he'd divorced her to marry Anne and care for their infant daughter.

Mary knew it wouldn't be long before she must keep a promise made by her father. She was destined to marry Prince Charles of Ghent, grandson of both King Ferdinand and Emperor Maximilian, son of Queen Catherine's elder sister Joan. Four years younger than her, he would be nine or ten years old now, although she couldn't recall when she'd last heard from him.

She had been betrothed before Christmas the previous year at Richmond Palace. The Lord of Bergues, chosen to stand in for young Charles at the ceremony, presented her with a velvet box containing a present from Emperor Maximilian, a gold fleur-de-lis glittering with fine diamonds, valued at fifty thousand crowns. Only the previous week Mary was annoyed to see Henry wearing her wedding present as a decoration in his hat.

Her betrothal didn't stop her dreaming though. Brandon's roving eye noted her admiration – and he'd encouraged her attention with his flirtatious words. Once he'd helped her down from her palfrey, as if she weighed nothing, and held her close for a moment longer than necessary.

She'd been born into great privilege, had the benefit of the best education, was graced by beauty and intelligence beyond her years, yet could never have the one thing she longed for.

~

Mary cursed as the sharp needle pierced her finger. She examined the spot of bright blood and called for a servant to bring a linen cloth. The hours of painstaking embroidery would not be ruined by a moment's carelessness.

She looked across to where Jane Popincourt sat working on a tapestry. Originally from France, twenty-six-year-old Jane had been retained by Mary's father as her French tutor and had once served at the court of the French king, Louis. She'd been appointed a maid of honour to Queen Catherine before becoming one of Mary's most trusted ladies-in-waiting.

'Life seems so different, Jane, since my brother became king.'

Jane smiled. 'I wonder what your father would have said about what happened on Henry's eighteenth birthday!'

Mary laughed in agreement. She'd been made to defend a wooden castle with her ladies-in-waiting while Henry besieged it with his companions. The masque degenerated into a drunken revelry, with Mary and her ladies ordered to dance until they were exhausted.

'My father encouraged Henry's love of disguisings, but now we never know what to expect.' Mary lowered her voice so the servants couldn't hear. 'Last night they all dressed as vagabonds and were nearly arrested by the royal guards.'

A liveried servant carrying a folded note on a silver tray interrupted Jane's reply. He bowed and offered the note to Mary. She took the note with a sense of foreboding and broke the red wax seal to unfold it. She studied the contents with a frown and looked up at Jane.

'It's from Bishop John Fisher. My grandmother is gravely ill and he asks me to come at once.'

'Would you like me to come with you?'

Mary hesitated. 'It's getting late – but you could have my escort prepare fast horses while I change from this gown into something more suitable for the journey.'

'You're not going by river?'

'Henry has taken the royal barges to Greenwich. I'd not like to rely on a wherry at this time of night.'

A heavy shower of rain turned the dusty roads to mud and slowed the ten-mile ride from Richmond Palace to Lady Margaret's house at Westminster. Mary wished she could have made the journey by river in her father's gilded barge with its covered cabin but, like everything, the barge belonged to Henry now.

John Fisher, Bishop of Rochester, welcomed her to the poorly lit manor house which Lady Margaret referred to as her 'cottage', his face grave. He kept his voice low and spoke in a broad northern accent.

'Lady Margaret has been asking for you, Princess Mary.' He glanced back over his shoulder at the door to her grandmother's bedchamber. 'You should prepare yourself. She will soon be with God.'

An elderly servant unfastened her wet riding cloak as Mary struggled to understand the dreadful news, delivered so bluntly. Bishop Fisher was unlikely to be mistaken. He'd been her grandmother's priest and confessor for many years and the sadness in his dark eyes confirmed the truth of his words.

'My grandmother seemed quite well when I saw her last, at the coronation banquet.' Mary clung to the slender thread of hope.

Bishop Fisher shook his head. 'Lady Margaret places her duty before her health – as is her way.' He frowned but Mary heard the admiration in his voice. 'I must tell you the coronation has taken its toll on her. I summoned your father's physicians but they are of one mind. Lady Margaret is beyond any help their potions can offer now.'

Mary nodded in understanding. 'May I see her?'

'She is sleeping but I know she will wish to be woken – if you will permit me a moment, Your Grace?'

Mary nodded and watched as he left to wake her grandmother. A sharp memory of her mother's death returned as she waited, trying to come to terms with her loss. It had been on her mother's birthday, one month before her own seventh birthday, when everything changed. Her brother Henry, always so strong, wept openly. Her father's heart hardened and he'd never been the same again.

Mary knew she'd lost her childhood and grown much wiser than her years after her mother's death. She had her own household and ladies-in-waiting from her seventh birthday and did her best to watch over her brother and her father. Her only friend was her eldest brother's widow, Princess Catherine, although she was eleven years older, with her own problems.

Her grandmother had always been there, ready to guide her, first taking her mother's place and now filling the void left by her father. Bishop Fisher had told her to prepare herself, yet she couldn't think how to prepare for what might be her last words with her grandmother.

She recalled her last meeting with her father. He'd been barely able to speak as she'd tried to comfort him. Like a stupid girl, she'd read a letter from Prince Charles in French in an effort to cheer him. Now she realised she'd wasted those last precious moments. There were so many questions she could have asked. Worst of all, she had not told her father how much she loved him.

As her eyes became accustomed to the poor light she looked around the room. Her grandmother lived simply for one of the wealthiest women in England. The table and chairs were well made but functional and no rushes softened the cold flagstone floor. The only decoration was a simple crucifix and the Beaufort portcullis carved into the empty stone fireplace.

At last a servant bowed and led her to Lady Margaret's bedchamber. A single beeswax candle flickered, casting long shadows and the scent of lavender failed to mask the mustiness of the room. Her grandmother looked up at her with dark-ringed eyes. Mary sat in the chair at the side of the canopied bed and heard the latch as the bishop closed the door behind him.

'Thank you for coming, my dearest Mary.' Her voice sounded weak, each word an effort.

Mary struggled to think what to say. As with her father, she had many questions but now they all seemed irrelevant. She took her grandmother's hand in hers and held Lady Margaret's thin fingers to her lips. The candlelight shone on pale, waxy skin lined with dark blue veins.

'I want to thank you, Grandmother, for your great kindness towards me during such a difficult time for us both.'

Lady Margaret closed her eyes as if in pain before opening them again and staring at Mary. 'I was your age when your father was born.' Her voice was more determined now. 'I thought I would die, yet that proved to be the moment I treasure most in my entire life.'

Again, Mary was at a loss for words. 'We all owe you a great debt for your sacrifices.'

'No. My life has been too easy. Your father...' Her eyes brightened at the thought of him. 'He spent more than your lifetime in exile, in fear of his life, yet he had the courage to return, to restore this country.'

'I pray for my father, and my mother, every day.'

Lady Margaret smiled. 'You are a credit to them both. Now I must ask you a great favour.'

'Anything, Grandmother.'

'Will you pray for your brother, and persuade him to take John Fisher as his confessor, to guide his path?'

Mary nodded. 'I will.' Almost as an afterthought she added. 'Do not worry yourself about Henry. He is a Tudor – and as my father often reminded us, we have Beaufort steel in our blood.'

Lady Margaret gave a weak smile at her words. 'Thank you, dearest Mary. May God be with you.'

Mary remained at her bedside until Bishop Fisher returned and saw her grandmother sleeping. He ushered her back to the outer room where a servant waited with a lantern.

'The hour is late, Princess Mary. I have arranged for a bed to be made ready.'

'I wish to remain with my grandmother.'

Bishop Fisher nodded. 'Permit me to sit with her through the night and you can take my place in the morning.'

Mary knew she should respect the bishop's suggestion. 'You will wake me if...'

Bishop Fisher nodded to the servant, who opened the door. He turned to Mary. 'Of course.'

Mary woke at dawn with a sense of foreboding. She dressed in the travelling gown she'd arrived in the previous night, noting it had been cleaned of the mud from the road and looked as good as new.

Bishop Fisher met her in the outer room. One look at his face told her why he wasn't at her grandmother's bedside.

'It was in the early hours, Your Grace. There was no time to wake you.' His voice choked with emotion. 'She passed as I was giving her the last rites.' He placed a gentle hand on Mary's shoulder. 'Your grandmother is at peace with God.'

Mary prayed on her knees in the cold chapel rebuilt by her father after the fire at Richmond Palace, her grandmother's favourite place. Like her grandmother, she'd chosen not to use a cushion and the numbing coolness of the hard stone floor drained the feeling from her knees.

A memory of her grandmother's words in Westminster Abbey echoed in her mind. Too late, Mary wished she'd asked her why she'd feared some adversity would follow Henry's coronation.

Raising her eyes to the tortured figure of Christ on the cross she wept with an overwhelming sense of loss. She was the daughter of the first Tudor king and now she was the sister of the next. Mary recalled her promise to pray, to make her brother accept Bishop Fisher as his confessor, to guide his path. She suspected it might be a difficult promise to keep.

2

FEBRUARY 1510

The cry of anguish carried in the freezing dawn air, waking Mary. She lay still for a moment, considering the possible consequences, before dressing in the dim light. She called out to the men guarding the long corridor outside her room and one of her guards appeared.

'My lady?' There was a note of concern in his deep voice.

'I wish to see the queen – straight away.'

'Yes, my lady.' The guard seemed unsurprised. This was not the first time she'd had to comfort Catherine at an unusual hour. He lit a lantern and led her down the wood-panelled passageway. Built for use by servants, the narrow passage offered a useful connection between her rooms and Catherine's confinement chamber.

Mary shivered and pulled her woollen cloak more tightly around her shoulders. She disliked the Palace of Westminster, haunted by the chill presence of ancient ghosts. The panelling was infested with woodworm and the dark corners were festooned with cobwebs. She'd heard something scuttle under her bed the previous night, too heavy to be a mouse.

She'd told Henry she thought Westminster a poor choice

for Catherine's confinement yet as usual he'd ignored her. Mary preferred the refinement of Richmond Palace, with its flower gardens and the fountain her father had dedicated to her mother. She'd adopted Richmond as her home, although she knew Henry, who preferred Greenwich, could move her from there at his whim.

An unearthly wail echoed down the passageway, startling Mary from her thoughts. 'We must hurry!'

The guard quickened his pace. She'd become used to Catherine's vocal Latin temperament over the years but this was different. This time Catherine could cry out as much as she wished, as her condition was a matter of life and death.

The whole country celebrated when Henry announced that Catherine carried his heir the previous August. Cannons roared at the Tower of London and the taverns had never been so busy. Henry even sent an eloquent letter to Catherine's father, King Ferdinand, to confirm the good news.

Mary knew this was too soon if the child was conceived after their marriage last June. Her own mother died of a fever after giving birth too soon to her last child. Mary's younger sister lived for only eight short days, long enough to be given a name. They'd called her Catherine.

She pushed the painful memory away as she reached the confinement chamber. By tradition, Catherine should be supported by the women of her family, but her mother was dead and her sister Isabella died in childbirth. Of Catherine's surviving sisters, Joanna 'the mad' was confined in a nunnery for life and her sister Maria was queen of faraway Portugal.

Catherine had eight ladies-in-waiting but Mary was the closest she had to family in England, and she knew her duty. One of the few good things that followed the tragic death of her brother Arthur had been her close friendship with her Spanish sister-in-law.

The midwife cast Mary a concerned look as she entered

the room. A fire blazed in the hearth and the delicate scent of rose water mixed with herbs, strewn on the rush-covered floor. Catherine lay in her bed, supported by colourful silk pillows, her pale face framed by her long auburn hair. Maria de Salinas, the most loyal of Catherine's maids of honour, sat at her side reading a Latin prayer aloud in her soft Spanish accent.

Maria stopped in mid-sentence and Catherine turned her head as she heard the door open and saw Mary. 'Thank the Lord you've come.' She glanced at the midwife. 'I've lost ... our child.'

Mary froze to the spot as she struggled to find the right words. Although she'd feared the worst since she was first woken, she had no idea how to help. She reached out instinctively and placed a hand on Catherine's shoulder. 'I'm so sorry.' Her words sounded inadequate for such a disaster.

Maria stood and offered Mary her chair, then made her excuses and left with the midwife. Mary turned to watch them go. She noticed bloodstains on the heavy bundle of white linen the midwife carried and wondered what they'd done with the baby. After they closed the door Mary turned back to Catherine.

She wished she knew what to say. 'Do you know the cause?' She regretted her question as soon as she asked it. Whatever the reason for Catherine's child, it was irrelevant now.

Catherine shook her head, unable to reply, then with some effort managed to compose herself. 'This is God's punishment on me.' Her voice sounded bitter, her Spanish accent returning.

'No!' Mary surprised herself with the force of her denial. 'You know as well as I that childbirth has its dangers.'

'I had a pain.' She closed her eyes at the memory. 'I called for the midwife and then...' Overcome with emotion, her words tailed away.

Mary placed a hand on Catherine's forehead. 'I'm afraid I

know little enough of these things but I will pray for you, Catherine.'

'Thank you, Mary.' She wiped a tear from her eye.

A thought occurred to Mary. 'Has anyone been sent to tell my brother?'

Catherine looked alarmed at the thought. 'He will take this badly.'

Mary shook her head. 'You misjudge Henry. He loves you greatly.'

A silence descended over them both as they began to think about the implications. Mary prayed she was right. Henry became more unpredictable each day and she'd seen the looks he had given her ladies-in-waiting after Catherine entered her confinement. He'd been so proud of his impending father-hood, making plans and counting the days.

'It was a girl.' The sadness in Catherine's voice brought tears to Mary's eyes.

'Have faith, Catherine. Your time will come.'

She turned her head at the sound of footsteps and the metallic clink of rattling swords in the corridor outside. Men with heavy boots were approaching Catherine's sanctuary where only women and priests were allowed.

Mary stood. 'I think my brother has already been informed.' She placed an affectionate hand on Catherine's arm. 'I must leave but I will return soon.'

She slipped back through the narrow door into the passage-way. As she followed her guard, Catherine's words echoed in her head. It was a girl. Mary should have stayed and supported Catherine but couldn't face her brother. She missed her grand-mother, who would have been there now, taking charge and dealing with Henry.

~

Mary laughed with exhilaration as she urged her powerful horse into a canter. Despite her gloves the cold numbed her fingers but she loved to ride in the grounds of Richmond Palace. She'd not followed Catherine when she returned to Greenwich, and couldn't wait to be out riding after the musty atmosphere of Westminster.

Her horse's breath froze like a dragon's smoke in the still air, its hooves pounding the hard ground which glistened with frost in the dazzling early morning sunlight. Glancing back, she saw she'd already put some distance between herself and her ladies, who followed with her escort of royal guards.

By chance she'd overheard the stable boys talking about Charles Brandon taking his black destrier for exercise a short time before. She knew it was improper to meet him unchaperoned but there was no one to stop her.

She spurred on her mount as she spotted him in the distance. He stopped and turned in the saddle as she cantered closer. Mary smiled at the genuine surprise on Brandon's face as he recognised her and raised a gloved hand in welcome.

'Good morning, Your Grace.' He glanced back at the distant followers as if making a judgement, then ran an expert eye over Mary's horse before resting his gaze on her. 'You ride well – and like its rider, your horse is a beauty.'

Mary smiled at his compliment and patted her horse. 'She's Arabian, descended from horses brought back from the crusades, a gift to my father.'

Brandon looked down at his own mount. 'I doubt I'd be able to keep up with you on a run. These heavy horses are only fast over short distances.'

Mary's mind raced with questions. There were so many things she wished to say but could not. 'What news is there from Greenwich?'

'Your brother is back in good spirits – now the queen has

returned to confinement.' He grinned and urged his mount closer.

'She cannot be...'

'The child she lost has a twin, which her physicians confirm will reach full term.'

'Praise God – it is a miracle!'

'God works in mysterious ways, Your Grace.' His blue-grey eyes sparkled as they fixed on hers. 'And you – why do you hide yourself away here at Richmond instead of following the court?'

'I'm not hiding.' She heard the defensive note in her voice and smiled at how easily he'd tricked her. 'What brings you here, Charles Brandon?'

'I had to stay on after the jousting. Did you not hear what happened?'

Mary was confused by his answer. 'I've been shut away with the queen at the Palace of Westminster.'

He gave her a look of mock disbelief. 'I thought your ladies were the greatest gossips in the country?'

'You do them a disservice, sir.'

'My apologies, Your Grace.' He grinned again, a twinkle in his eye. 'Your brother entered a private joust here in Richmond last week.'

'His first time as king?'

Brandon nodded. 'The king jousted in disguise with William Compton – and Compton was badly wounded with a broken lance.'

'By my brother's hand?'

'It was Sir Edward Neville's lance, although he's not to be blamed.' His face became serious for a moment. 'The price we have to pay for jousting can be high.'

'Does William live?' He'd been her father's ward and Henry's companion since their days at Eltham Palace and always had a kind word for her.

Brandon gave a wry smile. 'We all thought Compton mortally wounded but he's as strong as an ox, although I doubt he'll wish to joust again soon.' He lowered his voice, even though there was no one to hear. 'I understand Henry is to make him Groom of the Stool, an unusual reward – and of course a great honour, to wipe the royal behind.' He grinned at his own joke.

Mary laughed. 'You know full well William Compton will be the eyes and ears of the king.'

Mary's ladies and escort approached before Brandon could reply. They both turned their horses and rode to meet them. He gave her what she thought might be a wistful look. She regretted her missed opportunity although she had no idea of what she could have said. At least the news about Catherine was good.

Mary strolled in the gardens at Richmond Palace in the warm August sunshine with Jane Popincourt. The gardens had once been her mother's pride and joy, as she'd created them from an overgrown wilderness before the old palace of Sheen was destroyed in the fire.

After her father's death Mary persuaded Henry to employ a team of gardeners to restore the grounds to their former glory. Now flower borders filled with red and white roses replaced the wild tangle of brambles and stinging nettles.

The scent drifted on the warm summer air as they made their way down a narrow path to one of Mary's favourite places, a secluded bench-seat in the shade of an ancient oak. The seat overlooked the river and her father once said her mother called it her sanctuary. She could imagine this was where her parents would sit, watching the swans and planning their future together, so long ago.

Now Mary and Jane sat there, enjoying the sunshine and watching the river. In the heart of the city the Thames was a foul-smelling sewer, bustling with barges and boatmen clamouring for fares. At Richmond the water was tranquil, with the occasional boat drifting past. The swans were gone but once they'd seen a kingfisher, flashing turquoise and orange as it plunged into the river to emerge with tiny fish.

Jane fanned her face with her hand, then pulled off her close-fitting French style hood and cowl to free her long hair from its silver pins. 'Sometimes I wish I could wear my hair down, like the queen.'

Mary nodded and followed Jane's example. She unplaited the long strands of her golden hair, using her slender fingers as a comb. 'Catherine says it is the fashion in Spain – and no one wants to disagree with her.'

'I'm glad she's with child again, after that strange business of the twin that never existed.'

Mary heard the critical note in Jane's voice. 'It wasn't Catherine's fault the physicians were wrong about there being a twin. At least my brother was understanding.'

'And wasted no time in putting matters right.' Jane smiled at the thought.

Mary nodded. 'Catherine said she plans to name the child after me if it's a girl – and Henry if it's a boy.'

Jane gave her a quizzical look. 'I heard Charles Brandon named his daughter Mary. Would that also be after you?'

'How can you suggest such a thing, Jane Popincourt? I've known Brandon all my life but I hardly think he'd choose to name his daughter after me!'

She surprised herself at the strength of her denial. In truth, she'd wondered about his choice but Mary was a popular name. She also had to confess to her priest the sin of jealousy. Now Charles had two children she knew she must forget her feelings for him.

Mary had always been a little in awe of the black-garbed, crowlike Richard Foxe, Bishop of Winchester. He'd been her father's most faithful advisor since his days in exile. She remembered how her father relied on him, so agreed to his mysterious request to meet with her in private. Now his dark, impassive eyes – which never gave anything away – fixed on hers.

'I need to ask for your help, Your Grace.'

It was the last thing she expected him to say and she wondered if this private visit concerned Prince Charles. She knew Bishop Foxe arranged the marriage of her sister Margaret to King James of Scotland. Although there'd been the occasional letter, Mary doubted she would ever see her sister again.

'What is it, bishop?' She studied his face and saw his hesitation, as if what he was about to say would commit him to something he might regret.

The bishop took a deep breath. 'Two men, loyal to your father, were arrested three days after his death. Their names are Sir Richard Empson and Edmund Dudley.'

'It was for treason.'

Bishop Foxe shook his head. 'They served your father doing often difficult work which made them unpopular with the people.'

'I was told they were raising men against my brother.' Mary remembered being relieved when Henry acted quickly to deal with the threat.

'After your father died they feared their neighbours would turn against them.' The bishop's eyes showed he believed it to be the truth. 'The men were their retainers, brought to London to protect their property.'

'I wonder what this has to do with me, bishop?'

Foxe looked uncomfortable now. 'I understand they are to be publicly executed. I must tell you, Your Grace, that, before God, my conscience and loyalty to your father's memory demand I do whatever I can for them.'

'You've spoken to my brother?'

'I tried, Your Grace. I christened the king as a baby yet, to my regret, now cause him to raise his voice to me.' He looked deep into her eyes once more. 'I pray he might listen to you, his sister.'

'You wish me to ask him to spare these men?'

Foxe nodded, his lined face impossible to read.

'I could not, bishop.'

'Their only crime was to implement your father's wishes, as his loyal servants. I'm not asking for them to be released from the Tower, only a stay of execution.'

'It's not my place.' Mary heard the firmness in her voice. 'In truth, my brother never involves me in such matters.'

'I understand, Your Grace.' He looked as if he was about to try to persuade her but thought better of it. 'I thought it worth meeting with you but I'll wish you good day.' He turned to leave.

'Wait, bishop.'

He stopped and turned back to study her face with his deep-set eyes. 'Your Grace?'

'My father would have wished me to speak to Henry about this. I will have to choose the right moment, although I can make no promise to you.'

'That is all I ask, Your Grace.' He almost smiled. 'Although you are much like your mother, you have many of your father's qualities. I shall pray for you – and for those unfortunates held in the Tower.'

As Mary watched him leave she wished she'd never agreed to see Bishop Richard Foxe. If she failed to persuade Henry, the lives of two innocent men would now be on her conscience.

Henry seemed in good spirits after a successful hunt and hugged her warmly. 'I see too little of you, Mary. You've become a presentable young woman while my back has been turned. What have you been up to?'

'I keep myself busy enough at Richmond, dear brother.'

He looked at her as if he doubted it. 'We must discuss your marriage. How old is your young prince now?'

'Nine or perhaps ten years old.' Mary shrugged. 'I confess I'm not sure.' She couldn't remember when Charles had written one of his formal letters but decided to keep that information to herself.

'Well, it's time we made a man of him, don't you think?' He laughed and called for wine. 'I tell you what I'll do, Mary. I'll ask them to send a portrait of how he looks now. It will help you prepare for your life together.'

'Thank you, dear brother, you are too kind to me.'

Henry gave her a quizzical look. 'I am intrigued. What brings you to Greenwich this fine day, asking to meet with me in private?'

Mary took a deep breath. 'I've come to plead for the lives of our father's servants.'

Henry's eyes narrowed. 'You cannot.'

'I think...' She summoned up her courage as her voice faltered. 'Father would have wished me to speak on their behalf.'

He glowered at her. 'I forbid it, and that's the end of it.'

'I only ask for their lives to be spared, for our father's sake.'

'You're too late. They have been found guilty and sentenced. My mind is made up.'

'I thought...'

'Keep to your embroidery, sister. You know nothing of these men, but I shall educate you.' Henry gave her a questioning stare. 'Have you even heard of recognisances?'

Mary had not. She shook her head, like a small child again. Except that her brother now towered over her, barely able to control his annoyance at her foolishness.

Henry gestured for her to sit and pulled a second chair closer. His keen eyes studied her appraisingly for a moment.

'Our father's advisors found a legal way to rob noble families of their fortunes. They turned his insecurity to advantage and proposed these fines they called recognisances. They demanded payments of hundreds of thousands of pounds in our father's name.'

'I didn't know.'

'There is no reason why you should but I can tell you it blackened our father's reputation.' Henry shook his head. 'I resolved to deal with the ringleaders, two lawyers named Empson and Dudley. They confessed to embezzlement, as well as other crimes against the Crown.'

'Did our father know what they did in his name?' Her voice sounded small in the high-ceilinged chamber.

Henry nodded. 'He recorded every penny in his ledgers.'

Mary sat in silence while Henry's news sank in. She could see he told the truth and understood why he'd been angry.

Henry sat back in his chair. 'They plotted against us, Mary, and cheated the people to line their own pockets. I must make an example of them.'

Mary heard the threat in Henry's voice and knew better than to pursue it.

Her brother leaned forward and fixed her with a shrewd look. 'I've troubled to explain my reasons to you – now tell me, who put you up to this?'

With a jolt Mary realised she held Bishop Foxe's future in

her hands, possibly his life. Henry's tone demanded an answer but she couldn't think what to tell him.

'No one.' Her lie echoed around the empty chamber. 'I didn't understand.'

Henry nodded. 'Learn from this, dear sister,' he placed his hand on her arm, 'and be wary of those who would try to use your good nature, as they did with our father, God rest him.'

3

NEW YEAR'S DAY 1511

Bonfires crackled, sending orange flames and sparks high into the air and plumes of grey smoke across the city. New Year's Day was always a time for celebration and now cannons thundered at the Tower Wharf and the bells of every church in London pealed incessantly.

Mary watched as Henry held up his swaddled infant son for the world to see the future King of England. After all the hardship, tragedy and waiting, Queen Catherine, surrounded by her coterie of ladies, beamed with pleasure – yet her acknowledgement of Mary was reserved.

Mary curtseyed to show her respect for Catherine's new status and sensed their relationship had shifted. When Catherine finally spoke to Mary, it was to surprise her. 'You must represent me at the christening, Princess Mary.'

'It would be an honour. Will you still be churching, as in my grandmother's ordinances?'

'Of course.' Catherine's voice carried a new confidence, so different from the last time they met. 'The silver font of Canterbury has already been sent for, and the king has decreed no expense is to be spared.'

Mary smiled with relief that Catherine's earlier distance hadn't been because of the secrets between them. She'd been told never to speak of the lost child. Then there was Catherine's great secret, which had become even greater now she was mother to the heir to the throne.

Snowflakes drifted from an ashen sky as the slow-moving christening procession approached the old church, built in the lee of the ivy-covered walls of Richmond Palace. Mary walked behind the bishops on a path strewn with fresh rushes, leading the queen's ladies-in-waiting and thirty maids of honour. She looked back at the gaudily dressed ambassadors of Spain, Venice and Rome who followed her, complete with grand delegations of priests and nobles.

Her fears of rebuke from Henry proved unfounded. There had been no consequences of asking him to spare the lawyers. Edmund Dudley and Richard Empson were marched to Tower Hill on the appointed day. Henry had been right, as she'd heard that the people, gathered in great numbers, cheered when the men were executed.

Mary learned from her attempt to interfere with matters of state. Although she knew great secrets, many more had been kept from her. In her heart, she knew her father encouraged Empson, Dudley, and others to relieve the rich of their wealth. She'd also learned her brother now had the power of life and death – and was prepared to use it.

A bitter breeze tugged at her fur-trimmed cloak and she glanced at Jane, who shivered at her side. 'There are too many guests.' She glanced back at the queue of people disappearing into the distance. 'They will never all fit inside this little church.'

'The king has been generous with his invitations.' Jane smiled. 'I've never seen him look so pleased.'

Mary agreed. 'He's already appointed forty staff for the prince and spent a fortune on the new nursery.'

She smiled as they reached the church, decked out in brightly coloured cloth of Arras, glowing in the light from more candles than she could count. 'My father would have been so proud to have seen this day – as would my grandmother.'

They entered the church, already filled with guests and squeezed into a narrow space. Mary's spirits lifted as the little child squealed a protest, his shrill voice echoing from the rafters. A choir sang a *Te Deum laudamus* as he was held over the gleaming silver font and named Henry Tudor, Prince of Wales, the next generation of the Tudor line and future king.

The celebratory joust at the Westminster tiltyard was the greatest spectacle ever seen in England. The queen sat with her ladies-in-waiting in an elaborate wooden gallery hung with cloth of gold under a canopy of state. Mary sat a little distance away with her ladies, glad of their thick furs and the velvet cushions they'd brought to make the hard oak benches more bearable.

Her grandmother would have been pleased to see her golden Beaufort portcullis badge given such prominence on the banners around the grandstands. Mary realised this was Henry's way of acknowledging her, although as far as she knew he'd been too busy to visit her before she passed away.

Before the fanfares to announce the start of the festivities a strange hermit, dressed in a plain brown habit, rode up to the queen. The curious crowd watched in silence as he made the sign of the cross, then threw back his hood to reveal his true identity. Charles Brandon requested the right to defend the queen's honour as her champion. The crowd cheered and applauded as she accepted.

Mary resolved to forget any feelings for the handsome knight in his burnished armour. She'd received a small gold-framed portrait of her betrothed from Ghent which she kept on display by her bed. She went to sleep each night studying his pale expressionless face, although the Spanish envoy, Gutierre de Fuensalida, told her he thought it a poor likeness.

She'd also written a long letter to Prince Charles, affirming her love, and awaited his reply. He was young and wealthy with an empire to inherit. She found it hard to see her future through the mists of half-truths and third-hand information. She was sceptical of Ambassador de Fuensalida's description of the prince and began to wonder when she would ever meet him. A touch on her arm broke through her reverie.

'Do you not think he makes a handsome hermit?' Jane had a mischievous note in her voice.

'I cannot agree.' Mary shook her head. 'It's silly theatre, to amuse my brother.' She noted that Brandon didn't once glance in her direction and only had compliments for Queen Catherine.

A shrill fanfare of trumpets from green-garbed foresters announced the arrival of a huge pageant of a forest, pulled by a golden lion and a silver antelope. Topped with a golden castle garlanded with roses, the pageant was wheeled in front of them. At another trumpet blast the sides of the castle flung open to reveal the king, with his fellow jousters, dressed in bright-green satin edged with scarlet.

Mary recognised Henry's accomplices, despite their disguises, grinning like court jesters at their deception of the queen. Thomas Boleyn, Edward Howard and Thomas Knyvet, who sported a gold codpiece and proclaimed himself Sir Valiant Desire. Henry raised a hand for silence and announced he was to be known as Sir Loyal Heart for the duration of the tourney.

Catherine seemed to be enjoying the spectacle in her honour. For the first time Mary realised her brother might be in love with her, despite his bluff antics. She recalled how proudly he'd escorted the exotic Spanish princess to her wedding with Arthur. It had been their father's wish but he could have sent her back to Spain. Instead, he'd married her as soon as he could.

When the jousting began the tilt barriers were so close to where Mary sat she could almost taste the sweat of the horses. As the knights charged, her seat reverberated with the pounding of hooves on sawdust-covered cobbles. Once she jumped as a broken shard of lance struck the side of the grandstand in front of her with a hollow crack, too close for comfort.

Charles Brandon defeated yet another challenger and Mary had a sudden realisation. She turned to Jane Popincourt. 'He's going to ride against my brother.'

Jane frowned. 'Don't they both claim to be fighting for the honour of the queen?'

'It's another of Henry's games. You can rest assured he'll win.' Even as Mary said the words she doubted them. She'd watched the dangerous sport too often and knew how competitive both Henry and Brandon could be.

As she'd predicted, the jousting ended with Brandon facing up to Sir Loyal Heart, whose warhorse was caparisoned with golden hearts. Mary raised her hand to her mouth as they clashed in front of her, Henry's lance shattering on Brandon's chest. Few would guess it was anything other than proof of her brother's prowess, yet Mary knew Brandon. He'd allowed the king his moment of glory.

The celebrations continued after evensong in the White Hall of Westminster Palace. Henry's musicians played lively dance music on horns and drums, and fine wine flowed like water. Mary and her ladies joined in with the singing but she was glad they'd resisted demands to join the dancing, which soon degenerated into drunken brawling.

Henry shouted to the staff of the visiting ambassadors to try their luck against his valiant knights. They took this as an invitation to start a melee, ripping at each other's clothes, pulling open the gowns of the dancing ladies and even tearing the gold ornaments from Henry's doublet. Mary decided it was time to leave when Sir Thomas Knyvet was stripped naked after losing his gold codpiece to a triumphant Spaniard.

Henry had to call for his guards to intervene. He'd laughed it off as nothing more than high spirits, but ribald, drunken shouts followed Mary, echoing down the corridor as she returned to her rooms with her ladies, in fear of their virtue.

Bad news travelled through the long corridors and winding back stairs of Richmond Palace like a forest fire, touching the lives of everyone. Little Henry, the future of the Tudor dynasty, heir to the king, was dead. Mary stood by the mullioned window, looking down into the courtyard where she'd played as a girl, and wept.

She cried for her brother, who had been the proudest father in England. Tears ran down her face for Catherine, her friend, who'd suffered enough tragedy and did not deserve more. She wept for the innocent little child, who would never now be king. He had seemed so bright-eyed and happy, the whole world within reach of his tiny, grasping fingers.

In that moment, the last traces of the girl she had been slipped away. She would be strong for her brother, a good sister. She would put his wishes before her own and marry her mysterious young prince. She would become a powerful empress and help Henry keep the fragile peace her father worked so hard to secure.

Mary once confessed the sin of envy to her priest, although she didn't name Anne Browne. She'd often dreamed of life with Charles Brandon, yet didn't bear his wife ill will. They had two young daughters, one named after her, and Mary knew her own duty was to marry her foreign prince.

Then came the shocking news. Brandon's wife Anne had died of a mysterious fever, a dreadful, short-lived affliction that took rich and poor, young and old. Lady Elizabeth Boleyn brought the news. One of Catherine's ladies-in-waiting, Lady Elizabeth always showed Mary kindness, having two daughters of her own.

Mary stared at her as the implications of her news sank in. 'I am so sorry for those poor girls.'

Lady Elizabeth nodded. 'I understand they are both well, thank the Lord, as is their father.' She placed a comforting hand on Mary's arm. 'Charles Brandon will remarry soon enough – and is a wealthy man now he's inherited his uncle's fortune. You know he's been made Marshal of the King's Household?'

'No, although it doesn't surprise me. Those two have been like brothers since Henry was a boy.' She looked at Lady Elizabeth as she made a judgement. 'May I confess something to you, in confidence?'

'Of course, Your Grace.'

'I would like to ask my brother if he would consent to ending my betrothal to Prince Charles – but I've no idea how he might react.'

Lady Elizabeth raised an eyebrow at the suggestion. 'Has he mentioned your betrothal lately?'

'Not since I showed him the little portrait,' Mary frowned, 'and I've had no reply to my letters to Prince Charles.'

Lady Elizabeth thought for a moment. 'I expect the king places great store on the advantages of uniting his family with Emperor Maximilian's.'

'But I wish to marry Charles Brandon.' Her words hung in the air like a heady, exotic perfume, her dreams and dangerous desire crystallised now they were tantalisingly within her reach. It was the first time she'd said them aloud to anyone – or even admitted them to herself.

'You wish to marry Brandon?' Lady Elizabeth stared at her in disbelief, then her expression softened and she looked amused at the thought. 'I've seen how he flatters the ladies, Your Grace. You would never know what he was up to.'

'I would wait until after a suitable period of mourning...' Her words tailed off. She knew it was a futile idea. Henry would never change his mind.

Lady Elizabeth studied her for a moment, as if realising how much this meant to her. 'You would need to choose your moment with great care.'

Mary nodded. 'Henry is quite different since the little prince's death. He dresses in sombre mourning clothes and acts,' she struggled to find the right words, 'more like a king.'

Lady Elizabeth lowered her voice in case the servants overheard. 'At least he's put an end to all these disguisings and capers at court. The queen told me he hasn't blamed any of the staff who cared for his infant son.'

'I'm glad my brother has shown understanding towards poor Catherine.'

'He has been most caring after her loss and openly shows his love for her.' Lady Elizabeth leaned forward in her chair, as if sharing a great secret. 'I understand the king has also joined the Holy League.'

'The pope's alliance?' Mary struggled to keep up with the politics of state, although from the way Lady Elizabeth spoke she could tell it was significant.

'The Holy League includes Spain and the Venetians. They band together against King Louis of France.'

'I thought we were at peace with France? King Louis was a sponsor at little Henry's christening.'

Lady Elizabeth looked at her as if she was an innocent child. 'The French would invade us tomorrow if they saw the opportunity. Your brother does well to keep them at bay, although I fear it's simply a matter of time.' Her voice carried a note of bitterness which surprised Mary.

'Forgive my ignorance, Lady Elizabeth, but I had no idea.'

'You should be glad the king has chosen so well for you, for such a marriage is a great blessing. Young Prince Charles is heir to the House of Valois-Burgundy and the Holy Roman Empire. When he inherits, he will become one of the most powerful men in the world.'

Mary ran through their conversation that night alone in her bed, staring as usual at the miniature pale-faced portrait. Lady Elizabeth Boleyn was right; she should be grateful for what she had. Even if Henry approved her request, she had no idea of Charles Brandon's feelings towards her. She'd been touched by his compliments, yet she'd seen the way he used his natural charm with all the ladies.

She reached out and touched the gold-framed portrait, a nightly ritual. 'Goodnight, my Charles.'

As she blew out her flickering candle the image forming in her mind was not the pale boy from Castile. Despite the promises she'd made to herself, the picture in her mind was of an older, laughing Charles, his face tanned by the sun, in full armour of burnished gilt. A daring plan stole into her thoughts. It seemed so obvious it was a wonder she'd not thought of it before. Somehow, she must find a way to let Charles Brandon know she would willingly marry him.

Mary lay back in the darkness, wide awake as she ran through the possibilities in her mind. He might admit he'd always secretly loved her. He might be shocked at her presumption and say he thought of her as a sister, although she doubted it. Even if he didn't have feelings for her, he was ambitious enough to see the advantage of marriage to a Tudor princess, the sister of the king.

She would wait until he'd buried his poor wife. Then she would make one last roll of the dice and find an opportunity to confront him. Whatever the outcome, she swore to believe it to be God's plan for her.

Many weeks passed before her chance came. Mary made it her business to learn when Brandon would next visit the king's stables at Richmond. The stables offered more privacy than meeting in the palace and she hoped the stable boys were more discreet than her gossiping servants. She rode every day, so it was easy enough to contrive to visit the stables once he arrived, but she was surprised by his greeting.

'You've come to see me off, Princess Mary?'

'You are leaving? You've only just arrived.'

'I'm off to fight the French!' He smiled at her puzzled expression. 'Surely you know?' He shook his head in mock disbelief. 'You do live a sheltered life here at Richmond!'

Mary stared at him, recalling Lady Elizabeth's dire prediction. 'We are at war with France?'

'A holy war, now Pope Julius has sided with us. He promises your brother the crown of France once King Louis is defeated.'

'I thought the king had made you marshal of his household?' She'd never thought of Charles Brandon as a soldier, despite his prowess at the jousts.

'He has, but we've all been made sea captains, not only me – Edward Howard and that scoundrel Thomas Knyvet too.' His eyes flashed with pride. 'I've been given command of your father's old flagship, the *Sovereign*, to keep the English Channel free from marauding Frenchmen.'

'Do you know how to command a warship in a sea battle?'

'In truth, she already has an experienced captain and crew.' Brandon grinned. 'It's my duty, Princess Mary. The king would wish to take command himself but he's chosen those he can rely on, so I consider it an honour.'

Mary could imagine how they'd come up with the plan during one of their drinking bouts. She consoled herself with the knowledge Charles Brandon was safer at sea than in a land campaign. The French would probably run at the sight of the *Sovereign*, with her array of fine cannons.

A stable boy brought her saddled horse and handed her the reins. Mary had almost forgotten her pretext for visiting the stables. She smoothed the horse's flank as she tried to recall her well-rehearsed words, then realised this was neither the time nor the place for such speeches.

She turned to Brandon. 'My brother tells me nothing, so will you let me know when you return?'

'Of course, Your Grace,' he gave her a wry look, 'although I didn't think you cared, now you are to marry your little prince?'

She glanced to be sure the stable boy had gone. This was her moment, the reason she'd gone to so much trouble to meet with him, yet something in his tone made her hesitate. 'Have you heard something?' She studied his face for any clue. 'Has my brother mentioned the wedding?'

'This war,' he became serious for a moment, 'it makes our alliances more important. The king is keen to secure the support of Emperor Maximilian.' He smiled. 'He may not wish him as a friend but he certainly doesn't want him as his enemy.'

'I will pray for you, Charles. I will pray for your safe return.' She led her horse to the mounting block and climbed into the saddle, urging it forward before he saw her tears.

4

SUMMER 1512

Mary tasted the salt in the fresh sea air and looked out across the sparkling blue-green waters of Portsmouth harbour. She'd made the seventy-mile journey from London with Queen Catherine and her ladies to watch the king's fleet sail for Brest. Now she could see how her father's modest royal fleet had grown, thanks to Henry's spending.

She counted seven high-masted ships at the quayside and another eighteen sitting at anchor. Some, like the *Regent*, had once been her father's ships. Others were converted carvels and merchantmen, commandeered in the king's name and fitted with guns fore and aft.

In front of them, Henry's colourful royal standard and banners flew from the topmast of his magnificent new flagship the *Mary Rose*. A floating fortress, she bristled with the latest guns and was the pride of England's growing fleet. Henry told her over six hundred oak trees were used in her construction, making her the most expensive warship ever built.

The shouts of sailors, clambering precariously high in the rigging, carried on the light June breeze as they prepared huge canvas sails. Teams of men sang out in deep voices as they hauled on ropes and great wooden cranes hoisted the last supplies aboard. Crates and casks littered the quay and a live pig squealed in distress as it was lifted high into the air and lowered into the dark hold of a ship.

The crowds who'd gathered to see the fleet sail cheered and shouted as the last of five thousand soldiers queued at gangplanks, the sun glinting off new armour and weapons as they waited to embark. The decks of the ships closest to her were already crowded with archers. They'd marched from all over England to fight for their king and country. Each carried a longbow and quiver of at least thirty arrows with sharpened iron tips.

Street vendors called out to customers as they sold cups of ale and cakes. The king's musicians played lively tunes and some of the onlookers danced on the quayside, creating a cheerful atmosphere while all around them prepared for war.

Only Mary knew the real reason she had come. She'd promised to accept whatever happened as God's will, and this was her last chance to say goodbye to the man she'd dared to dream of marrying. She scanned the ships, trying to identify the distinctive high sterncastle of the *Sovereign* among the forest of masts but there were too many.

In her mind she'd envisaged Charles Brandon looking into her eyes and perhaps kissing her hand as he promised to keep safe. It was difficult to tell one ship from another in the crowded harbour. For all she knew Brandon might be watching her, perhaps raising a hand in farewell.

'Look – the king!' Catherine pointed as the tall figure of Henry appeared on the deck of the *Mary Rose*, talking to Sir Edward Howard.

A thought occurred to her as she watched her brother strutting on the deck of his grand flagship. 'I know Henry would dearly wish to sail with them.' Mary turned to Catherine. 'What is there to stop him?'

Catherine smiled. 'Me, for one. We couldn't risk the king in the first raid on Brittany.'

'Surely this fleet is more than a match for any French ships?' Mary studied her friend's face, hoping for confirmation.

Catherine's face became serious. 'The French fleet numbers more than thirty-five ships, Mary, with captains and crews far more experienced than ours.'

'You think this a dangerous expedition?'

Catherine nodded. 'You risk your life whenever you put to sea, Mary. When I sailed from Spain the weather was fine – but we suffered a terrible storm in the Bay of Biscay.' She shuddered at the memory. 'My ship began to take on water and I feared we would all drown.'

Mary stared up at the clear blue sky and said a silent prayer for the fleet's safe return. When she'd last seen Charles Brandon he told her it was his duty, yet in her heart she knew he sailed today for the adventure and would not have missed it for the world.

At last she identified the *Sovereign*, hidden behind several other ships. Mary thought she could make out the figure of Brandon at the rail, gazing in her direction. She resisted the urge to call his name or wave, yet all her resolve to forget her feelings vanished in that instant.

As the weeks passed she did her best to follow news of the war with France. Queen Catherine proved well informed and Mary was surprised to learn she had acted on behalf of her father, King Ferdinand of Spain, to encourage Henry's invasion.

'The pope will make your brother the most Christian king,' Catherine's eyes flashed with ambition, 'and I will soon become Queen of England and of France!'

Catherine called for one of her ladies to bring a parchment map, which she spread out in front of them. Mary studied the turquoise blue of the English Channel, which an imaginative scribe had embellished with sea monsters.

She looked up at Catherine. 'Forgive me, I don't understand. We were at peace. What was it that started this war?'

'King Louis accused Pope Julius of corruption.' Catherine spoke with a note of contempt in her voice. 'He tried to blacken the name of our Holy Father.'

Mary studied the brightly coloured map again. It amazed her to see how close France was to England and how narrow the Channel looked on a map, considering how long it took to sail to Calais. 'It seems strange to me that we declare war on France for such a thing.'

Catherine gave her a wry look. 'It was an excuse for King Louis to keep his army in Venice. His real reason was to be ready to invade my father's lands,' she tapped the parchment map with a gold-ringed finger, 'and the people of England have a score to settle with the French.'

'My father used to say war is the last resort, after diplomacy has failed.'

Catherine studied her for a moment. 'Your father's men on the king's council, Archbishop Foxe and Bishop Fisher, tried to intervene in the king's plans. They urged him to reconsider – but they still don't see that if we show weakness now, the Scots and the French will join forces.'

'They could invade England?' The war which had seemed so distant to Mary was suddenly close to home.

Catherine stared at her. 'This is how Henry will make his name in the world.' Her tone became conspiratorial. 'Bishop Foxe put his own man, a cleric named Thomas Wolsey, into Henry's service, yet he's been more than willing to implement the king's wishes.'

Mary understood. She'd heard about Wolsey from her

ladies. In no time he'd become her brother's chief administrator. She also understood this latest fleet was a show of English strength after the failed expedition in the spring led by Thomas Grey, Marquess of Dorset. Mary had heard her brother cursing his mutinous soldiers and their disloyal leaders.

The fire at Westminster Palace in April also unsettled Henry. He was at Greenwich and she'd been at Richmond when Westminster burned down. The great hall and the jewel rooms survived but the flames destroyed her father's ancient chambers and most of his precious library. The fire started in the palace kitchens but the superstitious people of London were saying it was a bad omen, a sign of misfortune to come.

Henry wished to prove them wrong and win public support with a great victory over their old enemy, the French. The idea that this war was caused by an insult to a pope who was now dead made no sense. The truth was as simple as it was shocking to her. If what Catherine told her was true, more was at stake here than Henry's pride, as both Scotland and France stood poised to invade.

Mary tuned her lute, her deft fingers adjusting each of the five pairs of strings. She sat alone in the queen's presence chamber at Richmond Palace. The room was special to her, as it had been her mother's. Mary had only been six years old when her mother died. The memory of her was fading, although she thought she could sense her presence in the room.

The fine instrument was one of her most prized possessions. Decorated with an inlaid Tudor rose, the lute had been a gift from her father, who'd always loved to hear her play. She tried a few experimental runs and smiled to herself as the notes rang clear and true.

She'd learned a wide repertoire of tunes by heart and practised often, although she frowned as she studied the sheet music on a silver stand in front of her. Henry had taken to composing new works and wished her to play them for him. He treated her with a little more respect now she'd turned sixteen. He also seemed pleased to have her at his side at banquets, often asking her to play and sing for his visiting dignitaries.

This time the occasion was to impress scarlet-robed cardinals, envoys from the Vatican, and the flamboyant Spanish ambassadors of Catherine's father, King Ferdinand. Ambitious nobles and their gossiping wives crowded her brother's great hall. Mary found herself wishing Charles Brandon could have been among the guests. She had no idea if he was even still alive, although she prayed for him each day.

The entertainments began with the choir of the Chapel Royal, praising God and the king, their perfect harmonies echoing to the heavens. Then followed Henry's mummers, dressed as ancient Greeks in white togas and wearing green laurel wreaths, performing a play by Sophocles. It seemed the guests were growing bored of the well-intended moralising and cheered when at last it was Mary's turn.

She dressed as Euterpe, the Greek muse of music, in a long flowing gown of cream satin with a gold circlet on her plaited hair. As well as Henry's composition she sang a traditional Spanish lament, taught to her by Catherine, to rapturous applause and cheers from King Ferdinand's ambassadors.

Henry called out her name, summoning her to sit between himself and the queen as a reward. The colour rose to her cheeks as she realised she'd become the centre of attention.

'You've helped retrieve this evening's entertainment from those accursed mummers, dear sister,' Henry smiled, 'and ensured the ambassadors report the night as a success. At least one of my sisters knows how to please me.'

'Thank you, dearest brother.' Mary studied his face, trying to judge his mood. 'Is there news of Margaret?'

Henry nodded. 'We've had letters from our sister Margaret.' Henry shared a look with Catherine then drained his goblet of wine and gestured to his server for another.

The news was a surprise to Mary, who'd almost forgotten she had a sister. She'd only been seven years old when Margaret was sent to Scotland and could hardly imagine how she might look. Mary did a quick calculation. Her sister would be twenty-three now. She received a short letter from Margaret long ago and agonised over her reply, yet never received an answer.

'Is our sister well?'

'Her son lives.' Henry scowled as if the thought reminded him of his own situation. 'She named him James – and she's pregnant again.'

'Does this mean we are at peace with the Scots?' Mary found it hard to understand how their sister could be an enemy.

'Far from it!' Heads turned as Henry raised his voice. 'Her husband appointed himself as a peacemaker – but will support the French, given the chance.'

'Are we sure of this?'

Henry glowered at her question. 'Our sources are reliable.' He seemed to realise he'd spoken a little harshly. 'We offered to send Margaret the jewels our father bequeathed her, if she would only confirm the Scots would not attack England, yet she refused.'

Mary hesitated to ask more. She'd learned better than to press her brother on affairs of state, and fought back the frustration building inside her. Matters such as these affected them all, yet secrets were kept from her.

Queen Catherine filled the silence. 'The child she carries is too soon after the birth of her son. I've ordered the Abbot of Westminster to deliver the sacred girdle of Our Lady to comfort your sister in her confinement – other than that there is little we can do.' She put her hand on Mary's arm and lowered her voice to a whisper. 'Our agents in the Scottish court tell us she is not as well as her letters would have us believe.'

Mary wasn't surprised to learn her brother had spies in the Scottish court. Her father once bitterly complained that every foreign visitor was a spy at heart, looking for signs of weakness to turn to their own advantage. The ambassadors drinking his wine would report all they heard back to King Ferdinand. Even the visiting cardinals were no doubt spying for the pope in Rome.

What troubled her was this unexpected glimpse of her sister Margaret's life. Henry said King James wished for peace, so that could only mean one thing. He was prepared to risk all their father worked so hard to achieve, to win personal glory.

It seemed an eternity before Charles Brandon returned and Mary could tell his time at sea had changed him. His skin had darkened from the sun, his hair was cut shorter and his long beard neatly trimmed. He dressed like a wealthy merchant in a fine black velvet doublet with gold buttons. A heavy gold chain of office hung around his neck and he wore an engraved silver dagger with a jewelled hilt on a low-slung belt.

Mary had changed her mind several times before choosing a gown of rich crimson satin embroidered with gold thread. Her fashionable hood ringed with pure white pearls made her look older and her girlish figure had started to fill out at last. Her heart quickened as she saw a flash of appreciation in Brandon's eyes before he turned his attention to Catherine.

The queen dismissed her other ladies, who retired to a discreet distance, and held out her hand for him to kiss. 'Welcome home, Master Brandon. We hear so many rumours about events in France it is hard to tell the truth from speculation.' She smiled at him. 'Please be seated. We would like to hear your account first-hand.'

Brandon looked uncomfortable. 'The king asked for such matters not to be spoken of, Your Grace.'

'He would wish you to tell me, Master Brandon.' There was a firmness in her voice that demanded an answer.

'Of course, Your Grace,' he glanced at Mary, 'although as you will have heard, it is sad news I bring you.'

'We give thanks to God you have returned safely with the *Sovereign* – and we hear the *Mary Rose* is safe in Southampton.'

Brandon nodded. 'Others have fared less well, Your Grace, including our good friend Thomas Knyvet.' He shook his head, then continued. 'We engaged with pirates and sunk one of their ships before we encountered the French and Breton fleets. A cannon shot shattered the mast of the *Sovereign* and we had to withdraw to make repairs. Thomas Knyvet was aboard the *Regent*, which fired on a French warship, the *Marie la Cordelière*, and engaged her with grappling irons. There was a pitched battle and many men had crossed to the French ship when there was a great explosion.' He stopped talking, his face grave.

Catherine leaned forward in her chair. 'Please continue, Master Brandon.'

'I cannot be certain, Your Grace, but it's thought her gunpowder store caught fire. I regret to tell you both ships burned to the waterline and were lost.'

Mary raised a hand to her mouth. 'Thomas Knyvet burned to death?'

Brandon shook his head. 'One of the men we rescued told us he was killed by a cannon shot, but many of his crew were burned or drowned. We were able to pick up only a small number of survivors and most died before we reached home. Some six hundred men were lost, Your Grace, and twice that number of Frenchmen. We repaired our ship as best we could, then a violent storm forced our return to England.'

Catherine nodded. 'We understand why you've been asked not to speak of this – and shall pray for the souls of those lost in the service of the king.'

'Thank you, Your Grace.'

They sat in silence for a moment and Mary saw her chance. 'What is next for you, Master Brandon?' She tried to sound as if she was making polite conversation yet her future might depend on his answer.

He studied their faces as if deciding how much to tell them. 'The king has asked me to lead an invasion of Brittany. This must be kept a close secret.'

Mary nodded, her mind a whirl of consequences. 'Of course. When must you leave?'

'First, I have to recruit an army,' he looked serious, 'and I have some business to attend to. I plan to purchase the wardship of Lady Elizabeth Grey.'

Catherine nodded. 'Sir Thomas Knyvet was her stepfather – she must be no more than seven years old?'

Brandon nodded. 'The poor girl is left an orphan. It will cost me a small fortune – but the king is in agreement for me to have her father's title and become Viscount Lisle.'

'You would have to marry her first!'

'I am free to marry, Your Grace. I've been a widower long enough.'

Mary's dreams evaporated like the morning dew in summer heat. Charles Brandon hardly glanced at her throughout the exchange. All he cared for was his title and returning to the war. She bit her lip as she struggled to hide the painful sense of loss of what might have been. She must prepare for marriage to Prince Charles and forget her foolish ideas of a future with this incorrigible adventurer.

5

AUTUMN 1513

Their voices joined in angelic harmony as Mary and Jane Popincourt rehearsed for the concert to celebrate Henry's return from France. Mary played her clavichord while Jane sang in tuneful French of chivalry and courtly love. They laughed together as the song finished with the confession of a secret passion.

'If I know my brother he will take great delight in this.' Mary smiled as she looked through the sheets of music, trying to decide the order of songs. Henry could be the most difficult of men at times but no one showed more appreciation of her music and singing.

'We should choose a solo for you, Jane, your voice is too pure to always be with mine.'

Jane gave her a look of pretended shyness. 'Only if you join me on your lute, my lady, and it would have to be in English, as I think the king will have heard more than enough from the French.'

Mary's constant companion in Henry's absence, Jane helped improve her French and entertained her with scandalous tales of her time at the court of King Louis of France. Mary realised she'd led a sheltered life, despite her brother's youthful bawdiness, and pressed Jane to describe the most salacious stories of how the French king indulged his mistresses.

They were about to continue their rehearsal when a servant appeared to announce the queen's herald, delivering a letter for Mary on a silver tray. After five years of waiting she hesitated before breaking the dark wax seal on the letter.

Her betrothed, Prince Charles of Castile, had finally replied and her future hung in the balance as she turned the folded yellow parchment in her hands. He would be thirteen years old now, with less than a year until he'd be old enough to marry her.

She hoped the letter would confirm their wedding day and end the troubling rumours, but feared it would tell her otherwise. Even when her father agreed her dowry, as well as jewels and gold plate, he'd made provision for Henry to use the money to finance another marriage of his choosing, if he so wished.

There had been so few letters from young Charles she could hardly recall the last one. She'd sent the prince a finely crafted gold ring and agonised for days over the wording of the letter sent with it. After months of waiting she received a jewelled pendant in return.

She'd worn the pendant on a gold chain around her neck every day since, yet the letter accompanying her precious jewel was a terse note, answering none of her questions, merely confirming it was sent to her from the prince, who called her his *'Bon Marie'*.

She ran the tip of her finger over the elaborate seal of a royal crest, sensing something out of the ordinary, then she realised the significance of it being unbroken. Henry read any letters before her but he was far away with his army in France.

The last news was that they had besieged the city of Tournai, after taking Thérouanne.

For the first time, she might learn something before Henry. Breaking the wax seal, Mary began to read. Written in the monkish, regular hand of a scribe, the letter began with the usual formalities. She frowned as she studied the flamboyant signature at the end.

'It's from Prince Charles's grandfather, Emperor Maximilian – and he confuses me with my poor sister Margaret.' She handed the letter to Jane.

Jane read quickly, making short work of the formal French, then raised an eyebrow as she looked up at Mary. 'Are you certain this is meant for your eyes, my lady?'

'It was delivered to me by the queen's own herald – do you think she was supposed to see it first?'

Jane shook her head. 'I imagine the queen has more important things on her mind, my lady. The war with Scotland has been won but there are others who try to take advantage of the king's absence.'

Mary's eyes widened as a troubling thought occurred to her. 'Perhaps there has been a change of plan now my sister Margaret is able to remarry?'

Jane's face changed to a look of concern. 'Queen Margaret is hardly a suitable bride for Prince Charles.'

'You know the king's advisors have no concern with suitability, Jane, only political advantage. Now King James is dead, my sister's son inherits the throne of Scotland. Margaret rules the country in his name until he comes of age, so my brother has good reason to bring her back within the fold.'

'King James was misguided to risk an invasion of the north while the king is away.' She gave Mary a wry look. 'The people are calling Queen Catherine the new Saint Joan. She has become quite a hero.'

Mary nodded. 'She ordered a special suit of armour, complete with a fine jewelled helmet – then let the people's imagination and the gossipers do the rest. In truth, she never even travelled to the north.'

'I heard that she wished King James's body to be sent to the king in France.'

Mary nodded. 'It's true. She was persuaded to send his bloodstained coat instead, as proof he was dead and to be used as a war banner.'

'I always thought the queen so devout, yet she seems as warlike as her mother, Queen Isabella.'

Mary heard the note of criticism in Jane's voice. 'She sees my brother's adventures in France as a holy war, defending the good name of the pope.'

Jane looked puzzled. 'But Pope Julius is dead and the new Pope Leo wants peace?'

'Yes – but King James broke a sacred oath he made to my father. In return for Margaret's hand he swore never to invade England.' Mary shook her head. 'I was too young to understand but now I see my sister Margaret's marriage was my father's plan to preserve the peace.'

Jane refolded the letter and handed it back to Mary. 'At least the king will soon return from his adventures in France, so you will be able to ask him if Emperor Maximilian has confused you with your sister.'

Mary studied the folded parchment in her hand, which she'd hoped would provide some answers but instead raised so many questions. 'I pray you are right, Jane, but I've waited too long for news of my wedding. Please tell my servants I wish to travel to see Queen Catherine.'

Fallen leaves swirled in the autumnal breeze around the

ancient stone gatehouse. Mary shivered and pulled her cloak around her shoulders. She disliked the sinister Tower of London with its damp, dark rooms. Although Henry had the royal apartments refurnished and decorated with bright tapestries they were still haunted by ghosts of the past.

She recognised the white-bearded guard who showed her to the queen's apartments. He'd been a loyal servant to her father yet now he stooped over and seemed to struggle for breath as he climbed the stone steps in front of her. Mary realised her brother had taken all the younger men to France with him, leaving Catherine to govern a vulnerable city.

Mary had asked Henry to take her with him, so she could meet her young prince and learn something of the places she would live in the future. He'd dismissed the idea as too dangerous yet had taken his best bed, three hundred household servants, his musicians and the choir of the Chapel Royal, as if he was embarking on a royal progress, rather than leading an army into battle.

Her last memory was of him waving from the deck of his magnificent warship the *Mary Rose* and laughing with Charles Brandon as they sailed from Dover. He'd made Brandon one of his most senior commanders, despite his lack of experience in battle. Mary could not imagine Charles Brandon being content to wait in relative safety at the rear of Henry's army. He would want to lead from the front, with little regard for the dangers.

She dismissed the pang of regret that she might never see Brandon again as the heavy oak doors swung open and she entered the queen's chambers. The delicious spiced-orange scent of pomanders mixed with woodsmoke from the fire in the hearth and the honeyed fumes of beeswax candles. The guard bowed before announcing her and leaving, closing the doors behind him.

Queen Catherine sat reading at a desk cluttered with

ledgers and papers, bringing back a sudden memory for Mary of her father at his work. He'd liked nothing better than to spend long evenings checking his accounts, initialling each entry. Now she began to understand. He'd never trusted anyone to do it on his behalf and it seemed Catherine followed his example.

Several of her ladies-in-waiting seated around her stopped working on the tapestries they were sewing, as if glad of the distraction of Mary's visit. Catherine wore a plain gown of azure blue and a simple gold necklace glinting with diamonds around her neck. Instead of her formal hood a plain linen cowl covered her plaited hair, a sign she wasn't expecting visitors.

She looked up as Mary entered. Clapping her hands, she dismissed her ladies and gestured for Mary to take the chair closest to her. The duties of regency and her victory against the Scots had changed Catherine. The shadows which told of troubled sleep were under her eyes yet they shone with a new confidence.

'It's good of you to visit me, Princess Mary, with plague here in London.' Her voice sounded tired yet carried the warmth of friendship.

Mary curtseyed, feeling a flutter of uncertainty about how she should address Catherine. 'Thank you for agreeing to see me, Your Grace. I must confess I thought the plague had passed long since.'

Catherine looked surprised. 'I pray each day for it to pass yet over three hundred are reported to have died in London each day, may God rest their souls.'

'I am truly sorry to hear it.'

'The plague is only one of so many things I've had to deal with during Henry's absence. The Palace of Westminster is still a ruin,' Catherine shook her head, 'and both Greenwich and Richmond are too far from my ministers, so I've had to spend more time here at the Tower than I would wish.'

'These apartments once belonged to my mother.' Mary pointed towards an ornate carved wooden door. 'Through there is the chamber where she spent her last days. My father made little use of her rooms afterwards. They were filled with too many memories.'

'Of course, I'd forgotten.' Catherine looked around the small-windowed room as if seeing it for the first time. 'Your mother showed me great kindness when I first arrived from Spain. You must miss her.'

'I regret I was only six years old when she died, so my memory of her is fading, although sometimes...' Mary looked at Catherine, making a judgement. 'I believe she appears to me in dreams, like an angel.'

Catherine nodded in understanding. 'Henry told me once he could not speak of your mother, as it would open a wound which time has yet to heal.'

'Henry was closer to our mother than Margaret or I. You know she taught him to read and write? My father said she indulged him too much when he was young.'

'Your father indulged him once.' Catherine smiled but looked wistful, as if an old memory had been triggered by Mary's words. 'He chose Henry to escort me to my wedding to Prince Arthur.'

'Those were happy times at Eltham. I have a memory of him marching through the nursery in a suit of pure white silk, waving a real sword!'

'His suit was a perfect match to my wedding dress.' Her eyes twinkled as she recalled the day. 'Henry could not have been more than ten years old but he was so proud that day.' Catherine stared into the distance, lost in reminiscence.

Mary wondered how best to raise the question that had been troubling her. If Henry's plans had changed she was certain Catherine would know of it. Then she remembered her sister Margaret's situation was far worse than hers.

'What will become of my sister, now her husband is dead?' Her words carried an unintended suggestion of disapproval.

Catherine's eyes flashed with surprise at the question. 'You must not think I wished him killed, Mary. I sent your sister my condolences and asked her to help me achieve a truce with Scotland.' Her voice sounded defensive.

'Do you think she will wish to remarry?'

'I expect Henry will have plans to find her a more suitable husband, when the time is right.'

Mary took a deep breath. 'And what can you tell me of Henry's plans for *my* wedding?'

'I thought that might be why you came to see me.' Catherine smiled. 'I asked Thomas Wolsey to arrange for Henry to see Archduchess Margaret of Savoy and my nephew the prince before he returns from France.'

'Thomas Wolsey works for you?' Mary didn't understand. She hadn't liked the way Wolsey schemed and plotted when he served as her father's chaplain. Now he'd somehow become not only Henry's right-hand man but also Catherine's agent.

'Master Wolsey's a shrewd, ambitious man, Mary. He understands the advantage of your marriage to Prince Charles. He kindly keeps me informed of matters in France, which is just as well, for Henry seems too busy with his sieges to write.' Catherine shook her head. 'Henry sent me instead a trouble-some French prisoner, the Duke of Longueville, together with his servants.'

'I've heard of him. Duke Louis is a famous general.'

Catherine nodded. 'Henry demands a generous ransom for his return, but the duke's not pleased to be under guard here in the Tower.' She looked close to tears.

Mary studied Catherine with new concern. There had been a rumour she'd lost yet another child but this was not the time to ask about it. 'You should return with me to Richmond

Palace. The roses are in bloom and the gardens have never looked more beautiful.'

'You are right, Mary. My work here is almost over and we must prepare the welcome for Henry's return.'

~

Henry's army marched through London with a fanfare of trumpets. As well as victory in Thérouanne, Tournai had surrendered after eight days of siege. Stories were circulating about how the French had run off so fast Henry's soldiers could hardly keep up with them.

They'd captured some thirty French nobles, brought to England like the Duke of Longueville, to be held to ransom. The bells of all the churches in London pealed in celebration and people lined the narrow streets, cheering and calling out 'God save the king!' and 'Long live King Henry!'

Mary watched with Queen Catherine as the royal procession approached. Catherine looked pleased with herself and wore her finest jewels with a new gown of cloth of gold over a brocade kirtle. Mary wore a voluminous emerald-green gown with a tight-fitting velvet bodice which accentuated her slender figure.

Henry rode a heavy warhorse behind knights carrying his golden mace and sword of state. A white tabard covered his armour, adorned with the blood-red cross of St George, and in place of his helmet he wore a gold circlet, studded with rubies. Mary could see her brother's broad grin as he lifted a gauntleted hand in acknowledgement to the cheering crowds.

Catherine put her hand on Mary's arm. 'See how the people adore him?'

Mary had to agree. Her brother could have stayed safe at home, yet chose to risk his life in France. His great gamble had paid off, although she wondered at the cost. It had been the first English defeat of the French for sixty years and Henry acted like a great victory had been won, although Mary doubted it.

Her attention was caught by the sight of Sir Charles Brandon, now made Viscount Lisle, a knight of the Order of the Garter and Master of the Horse. Dressed in full armour he looked a striking figure, his black warhorse caparisoned with a long flowing cape of cloth of gold and adorned with trappings of gleaming silver.

Catherine's eyes sparkled. 'This is quite a show but I can tell you a secret – it's all staged, as Henry arrived here last night.'

'You've already seen him?'

'I have. The king rode to see me on a fast horse, with only a few trusted men as his escort.'

Mary's mind raced with questions. 'Can I ask – has he seen the prince?'

Catherine nodded. 'You must ask him yourself, but I can tell you all is well with my nephew, Prince Charles.'

'Am I still to be married in the spring?' Mary held her breath.

'You are. Henry spent three days as the guest of Margaret of Savoy and has promised her the wedding will proceed before the fifteenth of May.' She smiled. 'I shall make sure you have the finest trousseau any bride could wish for. We must send for the latest Flemish fashions.'

'You will help me prepare for my wedding?'

'Of course – we must choose which ladies should accompany you, and there is the matter of your new household. We shall make this a wedding they will talk about for many years to come.' Catherine smiled at her. 'It will be a welcome relief from dealing with matters of state.'

That night, before she went to sleep, Mary reached out for her little portrait of Charles and examined it by the golden yellow flame of her candle. The pale, serious face of a young boy stared back at her and the weight of uncertainty lifted from her shoulders.

Her whole future had hung in the balance since reading Emperor Maximilian's letter yet now she could dream of a wonderful future, far away from London with its plagues and foul, stinking streets. Catherine was already busy ordering her new dresses, deciding on her ladies-in-waiting and appointing her household.

Mary held the gold ring, set with diamonds and pearls, which Prince Charles sent at the time of their betrothal. It was incised with a quotation from the Gospel of Luke, *Maria optimam partem elegit que non auferetue ab ea.* Her lips moved silently as she translated the familiar inscription – *Mary hath chosen the best part, which shall not be taken away from her.* She'd had little choice yet now she knew her prince chose his words well, and the best part, yet to come, would not be taken away from her.

Henry had taken personal charge of the arrangements for the wedding, including planning for her triumphant arrival in Calais. He planned to make the event a state occasion and an opportunity to display his own wealth and importance to the prince's grandfathers, King Ferdinand and Emperor Maximilian.

As she closed her eyes a fleeting memory returned. As Henry's triumphal procession passed the queen's viewing platform Charles Brandon's eyes connected with hers. For the briefest moment something passed between them. He'd not smiled or raised a hand in greeting but his thoughts were unmistakable.

She'd heard from Catherine that Brandon caused embarrassment at the court of Margaret of Savoy with his flirtatious talk. He'd even removed a ring from her finger and placed it on his own, causing Henry to apologise to Archduchess Margaret's father, Emperor Maximilian.

She was going to be Princess of Castile and one day become an empress, one of the most influential women in the world. It was so typical of Brandon, now he was contracted to his young ward and could no longer have her. The man whose love she wished for looked at her with eyes full of desire.

6

SPRING 1514

Cheering crowds lined both banks of the River Thames on a bright May morning, jostling for a view as the king and queen, dressed in glittering cloth of gold, were rowed in their gilded barge of state, followed by a procession of the entire royal court and the ambassadors of all the allied countries.

Mary's barge was still decorated with her father's brightly painted badge of the red dragon of Wales and white greyhound of Richmond. Accompanied by her ladies, her escort included several richly dressed young knights, although Sir Charles Brandon was not among them. He'd been made Duke of Suffolk as reward for his exploits in France, much to the annoyance of the established peers.

Mary no longer cared. Her hand moved to where she carried a recent letter from her own young Charles. Addressing her as 'my good wife' he'd wished her true happiness and prayed the son of God would provide her with all she desired. This time the signature at the end looked childlike, although Mary guessed the letter was written by the prince's secretary.

She wished he would agree a date for their wedding. First

he'd been ill, then there were the worrying rumours that he thought her too old. More worrying were suggestions that he'd fallen under the spell of a maiden from the Flemish court. Mary refused to believe such talk yet prayed each day for an answer.

Her oarsmen strained against the choppy grey waves of the incoming tide, some grunting with the effort. Mary smiled as the master of her barge let slip a curse as he urged them on, the rhythmic motion of the long oars plunging into the murky water like the legs of some great sea creature.

Their destination was the royal dockyard at Erith, some ten miles downriver from Greenwich Palace, where the newly completed pride of Henry's navy, the *Henry Grace à Dieu*, already nicknamed the *Great Harry*, was to be launched by the king.

They made the slow turn around the final bend in the river and the *Great Harry* came into sight. The colourful royal standard flew from the towering topmast, with smaller pennants of countries represented by visiting ambassadors fluttering in the rigging. Henry intended to send a clear message with his costly investment.

As Mary joined the guests on board the new flagship her senses were assaulted by the sharp tang of freshly tarred ropes and the gaudy colours of new paintwork. Mary clasped her hands in prayer as Archbishop Warham led the long-winded blessing of the ship and all who would sail in her.

She glanced up as the prayers ended and her heart missed a beat. Tall and bearded, standing a little apart from the others, the new Duke of Suffolk, Charles Brandon, watched her like a hawk sighting his prey. He didn't approach, offering her only the briefest nod. Despite herself, Mary raised a white-gloved hand in acknowledgement.

Tearing her eyes from his gaze, she turned to congratulate her brother, expecting to see Henry beaming with pride at his latest achievement. Instead he regarded her with an ominous frown, as if she'd reminded him of something he must do.

The summons followed soon after their return to Greenwich. It was unusual for Henry to see Mary in his privy chamber, so she guessed it might concern her dowry. As she made her way to see him she fought off a dark foreboding. She suspected he'd already used the money provided by her father for some other purpose, such as paying for his fine new ship. If he had, it could mean delaying her marriage even longer.

Ushered into his tapestry-lined chamber, she found Henry seated at a polished oak table between black-garbed Archbishop Foxe and Thomas Wolsey, who'd recently been made Bishop of Lincoln. Wolsey wore a gold crucifix on a chain around his neck, a badge of his new status. As always, both men's faces were impassive, offering no clues to Mary.

She'd never liked the dour Archbishop Foxe, despite his kindness to her father. Now she sensed the same instinctive distrust of Wolsey, who'd wheedled his way not only into Henry's life but also Queen Catherine's and now, it seemed, hers as well. Although both men were unquestionably devout they seemed to be hiding behind the masks of their faith to keep the truth from her.

Henry's face looked grim and she guessed the news he was about to share was not good. His hands were clasped tight in front of him and his welcoming smile looked forced. She curtseyed and was offered the chair at the table opposite her brother.

Henry glanced at Wolsey then fixed his sharp eyes on Mary's. 'Dearest sister, your marriage to Prince Charles of Castile is to be revoked.'

Mary stared back, open-mouthed as she tried to make sense of his words. To Henry's annoyance the day of her wedding had been delayed several times yet the preparations were almost complete. Her seamstresses were putting the final touches to her dresses and gowns. Her gold and silver plate was packed into several oak chests and everyone waited, ready for the voyage to Calais.

She swallowed hard but tried to remain composed as her mind raced with questions. 'Why, Your Grace?' Her voice carried more of a challenge than intended.

Henry's hand formed a fist then relaxed and he leaned forward a little. 'King Ferdinand betrayed us again – and so has Maximilian. They've gone behind our back and agreed a truce with the French.' He made no effort to conceal the bitterness in his voice.

'Forgive me, Your Grace, but I don't understand.' Mary shook her head as her future plans unravelled like a spool of embroidery thread dropped on to a hard-tiled floor.

'It means we cannot allow your marriage to their grandson.' Henry shook his head.

Mary knew she should submit to his will yet struggled to comprehend such a change in her circumstances. 'But the preparations – and you've given your word to Margaret of Savoy?' She heard the note of desperation in her voice. Her trousseau was ready, her dresses made, regardless of cost, the staff of her new household in place. 'What reason would you give for calling off my wedding at such a late hour?'

Henry glanced at Thomas Wolsey, who cleared his throat, as if they'd anticipated the question. 'When you renounce this engagement, Princess Mary, you will state that the prince has failed to ratify the treaty as agreed at the time.' Although he must know she was eighteen years old he spoke as if to a small child.

Mary stared at Wolsey, at a loss for words, sensing his hand behind this turn of events. She recalled Catherine telling her he was a shrewd, ambitious man. 'Am I to expect that you have another suitor planned for me, Your Grace?' She addressed her brother but saw Wolsey's eyes widen for a second before his composure returned.

Henry's chair scraped the tiled floor as he pushed it back. Their meeting was over. 'One step at a time, dearest sister. First you must make the necessary renouncement, then we shall see.' He forced another smile but Mary knew it was achieved with effort.

Catherine's attempted cheerfulness failed to hide the signs she'd been crying. Mary found her alone in her private chambers and immediately guessed the reason. Henry was not beyond blaming Catherine for her father's treachery.

'My wedding is to be called off, Your Grace.'

Catherine nodded. 'Henry informed me this morning.' Catherine's new-found confidence was gone. 'I'm truly sorry for you, Mary. I knew how Henry would react as soon as I heard my father now sides with France.'

'He told me Emperor Maximilian also seeks peace with France—'

'As does, the pope,' Catherine interrupted, 'which means we can no longer see this as a holy war.' She studied Mary for a moment, as if making a decision. 'You must promise to keep what I am to tell you secret, even from those closest to you, before it is time.' It was an order.

'Of course.' Mary knew Catherine referred to her gossiping ladies. 'You have my word.'

'You are to become Queen of France.' She lowered her voice. 'We are in negotiations with King Louis of France. He desires you as his wife.'

Mary's heart raced as she struggled to think through the consequences. 'King Louis is a lecherous, decrepit old man, without morals.'

Catherine gasped. 'Who told you this?'

Surprised by her challenging tone, Mary answered without thinking. 'Jane Popincourt. She once served at the court of King Louis.'

'King Louis can choose whoever he wishes as his wife and he's chosen you. As for Jane, she is fortunate I care for her – and she has no right to talk of morals.' Her tone became conspiratorial. 'You know Jane has become the mistress of our French general, the Duke of Longueville?'

Mary sat back in her chair. Jane was the one person she trusted with her secret thoughts yet clearly she kept her own secrets. 'I had no idea.'

'Let me offer you advice, Mary.' Catherine spoke as if to a child, just as Thomas Wolsey had. 'You will marry the King of France in good grace – and be grateful for what you have.'

Mary studied Catherine's eyes and read the sincerity in them. She knew she had no choice. Henry could marry her to whoever he chose and there was nothing to be gained by making it difficult for him. She would have to forget the young prince and prepare for a new life, as Queen of France.

'In my heart I always knew it could be like this.'

Catherine nodded. 'The good Lord guides our destiny, Mary. Sometimes it is hard to know his purpose.' A note of sadness carried in her voice.

'You've been caught up in this row between Henry and your father?'

Catherine nodded. 'My father is right to seek peace with France – yet Henry sees it as betrayal.' She looked into Mary's eyes and brightened a little. 'I pray your marriage will bring peace to us all.'

Mary lay awake, running through the events of the day in her mind. She picked up the portrait of the prince who would now never be hers. King Louis was three times her age. She believed Jane Popincourt told the truth when she'd said he didn't have long to live. Perhaps when he died she would be able to marry her young Prince of Castile after all.

She resolved to take Catherine's advice and become a good Queen of France, not under duress from Henry but in good faith. She would continue her father's work in keeping the peace between France and England. She had chosen her motto, *La volonté de Dieu me suffit*, and would place her trust in the will of God. The peace of Christendom might depend on it.

A memory drifted into her thoughts as she recalled the handsome face of Charles Brandon, watching her with a deep longing. He was betrothed to marry his young ward, Lady Elizabeth, when she came of age. Perhaps if King Louis died she could marry for love, if she could only find a way for Henry to agree.

The elderly Archbishop of Canterbury, William Warham, stumbled with the words of a Latin address at Mary's wedding ceremony, on a warm August day at Greenwich Palace, earning a scowl from Henry. She'd renounced her compact with Charles. Taking it upon herself to announce that he had treated her poorly, she asked Henry's forgiveness, which he reluctantly granted.

Mary glanced at the Duke of Longueville, standing in for King Louis and dressed, like her, in cloth of gold and purple satin. She could see why Jane was so attracted to him. Suave and handsome, he'd been released from the Tower to become the ambassador of France and joined Henry's privileged inner circle.

The duke returned her glance, a twinkle of amusement in

his eye, no doubt in anticipation of the intimate moment they were soon to share. Catherine's well-intended warning of what was to come simply heightened her nerves and the prospect filled her with dread.

A polite clearing of the throat broke through her reverie. It was time to repeat her vows, in French as rehearsed the previous day. She spoke clearly and with as much sincerity as she could, for this was not the time to suggest she was anything other than a willing bride for so great a king.

The duke took her right hand in his and smiled as he placed a gold ring on her fourth finger, then kissed her. The heavy ring was a little loose and she made a mental note to have a goldsmith improve the size. The kiss surprised her with its tenderness and the sensation of it lingered.

Mary glanced at the watching crowd of guests and saw a satisfied expression on the face of Thomas Wolsey. Behind him, standing well back, was Charles Brandon. Their eyes met for the briefest moment before she turned her attention back to the ceremony.

Queen Catherine, proud to be pregnant for the fourth time, gave Mary a nod of approval. She had been right. A new peace treaty was already declared with France, and the reparation of a million gold crowns more than compensated for the expense of Mary's dowry.

At last the dreaded time came and she was led to the richly decorated bedchamber, followed by the guests who were to act as witnesses. Bishops and foreign ambassadors, knights and nobles, and even a scarlet-capped papal envoy thronged to watch the strange ritual.

She allowed her ladies to undress her, unplaiting and combing her long hair so it flowed over her shoulders, a sign of her purity. Standing in her white satin nightdress, she crossed her hands protectively over her breasts, then summoned all her strength of will and let her arms fall to her side. Mary did her best to stand straight and proud, despite the many eyes upon her.

Her handmaidens led her to the bed where she lay, eyes closed, trying to focus on repeating the words of her chosen prayer, *Deus in adiutorium meum intende Domine ad adiuvandum me festina.* O God, come to my assistance; O Lord, make haste to help me.

She opened her eyes in time to see the handsome Duke of Longueville place his bared leg against hers. The symbolic act of intimate contact drew a raucous cheer from some of Henry's lusty nobles and a blush to Mary's face. There would be no going back now her marriage was consummated before so many witnesses.

She closed her eyes again. No man had ever touched her like that before and she sensed her life would never be the same again. Mary continued her repeated psalm, *Confundantur et revereantur qui quaerunt animam meam.* Let them be confounded and ashamed that seek my soul.

An image drifted into her consciousness. The face of Charles Brandon after she'd said her wedding vows. The special bond shared between them should have meant at least a smile of acknowledgement. Instead all she'd seen in his eyes was a bleak, empty look of deep sadness.

Mary saw no sign of Brandon at the High Mass in the palace chapel, the lavish banquet or the dancing which followed. Even the sight of her brother's boisterous and increasingly drunken dancing failed to amuse her.

Unlike her young prince, Mary's new husband insisted she must travel to France by Michaelmas. He sent envoys with his wedding gift, a magnificent jewel with an impressive pearl pendant, the 'Mirror of Naples', which once belonged to Duke Francis of Brittany. Mary could hardly enclose the large pear-shaped pearl within her hand and Henry promptly had it valued at over sixty thousand crowns.

King Louis also sent a Frenchman, Jean Perréal, to paint a portrait of his new queen, together with letters proclaiming his ardent love and adoration of her. Although insistent on writing in her own hand, Mary's new secretary and French tutor, an ordained Cambridge scholar named John Palsgrave, helped her word a shorter yet equally passionate reply.

Mary frowned when Palsgrave read it to her. 'Do you not think it seems a little insincere?'

Palsgrave grinned. 'If I might quote Julius Caesar, Your Grace, *Fere homines libenter id quod volunt credunt.*'

'King Louis will believe that which he wishes?' She laughed. 'I must thank Queen Catherine for your appointment, Master Palsgrave. I will have need of your guidance.'

'Thank you, Your Grace, it is a great honour to be of service.' He smiled and gave a little bow.

Mary studied her cleric's face, trying to see the man behind the veneer of politeness. King Louis refused Jane Popincourt as one of her ladies and Wolsey replaced her with Lady Jane Guildford, brought out of retirement. Although Mary suspected the fault lay with the charming but married Duke of Longueville, she welcomed Lady Guildford to her household.

She would need someone else to act as her confidante, particularly as a concern lingered in her mind. Thomas Wolsey would have contrived to have an informant close to her and the engaging John Palsgrave would be an ideal candidate.

'Tell me – how did you gain your knowledge of Parisian manners?'

Palsgrave looked up in surprise at her question. 'I travelled to Paris before my ordination to study, Your Grace, and have an enquiring mind.' He smiled at the thought. 'You will find the French court quite different from anything you've experienced here in England.'

After a frenzy of packing, including sixteen new gowns and many fine tapestries, the entire court left Greenwich for the port of Dover. Cheering crowds lined their route from London to watch the spectacle of the grandest procession ever seen and call out their farewells and good wishes. Henry rode at Mary's side until it began to rain and she chose to keep Catherine company in her covered litter, drawn by six grey palfreys.

Behind them followed six hundred lords and knights of the realm and countless wagons, laden with Mary's ladies, luggage and provisions for the voyage. At the rear came a crowd of servants and retainers, opportunistic merchants and barefoot young boys, some struggling to keep up.

Heavy rain and blustery sea breezes forced them to seek refuge in Dover Castle when they finally arrived. Henry declared the storm too fierce for their flotilla to sail, so there was nothing to do but wait. Mary passed the long hours with Catherine, trying to learn what she could of the mysteries and dangers of childbirth.

'King Louis needs an heir, Mary, and soon.' The edge to Catherine's voice revealed what she might have thought of it. 'He has two daughters, yet unless he can produce a son, peace between our countries will again be put at risk by his son-in-law, Duke Francis.'

'That's why he is so keen for me to arrive in France?'

Catherine smiled. 'One of the reasons, Mary,' she caressed her swollen midriff as she answered, 'just as why I pray to provide your brother a son.'

'You think it might be a boy this time?'

'If it pleases God. I am certain a strong and healthy boy would restore Henry's faith in me.'

Mary understood. 'Henry loves you dearly, Catherine. You cannot be blamed for your father's actions.'

'How I wish that were true.' Catherine shook her head. 'Wolsey has been intercepting my letters to my father for some time. He knows too much.'

'Have faith, Catherine.' She smiled to lighten the mood. 'You can pray for this weather to improve – and I shall pray you have the son you long for.'

Henry's patience failed him after nearly three weeks in the confines of the castle, waiting for the storms to pass. By the start of October, he decided the fleet should sail, despite ominous grey skies. Mary said her farewells to Catherine and walked to the quayside with him at dawn's first light to catch the early tide.

Mary's grand ship strained against its mooring ropes as if eager to leave. Young sailors climbed recklessly high on the yardarms, readying the heavy canvas sails. She looked up and saw Henry's standard fluttering at the topmast. A dozen other ships waited at anchor, ready to sail as her escort. Henry had planned to accompany her aboard the *Great Harry* but there was no longer time. She must say her farewells to him.

'Godspeed, dearest sister.' Henry placed his hand on her shoulder. 'You will be the greatest queen France has ever seen – but you will not forget your brother?'

Mary stared into his unfathomable eyes. 'You will be in my thoughts and prayers always.' She made a judgement. 'I have only one request, if I may?'

Henry smiled, clearly in good spirits to see the fleet readying to sail after such a long wait. 'Name it, Mary.' He sounded curious.

'I ask you to consent to my choice of husband, if it is God's wish that I outlive King Louis?' She held her breath and watched for his reaction.

Henry hesitated for a moment, then nodded. 'Dear sister, you shall have my blessing.'

She embraced him for the first time she could remember, aware that it might also be the last, and placed a small kiss on his bearded cheek. 'Thank you, Henry.'

Mary turned for one last look up at the castle where Catherine waited with the next King of England. She said a silent prayer for them both before allowing Sir Thomas Howard, Earl of Surrey, to escort her aboard her ship. Her new life was beginning at last and a plan was already forming in her mind. One day she intended to hold her brother to his promise.

7

AUTUMN 1514

Mary leaned against the wooden rail, refreshed by the cool air of a stiffening sea breeze. The rail juddered under her hand as a wave slapped the side of the hull and she tasted bitter salt as the icy spray splashed her face. The ship tilted under her feet and she took a firmer grip on the rail to steady herself.

Thick ropes creaked in protest in the rigging high over her head as the wind veered, causing sails to flap like rolls of thunder. Sailors shouted to each other, hauling on sheets to trim the troublesome canvas and keep them headed for France.

Fourteen ships of her fleet flanked her in formation like flocks of migrating geese she'd seen pass over Richmond. Some flew the bright-blue flag with gold fleur-de-lis, her escort of French galleons. One of Henry's older ships, the *Great Elizabeth*, was wrecked on its way to join the others, with the loss of half the crew.

She studied the swirling grey-green waves with their foaming white crests and shivered at the thought. She'd never learned to swim but could imagine what it must be like to drown in the freezing sea. Although unused to sailing any distance, she sensed concern in the face of the captain when she asked about the risk of the storm returning.

'Rest assured, Your Grace, this ship has crossed the Channel many times in far worse seas.' The grey-bearded captain's eyes avoided hers. He pulled at his cap, as if uncertain how to address her and looked keen to return to his work.

Mary returned to the sanctuary of her small cabin and lay back on the narrow pallet bed, staring up at the creaking wooden ceiling. She no longer felt in control of her destiny, yet God had chosen this path for her and she must follow it in good faith. She'd had plenty of time to think about her new life as the Queen of France but her mind filled with questions and doubts.

It would have been easier for her with the young Prince of Castile. Instead, the shadowy figure of King Louis loomed large in her future. Mary found herself recalling Jane Popincourt's stories of him. She said he'd blamed his wives for failing to give him a son and openly cavorted with mistresses.

Crippled with gout and suffering from an incurable skin disease, it wasn't surprising this made him temperamental. Nevertheless, he'd outwitted King Ferdinand, Emperor Maximilian and even Henry, to become the most powerful Christian king.

Mary recalled Catherine's well-intended advice, yet her position seemed precarious, depending on providing Henry with an heir. She wished she'd been older when her own mother was alive, as her father often said she'd been the most perfect queen any king could wish for.

An idea occurred to her and she sent her servant to summon Lady Jane Guildford. With the informal title of Mother of Maids, Lady Guildford, often referred to as Mother Guildford, had known Mary all her life and served as lady-in-waiting to both her grandmothers. She would know how to deal with King Louis.

Lady Guildford appeared to be suffering with the movement of the ship. 'Please accept my apologies, Your Grace. I am not much of a sailor.' Her face looked deathly pale and she gripped the door frame as if expecting to lose her footing at any moment.

Mary offered her the only chair in her small cabin while she sat on the pallet bed. 'I pray the weather will improve, Mother Guildford, although there's little sign of it.'

Lady Guildford studied her face. 'You look pale, my lady. Is it seasickness – or is there some other reason you wish to see me?' Her tone softened, returning to the way she'd spoken when Mary was a girl.

Mary took a deep breath. 'I worry about becoming Queen of France. John Palsgrave has been helping me understand the ways of the French court but as the time draws closer...' She twisted the loose gold wedding ring on her finger as she struggled with the words. 'I cannot rest with worry about my first meeting with King Louis.' She spoke quickly, her voice echoing in the small cabin. 'I'm afraid I don't know what I shall do if my new husband... mistreats me.'

Lady Guildford held up a gloved hand. 'I understand, Your Grace. It is natural for a bride to be anxious about a husband she has never met.' She smiled. 'I shall act as your chaperone and help ensure King Louis behaves with proper decorum.'

Mary smiled with relief. 'It will only be until I become used to his ways.'

Lady Guildford nodded. 'I have a feeling this will prove an education to us all, Your Grace.'

The storm worsened as the day wore on. Lightning flashed across the ashen sky, followed soon after by the crack and boom of thunder. Blustery winds tossed and pitched the ship in the rolling seas. Mary and all her ladies succumbed to seasickness and took to their beds, while the crew fought to keep them on course.

Mary shivered in fear for her life, the shipwreck of the *Great Elizabeth* fresh in her mind. She tried to pray for the storm to ease before they reached the rocky coast of France. Curling up on her narrow bunk, she listened to the waves crashing over the deck and the incessant drumming of rain on the roof of her cabin.

After what seemed an eternity, there was a knock at her door and her chamberer, Mistress Anne Jerningham, entered with a cup of warmed mead. Like all of them, Mistress Anne looked pale and dark-eyed after less than a day at sea. Water stained the hem of her silk dress and she'd removed her fashionable French cowl, leaving a linen coif covering her hair.

Weakened by seasickness, Mary knew she must drink to keep up her strength. 'What news is there of our progress, Anne?'

'We are not far from France, but...'

'What is it? Are we blown off course?'

'I'm afraid I don't know, Your Grace. I heard the fleet is scattered by the storm, my lady. I think we are alone.'

A deep grinding sound reverberated through the ship, which shuddered like a dying beast. Mary listened for shouts of alarm but heard only a strange stillness. With a jolt she realised the tiresome rocking motion of the ship had stopped. They had run aground.

Pulling her cape around her she joined the others on the deck. The rain had eased a little but a bitter wind took her breath away. Gulls swooped and shrieked overhead and a little way off were the twinkling lights of a harbour. They had reached France yet an expanse of dark water still lay between them and safety.

A tall, well-built man wearing a black leather riding cape over his silken doublet approached her and bowed. 'Sir Christopher Garnish, Your Grace.'

'Tell me, Sir Christopher, is that Boulogne?' Mary looked out towards the seaweed-covered walls of the harbour.

Sir Christopher grinned. 'It is, my lady. We were beaten by the tide. The captain decided to put us aground, rather than risk the rocks.' He glanced to where sailors were lowering a longboat. 'We shall need you to take the boat ashore, my lady, if I might assist you?'

Choppy waves slapped at the side of the ship and cold rain made Mary wish for the shelter of her cabin. Torn between the comparative safety of the grounded ship and the short but risky trip by boat, she studied his face for a moment. He reminded her of Charles Brandon, who'd not even come to see her off from Dover.

Mary made a decision. 'I shall place my trust in the Lord – and your kind offer of help, Sir Christopher.'

He led her to where the longboat waited, with four sailors ready at the oars. Worried faces lined the rail as they pushed off. Each new wave began to swamp them, making the bow of the longboat rise high in the air before plunging into the trough of the next.

'There are breakers ahead!' Sir Christopher shouted. 'Pull hard men, we must not allow these waves to take us broadside!'

A great wave broke over the boat, soaking Mary to the skin and making her gasp with the shock of cold water. She glanced back at the ship and knew there was no going back. She shut her eyes and said a silent prayer.

As they neared the harbour Sir Christopher leapt into the sea and stood up to his waist, doing his best to steady the boat through the pounding surf. The oarsmen heaved one more time, then he lifted Mary in the air as if she weighed nothing and carried her in his arms, wading to the shore. He didn't set her down until they were safe on dry land.

He grinned as he looked down at their soaked clothing and the seawater running from his boots. 'Welcome to France, my lady!'

'Thank you, Sir Christopher.' Mary shivered with cold as she looked up at the lights and saw the delegation of curious French nobles already gathering to welcome her. 'This is not the grand arrival I'd planned, but I've never been so grateful to feel solid ground under my feet.'

It took a week for Mary's entourage to prepare for the fifty-mile journey south to Abbeville, where King Louis waited. She was saddened to learn that one of Henry's largest ships, the *Lubeck*, had been wrecked with the loss of several hundred souls. Four more of her fleet made it to Boulogne and the rest reached Calais and Flanders, from where they were able to join her.

At last, on the first day of sunshine since they arrived, their procession set out with Mary riding a fine white palfrey. Lady Guildford, now fully recovered from the trials of the voyage, rode at her side, and her entire household followed, with wagons laden with her possessions and supplies.

At Etaples they were greeted by dukes and the Governor of Picardy on behalf of the king. Their progress was delayed by a series of long-winded pageants. Mary appreciated the considerable efforts made by the local people to welcome her, the sister of a king who had so recently been their enemy. She was also conscious of the need not to keep King Louis waiting longer than necessary.

The next day as they reached the wooded outskirts of Anders forest a number of mounted men approached them.

Their leader rode directly towards Mary. Young and athletic, with a flamboyant ostrich plume in his hat, he dressed in black-and-silver silks and carried a gold-handled sword, low slung on his belt. Mary's yeomen of the guard were unsure of his intentions and formed a barrier across the road, weapons at the ready.

'I am Duke Francis, son-in-law of the king,' he called out in French and studied her with sharp eyes, as if making a judgement. 'King Louis grows impatient for your arrival, my lady.'

Mary recalled Catherine's concern that the duke, as heir presumptive, could threaten the delicate peace. 'Good day to you, Duke Francis,' Mary called back in her best French and glanced across at Lady Guildford, who nodded to reassure her. 'I am pleased to meet you.'

The duke rode closer and stared at the line of riders and wagons trailing far into the distance behind her. 'The king rides with a hunting party, so it is possible he might encounter you, by chance, of course.' He gave her a wry look. 'I must return to Abbeville to report your progress, my lady.' He gave a curt bow from the saddle. 'I look forward to becoming better acquainted.'

There was something about the glance he gave her that alerted Mary's instinctive defences. Unless Louis had a son, Francis would one day become King of France. It struck her as odd he should trouble to ride out in person, although she suspected there would be many things the French did that would surprise her.

Ten miles from Abbeville another, much larger, group of riders appeared in the distance. This time, outriders carried the flag of France and, as they approached, Lady Guildford turned to Mary.

'I suspect this to be the king himself. If I am not mistaken, your moment has come, my lady.'

'Surely he should wait for us to make our entry into Abbeville?'

'That is how we would do it in England, but it seems everything is done differently here.'

'What should I say? How should I greet him, Lady Guildford?'

'My advice is to let him do the talking.' She smiled. 'I suspect the king's impatience has got the better of him.'

They watched as the riders came closer. Mary spotted a figure riding a powerful warhorse, caparisoned with cloth of gold and black silk, flanked by French knights in silver armour with flowing blue capes. Behind him followed several hundred nobles dressed in colourful robes. This was not like any hunting party she'd ever seen in England.

Sir Thomas Howard rode to her side. 'I recognise King Louis, Your Grace.' He peered ahead. 'Would you wish me to announce you?'

Mary nodded. 'If you will, Sir Thomas.' Her dry throat muted her words and she glanced again at Lady Guildford for reassurance. 'Please convey apologies for our delay.'

They watched as Sir Thomas rode ahead and saw him nodding as he addressed the king. Henry chose the earl as his representative for good reason. As well as his impeccable French, he was an experienced commander and proving to be a skilled negotiator and diplomat.

Mary steadied her horse as the king approached, not sure if she should remain in the saddle or dismount. At last, after all the waiting, she would meet her new husband. She took a deep breath and attempted a smile, then on an impulse raised her hand to her mouth and blew him a kiss, as she'd done to greet her father so many years ago.

The king seemed confused for a moment, then grinned and

raised his hand to blow her a kiss in return, before riding up to her and bowing his head. 'We welcome you to France, my queen.' He spoke in French, with a cultured accent, and his blue eyes fixed her with an intense, piercing stare.

As she feared, Mary found herself unable to recall her rehearsed words of greeting. King Louis had a deeply lined face and looked older than she'd imagined. Although not as pockmarked as she'd heard, she found herself wondering why he chose to remain clean-shaven when a beard would hide the disfiguring scars.

A large fly buzzed noisily around her horse's head, breaking the silence. She swallowed hard and returned his bow.

'My husband. I have waited so long for this moment.' It was true.

Louis smiled, revealing a few blackened teeth and reminding Mary of her father. 'You are more beautiful than I hoped, my lady. I give thanks to God for your safe arrival.' He urged his horse closer as he spoke, then leaned across and embraced her, placing a kiss on her lips.

'I feared for your safety in the storm. There were reports of shipwrecks.' He remained close as he spoke, his sharp eyes appraising her as if she were some precious jewel offered for sale.

Mary struggled to compose herself. 'Two of our ships were lost, Your Grace.'

Louis nodded. 'We trusted in the Lord to deliver you to us – and now we must be married in the sight of God.' He raised a hand and beckoned one of his followers.

Mary was surprised to see Duke Francis ride forward. He seemed less arrogant in the presence of the king and acted more like his servant than the heir presumptive. Again, the duke bowed his head to her but this time there was a twinkle in his eye as he spoke in accented English.

'King Louis has given me the great honour of escorting you to Abbeville, my lady.'

Mary returned his smile. Despite Catherine's warning, she saw Duke Francis as a useful ally in this strange land. 'Thank you, my lord duke,' she replied in English. 'I shall be glad of your company.'

King Louis bowed once more and returned to his hunting party, which rode off as quickly as they'd arrived. Mary turned to Lady Guildford and saw her nod of approval. The first test had been passed. Now she must learn to become a queen.

～

Sir Thomas Howard brought Mary's entourage to a halt a short way from the gates of Abbeville. 'Curse this rain, will it never stop?'

Mary knew she wasn't intended to hear but looked up to the brooding skies. There was no break in the rainclouds and she shivered in a chill breeze. Jane Popincourt often told her how she missed the French sunshine but there was little enough sign of it now.

Henry's plan to provide the French with an impressive show of wealth would be undermined by the rain, which ruined silk dresses and meant misery to those caught without shelter. Mary had intended to ride in her litter, decorated with gold lilies and Tudor roses. Instead, a canopy of cloth of gold was raised on long poles and held high over her head.

They entered Abbeville to a noisy fanfare of her eight trumpeters and the discordant clanging of church bells. Musicians competed with pipes and lutes, drums and songs, creating an atmosphere of celebration, despite the rain.

The procession was led by the town mayor and local dignitaries, followed by the escort of the king's guard. Behind them marched the captain of the town with two hundred scarlet-clad

French soldiers carrying muskets and bows, then Mary's squires and heralds in green-and-white Tudor livery.

Mary rode her white palfrey, caparisoned with cloth of gold, under her high canopy, supported by four stalwart local men. Duke Francis rode at her side and they were followed by thirty of her ladies-in-waiting, riding in pairs.

Then came the ambassadors, knights of the realm and noble lords, all wearing gleaming chains of gold. The endless line of horse-drawn wagons was followed by the servants of Mary's household. Two hundred liveried archers, each carrying a longbow and quiver of arrows, marched in pairs at the rear of the procession. Henry would have his show of strength after all.

Mary turned to Duke Francis. 'The people of the town have turned out in great numbers.'

The duke grinned and replied in English. 'They've been preparing for weeks, my lady. It will take more than a rain shower to stop them having sight of their beautiful new queen.'

Mary carried a white sceptre in her left hand and raised her right, with the loose gold ring on her fourth finger, in acknowledgement to the crowd. Her reward was a rousing cheer, which echoed through the streets. She felt a million miles away from Westminster, the ghosts of Richmond or the scheming of men such as Wolsey.

Her only wish was that the charming, handsome young man now riding at her side was her king, and not the strange man, three times her age, who'd surprised her with his stolen kiss.

8

OCTOBER 1514

Bright sunlight shone through unshuttered windows and the tuneful dawn chorus of songbirds greeted Mary as she woke. She lay back in her sumptuous feather bed and stared at her unfamiliar surroundings – the grand apartments of the King of France.

Exhausted from her long journey, she'd done her best to remain attentive at the state banquet hosted by Louis. It seemed he wished to impress, with too many courses and overlong speeches which Mary struggled to follow. Then he surprised her by apologising for retiring early and asking Duke Francis to escort her at the evening entertainments.

The ball went on long into the night, an extravagance of music and dancing, fine wine and so many people whose names she would never remember. She smiled to herself at how Duke Francis flattered her with compliments and danced as if they were lovers.

Not yet sixteen, Princess Claude, the duke's wife seemed oblivious to her husband's flirtations. Shorter than Mary and a little overweight, the king's eldest daughter proved understanding and helped her with introductions, explaining and translating for her when she struggled to understand.

Countess Louise of Savoy, the formidable mother of Duke Francis, could not be more different. Mary sensed she could be a threat as soon as their eyes met. The countess spoke in sophisticated French which put Mary at a disadvantage. There was an edge to her words as she wished Mary a long and happy marriage, as if she had good reason to doubt it.

'I'm afraid you must be dressed now, my lady.' Her cheerful young maid of honour, Anne Boleyn, entered carrying Mary's voluminous wedding gown. A fluent French speaker, thirteen-year-old Anne had been sent from the court of Margaret, Duchess of Savoy.

'Have I overslept?' Mary rubbed her eyes.

Anne placed the gown on the bed and smoothed it out to prevent creases. 'We have a little time yet, my lady, although I wonder why your service has been set so early. I've never before heard of a wedding taking place at nine in the morning.'

Mary guessed the reason might be her husband's eagerness but decided to keep it to herself. 'I heard quite a commotion in the night.'

Anne took her bridal chemise and petticoats and satin sleeves from an oak chest. 'There was a fire in the town, my lady.'

Mary sat up in bed. 'Was anyone killed? Were we in danger?'

Anne shook her head. 'Not that I know of, my lady. The fire was on the other side of the Somme, in the poor quarter.' She lowered her voice. 'A maid in the kitchens said half of Abbeville is burned to the ground. It's a miracle the people escaped.'

'We must thank the Lord we were all spared, Anne, although I worry they'll see it as a bad omen.' Mary looked across at her. 'Do you think the French are as superstitious as the English?'

'Let us hope they are not, my lady,' she held up the fine linen chemise while Mary slipped it over her head, 'although I think we are more the same than most people would imagine.'

She helped Mary put on a pair of long white stockings and silk slippers embroidered with gold thread, then the white satin petticoats and kirtle, before dressing her in the heavy gown of gold brocade trimmed with ermine. Lacing it at the forebody with a spiral of gold ribbon, Anne tied the satin sleeves into place and stood back to admire the results of her work.

'It is truly a gown fit for a queen.' She smiled as she unplaited Mary's long hair and began to comb it over her shoulders. 'I feared this day would be ruined by more rain – thank the Lord I was mistaken!'

Mary agreed. 'My prayers have been answered, in that regard at least.'

Woken in the night by the clanging of distant church bells she'd lain awake wondering what had become of Charles Brandon. She'd hoped he would somehow confirm his feelings for her, yet she'd not seen or heard from him since her betrothal at Greenwich.

'My lady?' Anne interrupted her thoughts. 'Are you ready for your jewels now?'

Mary nodded and watched as Anne left the room to return with Lady Guildford and Sir Thomas Howard, followed by a burly soldier carrying her strongbox. Lady Guildford wore her best gown, with an English hood. Sir Thomas wore a doublet of black velvet with his heavy gold chain of office as the king's representative. The badge of the Order of the Garter shone on his shoulder and a gold-handled sword hung from his belt.

Sir Thomas stood for a moment, taking in Mary's long red-gold hair and golden gown, then bowed. 'Good morning, Your Grace.'

Lady Guildford smiled. 'You look beautiful, Your Grace. I know your father would have been so proud of you.'

Mary nodded. 'This was not his plan – but he would have approved anything which preserves the peace.' She regretted the note of sadness in her voice but knew she was among friends who would understand.

Sir Thomas took a key and unlocked the strongbox to reveal Mary's glittering jewels. He handed her gold coronet, sparkling with precious diamonds, to Lady Guildford, who placed it with great care on Mary's head. Then she fastened a gold necklace studded with diamonds and rubies around Mary's neck.

'Your escort is waiting, Your Grace. It is time.'

Mary took a deep breath to compose herself as Sir Thomas opened the door and led them out into the courtyard, where her knights and ladies, heralds and musicians waited for the grand procession the short distance to the Church of Notre-Dame.

King Louis grinned as he greeted Mary. He made a great fuss of fastening a necklace with a large pointed diamond and the biggest ruby Mary had ever seen around her neck before Cardinal de Prie, Bishop of Bayeux, could begin the formal ceremony of the Nuptial Mass.

The words seemed meaningless to Mary, still tired from the exhaustions of the previous day, yet she was ready for her cue to repeat her much-practised vows. The bishop gave them his blessing and King Louis took the opportunity to seal their marriage with a lingering kiss.

The banquet lasted until the early evening, when at last Louis loudly announced his intention to consummate his marriage. Mary blushed when she understood his public declaration, unsure if it was another French tradition or simply the king's way.

She retired to her chambers with her ladies, led by Princess Claude, who helped her remove her jewels and change into her new nightdress. They combed her long hair until it shone in the light of a dozen tall candles, and perfumed the linen bedclothes with lavender. Laughing, they scattered symbolic red and white rose petals before withdrawing to leave Mary alone.

Mary stood at the side of her bed, unsure if she should lie down or wait for Louis. A memory flashed into her mind, of praying while the charming Duke of Longueville placed his bared leg against hers. That seemed long ago now, and Greenwich so far away.

She wished she could return to the familiar peace of Richmond Palace. Tears formed in her eyes at the overwhelming sense of loss and longing for her previous life, so simple and free of care. Picking up a handful of red and white rose petals, Mary let them fall through her fingers. She doubted Henry would concern himself to maintain her mother's rose gardens.

The door opened and Louis stood looking at her for a moment. 'My beautiful queen.' He crossed the room and kissed her with great tenderness on the cheek, then pulled back the covers and gestured for her to lie down. 'I've told them we are not to be disturbed – even if the rest of Abbeville burns to the ground!' He chuckled at his own joke as he removed his robe and joined her in the bed.

Mary had reflected on this moment many times on the long journey from Dover. In the absence of her mother, Jane Popincourt once explained what to expect. She'd laughed at the sight of Mary's wide-eyed and open-mouthed reaction.

'Even *you* can't be that innocent – surely you must know? Have you not seen horses in the fields?'

'I have wondered,' Mary admitted, 'although I somehow imagined it would be different.'

Jane studied her face for a moment, then nodded. 'You are right.' She reached out and took Mary's hand in hers. 'You must not let any man treat you as if you are nothing more than a brood mare. You are a Tudor, the daughter of one great king and sister to another.'

'What do I do?' Mary thought she knew but needed to hear it from Jane.

Jane Popincourt smiled knowingly. 'The secret is to show him how wonderful he is. No man can resist – and he will treat you well as your reward.'

Mary pressed Jane for details and they had laughed together at how easily a woman could rule any man, yet now it seemed quite different. Mary stiffened as Louis climbed on top of her, first kissing her on the mouth, then on her breasts. She knew she must surrender to her husband's will.

With a grunt he rolled back off her and lay at her side in silence. Alarmed, Mary saw a tear glint in the corner of his eye in the candlelight. He stared up at the high ceiling in silence.

'I'm sorry.' Her voice was a nervous whisper. 'I want to be a good wife for you, Louis.' She wiped the tear from his cheek. 'I will do my best to give you a son, the next King of France.'

Louis reached out and took Mary's slender fingers in his mottled hand. 'You've heard stories about my past?' He nodded knowingly when she hesitated to answer. 'Permit me to tell you something of the truth.' He took a deep breath, as if what he was about to tell her would open old wounds.

'I was perhaps even handsome, when I was fourteen years old and my bride half that when they insisted on a travesty of a marriage. My first wife, my cousin Jeanne, was so deformed with disease the people could not look upon her.'

He closed his eyes for a moment, then opened them again and turned to Mary. 'When her feeble brother became king I foolishly challenged him.' He paused for a moment, lost in his memories. 'I ended up in a foul, rat-infested dungeon, where I lost my mind.'

Mary pulled him closer and he lay his head on her breast, like a child. His words carried such torment she was overcome with compassion for the real man behind the facade of kingship.

'Why did they make you marry her?' She spoke softly.

'For the same reasons they made you marry me. To safeguard their own power – and take revenge on others.' He cursed. 'They knew poor Jeanne could never conceive a child, so it was all a cruel trick.'

Mary was tempted to deny her brother's motives but knew Louis spoke the truth. She could imagine how his treatment would have turned him from an ambitious young man into a suspicious king, more than a match for her brother Henry, King Ferdinand or Emperor Maximilian.

'How long did they keep you in that prison?' She caressed his hair with her free hand.

'Three years, perhaps four. My time there left its mark on me.' He shuddered at the memory. 'When I became king the first thing I did was divorce my poor wife.'

'And then you married your cousin's widow, Queen Anne of Brittany?' She felt Louis tense at the mention of Anne's name.

'I needed her. She was loved by the people – and in the end by me too.'

Mary struggled to reconcile his story with the scandalous tales Jane Popincourt regaled her with. Then it began to make sense. She could understand why he would seek solace with mistresses.

Louis sounded tired now. 'She gave me two daughters, yet no son. When she died...' His voice tailed off and he lay in her arms in silence.

Mary realised from his slow and steady breathing that her husband had fallen asleep. She lay awake for hours, despite her tiredness, thinking about what he'd told her, and knew what she must do to protect his reputation.

Lady Guildford brought troubling news to Mary the day after her wedding. 'We are all ordered to return to England, Your Grace.'

'By whose orders?' She heard the amazement in her voice.

'King Louis requires us to be on the next available ship.'

'He said nothing of this to me.'

Mary struggled to think how she'd offended Louis. She'd remained silent when she heard how he'd bragged of his prowess on his wedding night. She'd begun to understand his quirky ways and even to see the good qualities of the man behind the rugged face.

'What reason was given?'

'The king does not need to give a reason, Your Grace.'

'Surely I deserve an explanation before I allow all my trusted companions to abandon me?'

'I would advise against it, Your Grace. I understand he is concerned to see so many English nobles at his court.'

'The knights and lords are due to depart within the week. I could ask him to allow me my ladies?'

Lady Guildford shook her head. 'I think you no longer need my services as chaperone.' There was an edge to her voice.

Mary sat back in her chair. 'You are the one person I can confide in, Mother Guildford. I shall write to Henry that you at least are allowed to remain – and Wolsey has influence with Louis, perhaps...'

'This must be handled with care, Your Grace. There will be consequences if King Henry regards it as an insult.'

Louis permitted Mary to retain six ladies of her bedchamber. These included her chamberer, Mistress Anne Jerningham, and young Anne Boleyn. It was some consolation to Mary that Louis appointed his daughter, Princess Claude, as her companion. The duke's mother, Countess Louise, also imposed herself on Mary and wasted no opportunity to promote the interests of her son.

Mary was allowed to keep her secretary, John Palsgrave, as well as a skilled physician and scholar named James Denton, who advised her he'd observed the king suffered with a recurrence of gout. 'The disease is progressive and will make the king's joints feel tender, Your Grace, to the point of being unable to bear anything touching him.'

'Are you certain there is no cure, Master Denton?'

'His case is too severe to be cured by a tea of meadowsweet, my lady. You will recall your father suffered with the affliction, which hastened his demise at the same age King Louis is now?'

Mary understood. Her physician was suggesting she should prepare herself. When she departed from Dover, she'd known her new husband would not have long to live, yet now she knew it was her duty to care for him, as she had for her father.

As soon as he seemed well enough they began the journey to Paris for Mary's coronation. After some sixty miles they stopped for Louis to rest at the bishop's palace in Beauvais. Mary was sitting at his bedside when Louis woke.

'Is it day or night, my queen?' He looked around the room and seemed pleased to note they were alone.

'It's late afternoon, Louis. Would you wish me to send for your servants? You will feel better if you eat.'

Louis held up a frail hand to silence her. 'Not yet. I wish to spend a little time with you before we leave for Paris.' He managed a smile. 'Did you know that an uncrowned queen is not allowed into the city?'

Mary nodded. 'My secretary is well advised of your customs, and Princess Claude said by tradition I am to be crowned at the abbey church, on the outskirts of the city.'

A flicker of a smile crossed his tired face. 'Listen to Claude, she is wise beyond her years, although she deserved a better husband than my cousin Francis.' He winced with pain then continued. 'Watch for his mother. I would have her burned as a witch!'

He coughed, reminding Mary of her ailing father, then fixed her with a questioning stare. 'Did you wonder how I managed to win you from under the noses of those scheming scoundrels Ferdinand and Maximilian?' He raised an eyebrow at her look of surprise. 'You didn't know both grandfathers of your young prince tried to secure you as a wife?'

'No, I did not.' She wondered how innocent she could be of such a thing and why no one thought to mention it while she was in England.

'No matter,' he grinned, 'it's too late for them both now. I was going to tell you.' He grimaced in pain again then composed himself. 'I promised Wolsey I would use my influence to secure him a cardinal's hat.'

Mary nodded. 'I thought Wolsey had a hand in this.'

'You must tell no one, Mary. Thomas Wolsey would make a dangerous enemy if crossed.'

A knock sounded at the door before she could answer and a servant spoke rapidly in formal French. Mary understood only that a visitor of some importance had arrived. She was surprised to see Louis sit up in his bed and ask the servant to arrange his pillows.

'You need rest, Louis.' Mary frowned. 'Are you sure you feel well enough to receive a visitor, however important?'

He gave her a wry look. 'This visitor is the envoy of your own brother, the King of England. I sent for him as soon as I was informed of his arrival in France.' Louis forced a smile. 'Would you now have me send him away?'

'No, you must see him now.'

Mary sat back in her chair and wondered what her brother was up to as the servant left, to return shortly afterwards followed by a tall man, made to look even larger by the rich furs he wore against the wintry chill. She gasped as she looked into the blue-grey eyes of the last person she expected to see.

'Sir Charles Brandon, Duke of Suffolk, Your Grace. It is an honour to meet you,' he addressed Louis in passable French, bowed deeply then turned to Mary, 'and to see you again, my lady.'

9

NOVEMBER 1514

It proved easier than Mary expected to arrange to be alone with Charles Brandon. The bishop's palace in Beauvais had extensive grounds, so she asked her secretary, John Palsgrave, to let him know when she would be taking her walk. Although her ladies were in attendance, they kept a discreet distance when Brandon contrived his chance meeting.

He stood in silence for a moment, as if trying to read her intention, then smiled. 'You've become a beautiful woman, Mary. The air in France must suit you.'

Mary blushed at his informality. His compliments gave her hope despite the mischievous twinkle in his eye. He'd changed in some subtle way. He had new authority and dressed like an ambassador, in rich furs with a heavy gold chain. His hair looked a little longer and his dark beard showed the first traces of grey.

'It's good to see a friend from England.' She smiled. 'I've missed you, Charles.' Her words carried a deeper significance she hoped he'd understand.

'You've been always in my thoughts.' He glanced back at

her ladies-in-waiting and lowered his voice. 'I thought it best to keep my distance.'

Mary understood. 'What brings you here now?' She studied his face. 'Not only the prospect of taking part in my coronation joust?'

'King Louis seems pleased enough I'm here – and someone has to represent England.'

'What was your true reason, Charles?' She moved closer and her white-gloved hand touched his arm.

'Henry wishes me to secure a new treaty with the French.' He spoke in a low voice. 'We had reports of the king's illness. He needed to know you are being treated well.'

'I was saddened when so many members of my household were sent away but Louis shows me great kindness. As for the treaty, do we not already have one?'

Brandon hesitated to reply. 'Henry is concerned about what will happen if King Louis dies.' His voice became serious. 'I haven't come here alone. We stand ready to return you to England if the worst happens.'

With a jolt Mary realised how foolish she'd been. He'd not come to declare his love for her but as her brother's spy. She remembered John Palsgrave's words, that in most cases men believe what they wish. It didn't apply only to men. She'd been more than ready to believe what she wished to hear.

Escorted by Duke Francis, Mary noted the absence of cheering crowds as she made her way to the old abbey chapel. The clanging bells had a mournful note and she shivered in the cold as ominous slate-grey clouds gathered overhead.

Once inside she was reassured to see a full congregation, although the contrast with her recollection of Henry and Catherine's coronation could not have been more marked. While they had more bishops than she could count, she had only the same glum-faced Bishop de Prie of Bayeux, who'd officiated at her wedding in Abbeville.

Every noble worthy of note witnessed Henry and Catherine's coronation, while she recognised few who'd troubled to make the long journey. She looked around for Brandon and frowned that he'd chosen not to attend, although she knew he was in Paris for the joust. Then she spotted him talking to Sir Thomas Grey, Marquess of Dorset, who'd returned with him on the pretext of also taking part in the jousting. He didn't look in her direction.

Charles Brandon had every chance to show his hand at Beauvais yet gave no sign of feelings for her. She glanced at the handsome Duke Francis at her side, magnificently dressed in glittering cloth of gold with a silver sword at his belt. Although married to Princess Claude, he'd made his desire for her evident. If she failed to provide Louis a son the duke would be the next King of France.

Her coronation ceremony, conducted in French and Latin, seemed interminable and the jewelled gold crown felt heavy on her head. Duke Francis gallantly supported it while the bishop anointed her and said the long Mass before giving her his blessing.

At last she was Queen of France, one of the most powerful women in the world. The income from her dower lands also made her one of the wealthiest. She owned more jewels than any woman could wish for – yet the celebrations had a hollow feel.

Rumours of the king's failing health spread through Paris, casting an ominous shadow over her coronation. She could imagine the conversations behind her back, people asking if there was any point in her being crowned. Despite her warm welcome, Mary knew the French had good reason to resent an English queen.

Duke Francis made no secret of the fact he saw the celebratory jousting as an opportunity to make his name. He would show the people he was young and athletic, virile and successful, everything Louis failed to be. At the coronation banquet he'd once again stood in for the king and gave an eloquent speech which made no mention of his cousin Louis.

A rousing cheer and fanfares of trumpets greeted his parade down the Parc des Tournelles. Marching men carrying the banners of the noble houses of France led the procession and the duke rode at the head of the French knights on their magnificent warhorses. Behind him rode the duke's brother-in-law, Charles, Duke of Alençon and Governor of Normandy.

The spectacle of the tournament seemed to have attracted most of the people of Paris, as well as many of the outlying districts. Mary had never seen so many gathered in one place and only now understood that Paris was more than five times the size of London.

The duke wore shining silver armour with gold fleur-de-lis on the breastplate, a helmet plumed with red-dyed ostrich feathers, and a flowing cape of azure blue. He raised a gauntleted hand in the air and bowed his head as he drew level with the royal podium where King Louis sat with Mary. She saw him smile at her as the king returned his salute.

Next came the English knights, led by Charles Brandon in armour of burnished gold, carrying Henry's royal standard of three lions quartered with the flag of France. It crossed Mary's mind that it was not beyond Henry to risk attending as an anonymous knight. She studied each of the Englishmen, looking for his familiar face but their helmets made it impossible to be certain.

Overcome with loyalty for her countrymen, Mary stood up as they drew level with her. She saw a nod of acknowledgement from Brandon, then someone in the crowd yelled out something anti-English, to ribald laughter and cheering from the other Frenchmen. Mary remembered they had been mortal enemies only six months before.

Louis, now so troubled by his gout he rested on a gilded couch, reached out and took Mary's hand in his. 'High spirits!' He gave her a wry smile as some of the crowd began to sing a patriotic French song. 'It seems my cousin Francis has made this personal.'

Mary returned her ailing husband's smile yet knew he was right. After drinking more than he should at her coronation banquet, Francis bragged he'd had the grandstands built high to give the nobles of France the best view of the lists. With sudden insight she realised he planned to ride against Charles Brandon. From what she knew of both men, neither would submit without a fight.

She studied the overcast sky as the first heavy drops of rain began to patter to the already wet ground. The royal podium had the benefit of a canopy suspended on gilded wooden poles. Mary smiled to herself as she realised the partisan French nobles crowding the stands would have their jeering rewarded by a good soaking.

A sharp blast of trumpets announced the start of the contest, with a flamboyant French knight promptly being unhorsed and crashing into the mud. Time and again the English proved superior, to the increasing disappointment of the crowd.

Charles Brandon seemed like an invincible force, unseating two more Frenchmen and scoring the highest number of points. Charles, Duke of Alençon, struck him on the helmet, winning a roar of approval from the watching nobles. Mary held her breath as Brandon took a moment to recover, then raised a hand to show he could continue.

After many clashes between French and English, the time came at last for the confrontation Mary dreaded. Brandon's distinctive armour glinted in the driving rain as he charged towards the duke, both of them shattering their lances with brutal force. On the second pass Duke Francis suffered an injury to his hand but, after discussion, the Master of the Joust declared the contest a draw.

The jousting continued for the rest of the afternoon, with Brandon emerging as equal champion with his long-time sparring partner Sir Thomas Grey. The heavy rain turned the Parc des Tournelles to mud, yet Brandon managed a grin as he rode to salute the king.

Louis called out his congratulations in French, so everyone within earshot could understand. He turned to Mary as Brandon rode off. 'I'd have enjoyed seeing your countryman unhorse my scheming cousin!' He chuckled at the thought. 'You know he's been saying I'm incapable of fathering a son?'

Mary pretended to be shocked at the suggestion yet could easily believe it. She'd been amused by the duke's flattery before feeling sorry for Princess Claude. Francis was always at her side, her over-attentive escort while Louis remained in his bed, behaviour which would fan the smouldering embers of inevitable rumours at court.

She played along with his games, for now, as she did with Louis. Laughing at the duke's witty remarks was a small price to pay for her future security if he became king. Sleeping in the king's bed while he snored at her side also seemed little hardship if it kept the myth of their happy marriage alive.

Duke Francis planned a shock for the English on the second day of the tournament. The Master of the Joust announced in French that Sir Charles Brandon, Duke of Suffolk, and Sir Thomas Grey, Marquess of Dorset, as joint champions, would take on all comers in courses on foot.

Mary turned to Louis in protest. 'This is unfair! Their skill is at the joust, not the melee.'

Louis lay propped up on cushions, no longer caring what his subjects might think. His red-rimmed eyes studied Mary's concerned face. 'Would you have me put a stop to it?' His voice sounded strained, as if even talking was now an effort.

She looked out into the field, churned to mud with the hooves of heavy warhorses, and knew she had no choice. One of the Frenchmen died fighting on foot the previous day and she was certain many more had been injured, including Duke Francis. Louis said the wound to the duke's hand was a sprain to his little finger, yet he'd decided to withdraw. Now, it seemed, he'd devised his revenge on Brandon.

Mary said a silent prayer as she watched Brandon and Thomas draw their heavy swords and stand back to back. They reminded her of stories her Latin tutors told her of the gladiators of Rome. There was a cheer as a dozen Frenchmen marched into the arena and began to surround the two English knights.

With surprising swiftness, Brandon swung his sword in a vicious arc, causing the nearest Frenchmen to spring back in alarm. Reversing the weapon in a fluid motion, he used the heavy pommel as a club to fell one of the men with a crushing blow to the helmet. Another took the opportunity to try to push him off balance into the slippery mud.

This time Thomas Grey parried the blow and forced the man back with the blunted tip of his sword. Mary knew they wore protective armour yet it was easy to be injured in close fighting. Working together, Charles and Thomas stood their ground, defending each other and defeating their attackers one by one.

French nobles called out to rally their countrymen and cheered as a thickset man, even taller than Brandon, entered the arena. Duke Francis had been keeping him back for his grand finale. Brandon didn't hesitate, sidestepping the newcomer's swinging blade and smashing his gauntleted fist into the man's face, breaking his nose.

With a surprised howl, the large man dropped his sword to the mud and fell to his knees. If it had been a real battle he would soon be dead. The French court rose as one and applauded as Charles Brandon raised his sword in victory.

~

Louis opened his eyes and stared at Mary, as if surprised to see she still sat at his bedside. Mary closed the velvet-bound book of poetry she'd been reading and smoothed his brow. 'How are you feeling, my king?'

Louis grimaced. 'I fear I pay the price for my indulgence.' He attempted a weak smile.

She understood his joke. Her ladies shared the gossip from chattering French courtiers. 'They are saying I've worn out the king with my excessive lovemaking!'

Louis grinned as if he approved of the idea. 'My physicians advise me to abstain.' He gave her a wry look. 'They suspect a plot by King Henry to destroy France through his sister's unrelenting passion.'

Mary knew she should be outraged yet smiled at the thought. Nothing could be further from the truth. The only way to deal with rumours was to ignore them.

'Will you play for me?'

'I have some French music. Jane Popincourt—'

Louis cursed. 'Don't mention that woman!' His voice rasped like old parchment.

Mary shook her head at the unfairness of it and went to find her lute. Christmastide had passed without celebration and it seemed her first New Year's Eve as queen would be the same. Louis remained in a temperamental mood. His physicians were at a loss to know what to do and their attempted

cures with fat leeches, bleeding, and foul-smelling potions ma
him worse.

She'd seen little of Paris, which seemed a city of dungheaps and danger, as she spent every waking moment at his bedside. She entertained Louis, reading and singing to him, telling him stories of life at Richmond Palace. He laughed for the first time in ages at her tale of the time her father's pet monkey tore up his precious diaries.

She carried her lute back to his room and improved the tuning before she began to play. She chose a slow English melody she'd played as a young girl at Eltham Palace, so long ago. The soft music brightened the king's eyes but he held up a hand to interrupt her.

'Will you play my favourite, Mary?'

She smiled at how the relationship between them had shifted since he'd become bedridden. She nursed him as she had her father, who'd been the same age as Louis when he died a painful death of the quinsy. Now Louis had come to depend on her. Even a king was at the mercy of those who cared for him.

'Sweet pretty lady?' She knew yet waited for his answer.

Louis nodded. '*Je t'aime, mon ange.*'

He lay his head back on his satin pillows in expectation, the faintest smile on his face. She picked the notes of the introduction with the nails of her right hand, kept long for the purpose, and began to sing in French, her voice echoing in the stillness of the room.

'*Douce dame jolie, pour Dieu ne pensés mie, que nulle ait signorie, seur moy fors vous seulement.*'

She saw he'd closed his eyes again and sang the second verse more softly, this time in English. '*Sweet pretty lady...*' She heard him snore.

Her dreams were interrupted by Marguerite de Valois, one of the ladies of her bedchamber appointed by Louis after her own staff were sent home. A distant relation of Mary's Valois great-grandmother, Marguerite spoke English with a strong French accent.

'You must wake, Your Grace, it is most urgent.'

Mary sat up and rubbed her eyes. 'What's going on at such an early hour?'

Marguerite bit her lip as she hesitated. 'I regret to say, Your Grace, the king has died in the night.'

Mary stared at her in disbelief. 'He's dead?' The shock of grief mixed with the pang of guilty relief. It took a moment for the consequences to dawn on her. 'I was with him a short time ago. He seemed no worse than usual – in fact he was in good spirits.'

Marguerite shook her head. 'I am so sorry, Your Grace. You must be dressed please. Duke Francis wishes to speak with you.'

Mary stood while Marguerite helped her out of her long silk nightdress. Her mind began to focus as she struggled to understand. 'The duke is also here?' She'd not seen Francis since the sombre Christmas service. He'd barely spoken to her.

'Duke Francis was visiting the king.'

Something in the way she said it triggered a suspicion in Mary's mind. 'He was alone with the king when he died?'

Marguerite shrugged. 'I only know he demands to see you.' Her voice softened a little. 'I am sorry for your sad loss, Your Grace.'

Mary's mind raced with questions while Marguerite laced the bindings on her bodice, tied her sleeves in place and fixed her long hair under her coif with silver pins. She felt torn between the need to escape France while she could and her duty as queen, even if now she was only the dowager queen.

Duke Francis waited for her with his dark-eyed brother-in-law, Charles, Duke of Alençon, at his side. They both stood as she entered. 'I'm sorry to tell you King Louis passed away while you were sleeping, on the first day of this new year.' Francis shook his head. 'You can of course depend on our support during what will be a difficult time for you.'

Mary looked at their too innocent faces, trying to decide what to do. She had to play their game and thank her husband's murderers. Her instinct told her it could be dangerous not to. As soon as she could, she would share her suspicions with Charles Brandon, who would know exactly what to do.

'I am grateful to you.' She sat in the chair opposite them, still trying to comprehend such a sudden turn of events.

Francis nodded. 'My mother will act as regent while we wait to see if you are with child.' The coldness in his voice gave it a sinister edge.

Mary felt her face redden as she looked into his calculating eyes. 'I assure you, sir, I am not.'

Duke Charles answered. 'We must be certain, before the arrangements can be made for Duke Francis to become king.' He saw Mary's frown and added. 'It is the custom in France.'

Mary struggled to remain composed. 'First we must grieve, then my husband must have a state funeral.' She tried her best to sound firm. 'Only then will we talk of coronations.' Her words echoed in the empty room with the weight of a new widow's grief.

Francis placed a hand on her shoulder. 'I will ensure my good cousin Louis is buried with the full honours due to him.'

If his hand was intended to feel comforting it did not. Mary resisted the urge to shrug it off, to spit in his face, to call for the palace guards. She had no proof he'd been responsible for the death of Louis and was certain none would be found.

Mary noted the look of disdain from Countess Louise. Dressed in white mourning clothes, she'd wasted no time in taking control. The whole of Paris came to a standstill as the grand procession made its way to Notre-Dame, where Louis was laid to rest with undue haste at the side of Anne of Brittany.

'You must retire now to your mourning chapel, as is our custom.' It sounded like an order to a disobedient child.

Mary stared at Countess Louise. She had little time for French customs. 'For how long?' She tried to sound assertive yet it sounded petulant.

'Until it can be established that you are not with child.' Her tone suggested she doubted it. 'One month or two.'

'I refuse to be shut away. I must write to my brother the king, there is too much to do.'

'You cannot refuse,' Louise's voice sounded harsher now, 'and King Henry has of course been informed.'

Mary realised she could make a dangerous enemy by resisting the will of the countess. 'I agree on condition my secretary is permitted to see me to take letters to England.'

The countess gave a curt nod. 'I am pleased you respect our customs. You are the Dowager Queen of France and will want for nothing while you are in mourning.' She softened a little for the first time. 'You might pray for my son, that he will be a wise and noble king.'

Mary agreed. She had no choice. She entered the darkened rooms of Cluny Palace, overlooking the Seine, and heard the door close behind her with a thump. Looking around she saw an altar with a blue-robed statue of the Virgin and a few prayer books. Worst of all, the windows and walls and even her bed were hung with heavy black cloth, blocking the light.

She shivered in the cold, turned back and tried to open the door. It rattled in the frame as she shook the handle, realising it had been locked from the outside. She called out but heard no reply.

She'd been tricked. The duke's
sure nothing would stand in the wa
Even a king who clung to the last of
Mary crossed to the altar and kneeled b
she lit it from the solitary candle and lit a
she watched the yellow flame take hold she ī
words Louis said to her, '*Je t'aime mon ange*,' and wept.

Mary felt another stab of pain from her aching tooth, which seemed to be growing worse. She tried to put her father's smile of blackened teeth from her mind as she listened. Her secretary, John Palsgrave, read the long letter to Henry back to her. She'd no wish to compromise her position if the letter fell into the wrong hands.

Satisfied with the wording, she signed her name at the bottom and watched as Palsgrave folded the stiff new parchment. Melting a stick of dark sealing wax with the candle, he allowed it to drip on to the folded letter before pressing in her silver seal.

'I also wish you to take a message to Sir Charles Brandon. I need to see him before he leaves Paris.'

Palsgrave looked up from his work in surprise. 'The Duke of Suffolk left for England before Christmas, Your Grace.'

She bit her lip to conceal her disappointment. Brandon hadn't troubled to say farewell yet she realised there was no reason why he should. His work in Paris done, he would of course return home to report to her brother in person. She sat back in her chair and took a deep breath, determined to compose herself. She had important work to do.

Duke Francis visited every day now to enquire about her health. She understood his impatience, with the crown of France so close yet remaining out of reach of his grasping hands. She must put his mind at rest, so he could become king and she would be released from her dark confinement.

'What message would you have me give the Duke of Suffolk, Your Grace?' Palsgrave waited for her answer.

She looked into her secretary's hazel eyes and saw the questioning intelligence there. Duke Francis appointed Marie d'Albret, Countess of Nevers, to keep her company but Mary guessed the talkative countess was his spy, reporting back her every word. John Palsgrave was the only one of her original staff allowed to see her. She decided to trust him with her future plans.

'I need to know if Sir Charles Brandon will return to Paris – for me.'

Palsgrave looked down at the sealed letter in his hand. 'I will try my best, my lady, but it will be difficult for a poor cleric such as me to gain an audience with the highest ranking noble in England.'

'You are resourceful, John. I know you will find a way.' An idea occurred to her. She pulled one of her gold rings from her finger and held it in the candlelight. A token of her love, with her motto engraved around the inside: *La volenté de Dieu me suffit.* 'Take this – and have his squire give it to him as surety.' She smiled, pleased with herself, and handed him the ring.

'I suspect I know the answer, my lady, but might I know your purpose?' A twinkle of amusement flashed in his eyes.

'I need him to escort me back to England – and I plan to ask him to marry me.'

Duke Francis arrived in the early evening with French curses, stamping his boots and brushing flakes of snow from his hat and cape. Mary had her servant bring him a cup of warm spiced mead and invited him to sit in a chair by the hearth. He removed his riding gloves and held out his hands, warming them at her fire.

With the trials of Louis' illness and death she'd forgotten she married him to preserve the peace between England and France. She waited until the duke tasted the sweet mead then forced a smile. Her secret weapon would be informality, to disarm the arrogant king-in-waiting.

'It's good of you to visit me every day, Francis. It can be so lonely in this dark place, with no idea when it will end.'

It was true. There were times when she'd paced her dark-ened rooms like a caged beast at the Tower of London. She'd prayed at her altar until her knees ached on the cold stone floor. She'd wondered how she deserved the cruel twist of fate which caused her to be locked away from the world. Now she must smile at the man she cursed as the cause of it.

He turned from the warmth of the fire and looked at her white mourning dress, his appraising eyes lingering on her body a little too long. 'By tradition you should remain in your bed for six weeks.' He managed to make it sound salacious. 'It is only until there can be no question of a male child.' He looked away and changed the subject. 'I trust you are being treated well, Mary?'

'As your good lady mother promised. I want for nothing, except my liberty.'

Her well-rehearsed words made him look up at her face. 'I confess I am as eager to see you out of here as you are.'

She moved closer, speaking softly so her servants would not overhear. 'I give you my word of honour. You must know. I am *La Reine Blanche*. There is no child. There never could be.' Her tooth ached worse than ever yet she smiled.

He sipped the warm mead, never taking his eyes from her. 'I know. In truth, this is my mother's doing. She places great importance on the old traditions.' His dark eyes sparkled in the firelight. 'When I am king I will shake off these dusty cobwebs.'

'When you are king, my life can begin again.' She gave him a knowing look. 'Will you tell your mother it's a waste of our time for me to remain here? It is time to end our mourning – time for you to be crowned.' She saw his dark eyes shine with ambition at her words.

'I will!' Duke Francis drained his cup. He smiled at her as he stood and picked up his riding gloves from where they had been drying by the hearth. 'I bid you farewell – and thank you for giving me your word, my lady.'

He drew his flowing cape around his broad shoulders, fastening the silver clasp, fashioned in the shape of a salamander with sapphire eyes, his personal emblem. He pulled on his black gloves and left, without looking back, to arrange his coronation as King of France.

Mary dismissed her muttering French servants and sated her frustration at them by tearing down the black cloths covering the long windows. Shafts of bright winter sun lit up motes of dust drifting like tiny, glittering stars in the still air. Tears of relief ran down Mary's face as she looked out at the River Seine and the spires of Notre-Dame Cathedral. She was leaving Cluny Palace forever.

John Palsgrave returned with news that the waiting was finally over. Charles Brandon had sailed from Dover on the same ship and was meeting with Francis to negotiate her return to England.

Mary's mind raced with questions. 'Why must he negotiate? Of course I will return. Francis has no wish to hold me here. Is it the return of my dowry?' She recalled Wolsey's scheming before she'd left for France. He'd foreseen Louis' death and already planned for her return, wording the marriage contract to Henry's advantage.

John Palsgrave nodded. 'There is a considerable sum of money at stake, Your Grace, as well as the question of the jewels from the late king.'

'They were gifts!' She heard the outrage and frustration in her voice. Her confinement and aching tooth made her short-tempered. She saw her secretary's troubled look. 'I'm sorry. Does Duke Francis,' she corrected herself, 'does *King* Francis want them returned?'

'It seems, Your Grace, they were part of the crown jewels of France. I expect they now belong in law to Queen Claude.'

Mary understood. 'I have enough jewels. Claude is welcome to them after all she's been through – although I doubt my brother will take the same view.'

Palsgrave's troubled face revealed he had more bad news. 'You are right, Your Grace, which brings me to the other matter I must tell you.'

Mary felt the chill premonition of her plans slipping away yet again. 'My brother has already chosen me another husband?' She could picture Henry and Wolsey scheming as they weighed the usefulness of different suitors, with no regard for her.

'Not yet,' Palsgrave frowned, 'although it seems King Henry and the new King of France disagree over who has the right to choose on your behalf.' He smiled, for the first time since his return. 'King Henry has sent a delegation to resolve the matter – with the Duke of Suffolk as their chief negotiator.'

Mary groaned. 'Will you kindly take a message to my physician? Tell him his foul potion has done nothing to ease the pain from my tooth.'

Queen Claude shivered in the chill February air, despite her fur cape. She watched with Mary from the high balcony of her mansion as cheering crowds welcomed their new king to Paris. By tradition, neither of them were present at King Francis' coronation ceremony at the ancient cathedral of Notre-Dame in Rheims.

Neither of them cheered as King Francis rode through the crowds. He looked handsome and regal and wore a gold coronet. Behind him followed his flag-bearers with colourful banners, a cavalcade of mounted French knights and nobles, then five hundred marching soldiers in blue and gold.

Claude glanced over her shoulder at the waiting servants. 'I fear what kind of king my husband might become, Mary. He's made his scheming mother a duchess and his wastrel of a brother-in-law Governor of Normandy.' She frowned. 'Now he talks of reconquering Milan and spends his time hunting. I've hardly seen him since my father's funeral.'

Mary decided to remain silent about his daily visits to her in Cluny. Before leaving for his coronation Francis called late in the evening to propose a list of suitors. He promised Mary favours if she chose to allow him to decide for her. When she refused he'd warned her not to speak of his proposals. The threat in his narrowed eyes was unmistakable. Becoming king had changed him, as it changes any man.

Mary rode at the side of the queen on a fine white palfrey in a procession through the wintry Paris streets to the coronation banquet. When they arrived it seemed the new king had forgotten his wife, as he sat in a gilded throne with his mother on one side and his sister on the other, a sign of what was to come.

Claude was stoical and sat with Mary and her ladies, although she remained unusually silent. Watching the scene before her Mary realised it wasn't only Francis who had changed – the country seemed different now, as England had after the death of her father. Like Henry, Francis was abandoning the sedate atmosphere of Louis' old court. The grim-faced bishops and grey-haired advisors were nowhere to be seen.

Instead Francis surrounded himself with poets, musicians and his boisterous young hunting companions. Mary heard a crash of breaking glass followed by raucous laughter and turned to look. The rich wine flowed freely and the younger nobles were already playing noisy drinking games and singing bawdy songs.

Mary had little appetite for the rich platters of food weighing down their table and picked at the delicate bones of spiced quails in a sweet cherry sauce. She hoped none of the other guests noticed how she watched Charles Brandon. He'd arrived late and took his seat with the other ambassadors on the opposite side of the banqueting hall. She'd seen him studying her with a serious look on his face and worried about what it might mean.

She heard Duchess Louise's harsh laughter at her son's witty remarks and wondered at how their fortunes had changed in so short a time. She'd played along with Louise's demands yet the price had been higher than expected. The long lonely winter in the cold, darkened rooms of Cluny had left her pale and sapped her spirit.

She'd clung to her memories to survive the long dark days. She'd recalled her father's words of comfort when she'd fallen from her horse as a girl. 'Remember you are a Tudor,' he'd said. 'We Tudors are survivors in adversity.' She'd remembered the look in Charles Brandon's eyes, and dreamed of her knight coming to rescue his Tudor princess.

She took another sip of the sweet red wine, feeling it warming her throat as she tried to forget the scandalous rumours. She glanced at Claude's dish of gilt sugar plums and glistening pomegranate seeds. There'd been no sign Claude believed the speculation of gossiping courtiers that she'd been attempting to seduce Francis.

Mary only learned of it when she was reunited with her English ladies, who looked shocked when she told them the truth. She could imagine how Francis might have bragged to his companions after too much fine wine. It was also not beyond his calculating mother to encourage such talk.

Claude used the excuse of a headache to leave, after one last long look at Francis with his mother and sister. Mary was also about to do the same and was finishing her goblet of wine when she saw the tall figure of Charles Brandon approaching. Two well-dressed, middle-aged men she recognised as her brother's delegation followed close behind him.

Mary studied Brandon's face as he removed his hat and bowed to her, noting the changes since she'd last seen him. The gold chain around his neck looked heavier, a badge of his success. His beard had grown thicker and his eyes, which seemed to turn from grey to blue with his mood, hinted at concern.

'How are you, Your Grace?' His warm voice made her heart miss a beat.

'My time of mourning is over, Sir Charles,' she gestured towards the top table where Francis seemed to be enjoying another joke, 'and I must confess I'm ready to leave France. I pray to see England again, to walk in the grounds of Richmond, to take a barge down the Thames.' She realised she was babbling and put a hand to her mouth.

Brandon gestured towards the men at each side of him. 'You will know Sir Richard Wingfield, Lord Deputy of Calais, and our ambassador to France, Dean Nicholas West?'

'Gentlemen.' Mary smiled. 'It's good to see such a fine delegation come to speak on my behalf.'

She saw how they both looked at her with the shrewd eyes of men with questions that needed answers. Sir Richard Wingfield was her great uncle, through marriage to her mother's late sister Catherine Woodville. Her eyes went to his sword, the well-used weapon of a soldier, then returned to his grey-bearded, weather-beaten face, the legacy of his years in France.

'Sir Richard, you were my father's trusted courtier and arranged my betrothal to Prince Charles.' She shook her head. 'How different my life might have been if I had married him.'

Sir Richard removed his cap and bowed. 'At your service, Your Grace. Please accept our condolences on the loss of your husband. King Louis was a good friend to our country.'

Mary nodded in acknowledgement and turned to Nicholas West. A thin-faced man with white hair showing under his black velvet hat, he wore a cleric's dark robes yet their quality, and the gold rings on his fingers, suggested his legal expertise paid well. Mary knew he was Bishop Foxe's man, respected by Henry and Wolsey.

'Dean West, you have negotiated my betrothal twice now.'

Dean West didn't remove his hat but bowed his head and looked at her with his deep-set eyes. 'Indeed – and it seems you might have need of our services a third time, my lady.'

She forced a smile before looking back at Brandon, trying to read his thoughts. 'You must come to see me in the morning and tell me all the news from England.'

'Of course, Your Grace.' The faintest flicker of amusement passed over his face before he touched his cap and turned to leave.

Mary wasn't sure if she'd sipped too much fine wine but she didn't care who'd been watching or listening to their exchange. Her new life was about to begin and she returned to her chambers laughing at the comments of her ladies, in good spirits for the first time since she'd arrived in France.

It was noon the next day before Charles Brandon knocked at the door to her chambers. She led them into the next room where her fire still crackled in the hearth and signalled to Palsgrave to make his discrete withdrawal. Charles Brandon loosened his coat and sat in the chair she offered. He glanced back as Palsgrave closed the door behind him.

'At last we can speak freely.' He smiled at her, more at ease than she'd seen him since the jousting. 'The French think that holding you here strengthens their hand in these negotiations.'

'Can you take me with you?'

'Nicholas West cautions against it. We must secure a new treaty with King Francis first.'

Mary studied his face and made a judgement. This was her moment. 'Francis plans to marry me off before Henry can do anything about it, Charles. He warned me not to tell anyone – or there would be consequences.'

Brandon cursed. 'Wolsey predicted as much. Francis thinks he's been playing us for fools, wasting our time while he agrees a match for you.' He scowled. 'Did he tell you who he intends as your suitor?'

Mary shrugged. 'He mentioned his uncle, Charles, Duke of Savoy, and the Duke of Lorraine.'

'How did you reply?'

'I told him I would rather take myself to a convent.'

Brandon leaned forward in his chair. 'I have to ask you something which is not easy for me.'

Mary held her breath and stared at Brandon, knowing whatever he was about to ask could change the rest of her life. Her toothache returned, an unwelcome reminder of her time at Cluny Palace.

Brandon fixed his blue-grey eyes on hers. 'Has Francis ever taken advantage of you?'

It was the first time she'd seen him look embarrassed. Her first impulse was to laugh, then to cry. She'd feared this moment. Her word would be weighed against that of one of the most powerful and influential men in the world.

Mary returned his questioning stare. 'I give you my word that Francis has always treated me with the greatest of respect – except when he refers to me as his stepmother.' She leaned forward a little. 'You've known me all my life, Charles. Do you believe me?'

He relaxed. 'I do.' He gave her a sheepish grin. 'I promised Wolsey I would find out, but was halfway across the Channel before I realised there was only one way to be sure. Please forgive me.'

She reached out and placed her hand on his arm. 'Of course.' She gave his arm a squeeze and didn't remove her hand. 'There is a way to stop King Francis. There would be little he could do if I were already remarried.'

'King Henry would never permit it.' Brandon gave her a curious look. 'I don't think you have any idea—'

'Of course I do!' Her raised voice echoed in the high-ceilinged room. 'Which is why I extracted a promise from my brother before I left for France, that he will give his blessing when I choose my next husband.'

Brandon stared at her without answering for a moment, then grinned. 'I have a confession to make, Mary. Henry told me of his promise to you before I left – and that he suspected your intention. He had me swear an oath not to act on the information until you are returned safe to England.'

'And your intention, Charles? Is it your intention to obey your king or the Dowager Queen of France?' Mary held her breath for the second time, her pulse racing as she awaited his next words.

'I must be mad,' he placed his free hand over hers, 'bu
will risk everything I own, my reputation, my liberty anc
possibly my life to marry you, Mary Tudor.'

11

FEBRUARY 1515

Mary's plans for her new life began as a great secret, shared only with those she trusted most. She played her role as Queen Dowager, loyal supporter of the new king and close companion of his wife, Queen Claude. She learned the names of the new courtiers and John Palsgrave helped her to improve her French, as if she planned to stay.

She understood Brandon's view that he should only visit her in the course of his diplomatic duties, and even then would need a chaperone at all times. He'd also told her they must risk taking Dean Nicholas West into their confidence.

'Do you trust him, Charles?'

'Don't be fooled by his pious face. West's as sharp as a razor and will help us.' He grinned as a thought occurred to him. 'Although I'm certain it will cost me a great favour one day.'

'How can he help?' Mary placed her gold-ringed hand on Brandon's, her fingers as small and pale as a child's next to his.

He looked up at the physical contact, then leaned across and kissed her for the first time. A slow, lingering lover's kiss.

She was about to embrace him when he pulled back and sat up straight in his chair. 'We must be wary of your servants, Mary.'

She glanced back at the closed doors. He was right. Any of her servants could start rumours that would spread through the French court like a lit taper on dry kindling. 'I was asking what Dean West might be able to do...' Her voice sounded breathless.

'We shall see, as I'm bringing him here tomorrow.' Brandon leaned forward for one last kiss before leaving.

Mary breathed a sigh of relief that there seemed to be a glimmer of hope about her future. Then she sensed a deep misgiving. She'd lost count of the number of times her luck had changed for the worse. One malicious word in the wrong ear and her new life could unravel. She feared she could become an excuse for war between two young kings, both keen to prove their power, with her caught in the middle.

She kneeled on the cold, ancient stones of the palace chapel and prayed. She pleaded with God for good fortune, not only for herself but for Charles Brandon. She'd asked him to risk everything for her and he'd gladly accepted. She prayed he would never have reason to regret it.

A heavy fall of snow turned Paris white and froze overnight, making the paths treacherous and the icy roads impassable to horses. Mary watched from her high window to see if her visitors could still make it but the palace courtyard looked deserted.

As a precaution she'd dismissed all her servants except her loyal chamberer, Mistress Anne Jerningham. Mary trusted Anne and decided she should also be taken into her confidence but her response shocked her.

'I guessed as much, my lady,' Anne Jerningham smiled, 'from the way you look at Sir Charles.'

'Do others know?' Mary felt the cold stab of concern.

Anne shrugged. 'If they do not, it's only a matter of time. One thing I've learned in my time here in Paris is the courtiers love to gossip about such things – even more than those in England.'

Mary looked at her as she thought about the consequences of Anne's words. 'Please be ready for us to leave at short notice, Anne.'

'Are we returning to England, my lady?'

'God willing, although I pray we'll not have to leave before this snow has gone.'

Mary picked up her lute and ran her fingernail over the strings. Satisfied with the tuning, she began to play one of her favourite songs, an old English carol that reminded her of happier times.

'*There is no rose of such virtue,*' she sang slowly, her voice echoing and clear in the silent, high-ceilinged room, '*as is the rose that bore Jesu...*'

A tuneful tenor voice replied from outside her door. '*For in this rose contained, was Heaven and earth...*'

Mary sprang to her feet. 'Charles?' In a flash of recollection, she remembered a Christmas long ago in Richmond Palace, when Brandon and Henry dressed as minstrels and entertained her father with carols.

The door opened to reveal a grinning Brandon and sombre-faced West. 'Apologies for our lateness, Your Grace, we had to come here on foot.' He nodded to her chamberer and rubbed his hands together. 'A cup of warmed ale would suit us well, mistress.'

Mary waited until Anne left for the kitchens. 'Thomas Grey's son Edward has asked to marry her – but she's told me she wishes to stay in my service.' She looked from Brandon to the dean. 'I decided to tell her my intentions – and she'd already guessed!'

Dean West's eyes narrowed. 'She'll not be alone, my lady. We must act while there is time.'

They sat by the log fire while Anne returned with silver tankards of warmed spiced ale. Brandon took a sip and nodded in approval, wiping his mouth on his sleeve. He looked from Mary to Dean West, a twinkle in his eye.

'Nicholas has devised a plan,' he smiled at Mary, 'which requires a little deception.'

Mary raised an eyebrow. 'Is our situation not complicated enough?'

West sipped his ale before replying. 'I assure you my suggestion is nothing disloyal, my lady, but first I should say we have a number of difficulties to remedy.' He studied Mary, as if wondering where to start. 'We must secure a new peace treaty. Which means we have to win over King Francis.' West ticked off the points on his long fingers. 'We must of course placate your brother King Henry and,' he looked across at Brandon, 'not compromise the oath you swore before leaving England.'

Brandon leaned forward in his chair and looked into Mary's eyes. 'It's true your mourning left you in a state of some distress?'

Mary nodded. The memory of the dark chamber still haunted her. 'I felt I was being punished, although I'd done nothing wrong...'

'Then it will not be too hard to convince the king of your vulnerable state and appeal to his sense of brotherly duty?'

Mary understood. 'I'll write to my brother.'

Dean West nodded. 'It is fortunate the king agreed to bless your choice of husband. You could beseech him to honour his word – and must convince him this was your own initiative.'

'Yes,' Mary brightened, 'and I'll write to Thomas Wolsey. Henry listens to his counsel.'

Brandon's face became serious. 'There is another... problem, Mary. I regret to tell you Queen Catherine was delivered of a stillborn son.'

Mary raised her hand to her mouth. 'No! She longed to give Henry a son...'

Brandon shook his head. 'Queen Catherine was out of favour with the king because of her troublesome father, so the loss of this son is a doubly bitter blow.'

Mary looked up at them. 'We must pray for her – and for Henry but we don't have time to wait until they've finished grieving.'

Dean West agreed. 'You are right, which is why you need to ask King Francis to assist you.'

'He's the last person I would choose to confide in now.' Mary looked concerned. 'There's no telling what he might do.'

Brandon took another drink of his ale and leaned forward in his chair. 'King Francis has a keen sense of chivalry. Ask for his help. I think he'll surprise you.'

Mary felt doubtful but there seemed little alternative. 'What about your oath to Henry?'

'I shall write to him, after you have paved the way by making it clear this was your own doing.' He grinned. 'How could any man have refused you?'

Brandon was right. Francis surprised Mary by agreeing to her request to meet in private that afternoon. She'd expected to wait for days and planned to rehearse her words, yet now her only choice was to tell him the truth.

He wore a wide-sleeved black-and-silver tunic embroidered with gold. A white ostrich plume fluttered in his jewelled hat as he stood to welcome her. Mary noted how his hand rested on the golden hilt of a short sword.

'You intrigue me, my lady.' King Francis spoke in French

and bowed in greeting. 'Have you come to disc͟ betrothal?'

Mary gave a nervous smile as she returned his welcome with a curtsey. 'I've come seeking your advice, Your Grace.'

Francis gestured for her to sit and gave her a quizzical look. 'You wish to return to England?'

'I am in no hurry to leave France – but I have a dilemma. I wish to marry the Duke of Suffolk, yet my brother King Henry made him swear an oath not to marry me.'

Francis sat back in surprise. 'I was informed… by a reliable source, that the Duke of Suffolk had returned to Paris to seek your hand.' He frowned at her. 'When I confronted him with this, he told me he'd been charged to return you to England and his intentions were honourable.'

'I give you my word, Your Grace.' Mary placed her hands together as in prayer. 'As God is my witness, this was entirely my doing.'

Francis studied her with a disbelieving look in his sharp eyes. He seemed to be weighing up the truth of her words. 'The duke is a good man and excels at the joust – but I can find you a better match.'

'I am truly grateful to you, Your Grace, but I wish to marry the duke and he has accepted.'

Francis stroked his finely trimmed black beard as he considered the implications. 'What does King Henry have to say about this?'

'I will write to my brother but thought I should inform you first, Your Grace.'

'A wise decision, as there is more you clearly do not understand.'

His mocking tone put Mary on her guard. 'Your Grace?'

'My agents inform me the Duke of Suffolk plans to take you back to England so you can be married to the son of Emperor Maximilian.' He paused for effect, enjoying his power over her. 'He has no intention of marrying you himself. King Henry plans to secure further alliances by the duke's marriage to Archduchess Margaret of Savoy.'

'It cannot be true!'

'Has he professed his love for you?'

Mary hesitated. Brandon had not yet said the words, although she knew his feelings well enough. She had supposed he would, when he felt the time was right. Now she studied the young king's face and saw he felt he had the upper hand.

Francis tutted at her silence. 'I suspected as much.' He smiled as a thought seemed to occur to him. 'You have my blessing to marry him – here in France. If he finds some excuse, you will know I'm right.'

'I must wait for my brother's permission.'

'If you wait, you will live with the consequences.'

Mary hesitated again. 'You support my marriage to the Duke of Suffolk?'

'If your brother has his way it would strengthen his alliances against the interests of France,' Francis gave her a wolfish grin, 'and it amuses me to rob him of the opportunity.'

Mary sent for Brandon as soon as she returned from her meeting with King Francis. He arrived with Dean West and listened intently as she recounted what happened.

Brandon cursed. 'It's true I was sent to bring you back – but the idea of my ever marrying Margaret of Savoy was a joke.'

Mary stared into his eyes. 'Then will you marry me now, here in France?'

'Of course,' he stared back at her, a twinkle in his eye, 'if that is your wish.'

Dean West had been watching them in silence. 'You must be aware you both risk incurring King Henry's displeasure—'

'I know a certain way to win back his affection,' Brandon interrupted, 'with a token of our goodwill.'

'What do you have in mind, my lord?'

'You shall deliver my letter of explanation in person, together with the Mirror of Naples, which the king himself had valued at more than sixty thousand crowns.'

Dean West turned to Mary. 'Do you still have the jewel in your safekeeping, my lady?'

'I do – and I will gladly surrender it as the price of my brother's favour.' Mary looked back at Brandon. 'We must marry before Henry receives your letter, or he might forbid you to do so. It will be done in secret but with witnesses.' Her voice sounded more confident than she felt.

Dean West frowned. 'King Henry can still order such a marriage to be annulled.'

Brandon gave him a wry smile. 'He can – but I doubt he will if the marriage is consummated.'

Mary felt her face blush at his suggestion but knew it was the truth. Her hand involuntarily fell to her slender waist. Even better, she could be with child before Henry could prevent them.

The noon bell chimed with a dull, clanging tone and the serene figure of the Madonna smiled down at them as they stood together in the private chapel at Cluny. The elderly priest eyed the small congregation of the most loyal of Mary's ladies, and mumbled a Latin prayer.

Their secret, hasty wedding required little arrangement. Mary and her ladies dressed as if for any other Paris day in winter, with riding capes and furs over thick gowns instead of fine silk wedding dresses. It suited Mary when few heads turned as she rode past with her ladies, another reminder that being Dowager Queen of France counted for little now.

_red in the chill air as the priest muttered his way ₒn the order of service, uninterrupted by any music or ₒinging for fear of drawing attention. Her voice echoed in the emptiness of the old chapel when she said her vows, and she consoled herself with the promise of a grander wedding once they returned safely to England.

Charles Brandon smiled at her as he placed the gold ring on Mary's finger. She recognised it as the one inscribed with her motto. *La volenté de Dieu me suffit.* When she'd sent her ring to England with her secretary John Palsgrave she'd never dreamed it would be returned in such a way.

She stared adoringly into the grey eyes of her new husband as he swore to love and honour her. The will of God was a wondrous thing. He smiled, then kissed her. He bent closer to her ear and whispered, so only she could hear.

'I love you, Mary, with all my heart.'

Anne Jerningham held the lantern in the window, the signal it was safe for Brandon to enter Mary's apartments by the servants' stairs. For a moment Mary wondered if he'd seen it, then the door opened and he stood there, dressed in black velvet to conceal himself in the shadows.

She smiled at his look of surprise when he saw her dressed in a nightgown of lilac silk, her unplaited hair combed loose over her shoulders. She'd dismissed her servants for the night and now Anne had gone they were alone.

Brandon stared at her. 'You look ... beautiful, Mary.'

'Thank you. I was beginning to wonder if you'd forgotten me.'

He glanced back at the entrance to the servants' passageway. 'We shall have to declare our marriage soon. There are too many pairs of eyes on us to keep our secret for long.'

'It's only until our letters have arrived in England.'

Charles gave her a look of concern. 'Then it might be longer than I'd wish, as I struggle with the wording. It's no easy thing to tell Henry I've disobeyed his wishes.'

'My secretary has a way with words. I'll ask him to help you – but we needn't talk of such things now.' She took his hand and led him to the privacy of her inner chamber.

A dozen beeswax candles scented with the delicate perfume of lavender oil and a crackling log fire gave the room a warm glow. Mary closed the door behind them and slid across the bolt.

Charles took her in his arms and gave her a long passionate kiss that took her breath away. He finally spoke in a whisper, as if they might be overheard. 'Alone together at last.'

Mary put her arms around his neck and pulled him closer. 'As husband and wife.'

'Yes, as husband and wife.' He kissed her again.

She freed herself from his embrace and pulled at the thin ribbon securing her silk gown. It fell to her feet, leaving her naked before him.

Brandon lifted her in his arms and carried her over to the canopied bed, where he lay her down before unfastening his jerkin and linen undershirt. Pulling off his clothes he climbed on to the bed and lay at her side. Brushing her long hair from her face with his hand he looked into her eyes.

'I never believed this day would come.'

She ran the tips of her fingers through the dark hair of his chest. 'You used to think of me?'

'You were always so close, yet so far from my reach.'

'If two people are destined to be together, nothing can stand in their way.'

'Not even kings?'

'Not even the King of England – or the King of France.' She giggled at the thought. 'I remember seeing you when I was betrothed to Archduke Charles. You stood at the back, then left.'

'I could watch no more of it, Mary.'

She pulled him closer. 'Well, what will you do, now you have me in your spell, my lord of Suffolk?'

His answer left her breathless, like nothing she'd ever experienced before. Afterwards she lay on her back, her mind a whirl and her pulse racing. She finally understood why people were prepared to risk everything for love.

12

MARCH 1515

Mary guessed something was wrong as soon as she saw his face. Brandon's eyes revealed his thoughts to her more than any man she'd known. He waited for her to send her servants away then sat heavily in a chair. He pulled off his cap and ran his fingers through his unruly hair then frowned at a folded parchment he carried in his hand.

He'd been meeting with Francis and she guessed it had not gone well. The letter might be the reply he'd been waiting for from Henry, or another from Wolsey. She crossed the room, the hem of her emerald-green gown swishing on the marble floor tiles as she moved, then leaned down and kissed him.

'What's happened?'

He looked up at her, his face serious. 'King Francis demands the return of your jewel.'

She shrugged. 'It's not unexpected. He told me many of the jewels King Louis gave me now belong to Queen Claude, as the crown jewels of France.'

'He insists we return the Mirror of Naples.' He scowled. 'I realise now it was a mistake to send it to England.'

wels. You can give them all back to him if it
return home.'

don shook his head. 'Henry wishes me to return with
many of your jewels as I can. I told Francis I'll do my best to
retrieve the Mirror of Naples but he knows Henry will never
send it back.' His hand formed a fist in frustration. 'He's
playing games with us – and to make matters worse, my
enemies accuse me of being too lenient in my negotiations with
the French.'

'Your enemies?'

He looked at her, his eyebrows raised in surprise. 'You don't
know? Ever since I was made Master of the Horse, the old
families of England call me Henry's stable boy. They resent my
title and look for any chance to ruin my reputation. There have
always been whispers behind my back at the council – but now
they could turn the king's mind against me.' He frowned.
'Against us, Mary.'

She heard the note of bitterness in his voice and remembered how her ladies once joked about Brandon's rapid rise.
She'd reprimanded them but this was different. If enough
nobles of the council sided against him, Henry would be
bound to listen, with dire consequences for them both.

'I've made it worse for you.' She placed a hand on his arm
and noted he didn't deny it. Mary sat in silence for a moment
as she struggled to think what she could do. 'I will meet again
with Francis, tell him about our secret marriage – and that it
was me who sent the jewel back to Henry.'

'You should read this letter.' He handed her the folded
parchment.

Mary unfolded the parchment and began to read. From
Thomas Wolsey, it confirmed her worst fears. Brandon was to
discontinue his ambassadorial duties and there seemed to be
no prospect of the king's forgiveness.

She stared at Brandon, understanding in her eyes. 'So, even

if you can restore the French king's goodwill, others will take credit for any treaty.'

He nodded. 'Wolsey's tone has changed – and if he sets himself against us we are ruined.'

'Then we shall have to make sure he does not.' Her eyes narrowed. 'Whatever it takes.'

'He hints at a remedy, although there is no promise of success and it will cost us dearly.'

Mary studied the letter a second time. 'The price of my brother's forgiveness is that we must return my dowry in full?'

'Two hundred thousand crowns, as well as all your gold and silver plate and every one of your jewels. It's impossible, Mary. Everything of value we both have will not be enough to satisfy him. Could you live without all this?' He gestured at the grand furnishings that graced the luxurious royal apartments.

Mary refolded the parchment and looked into his troubled eyes. 'When my father was my age he had nothing, yet he confessed to me once that his years in exile were some of the happiest of his life.' She smiled. 'You've risked everything for me – and I will happily sacrifice everything for you, Charles Brandon.'

Their secret was out and the Paris court buzzed like a nest of hornets at the news. One advantage of Brandon no longer being an ambassador was that he could spend more time with Mary. This also meant more opportunity for them to be seen together. King Francis ended the speculation of his courtiers by blessing their union at a special service, followed by an extravagant banquet.

For once, Queen Claude sat at her husband's side. She wore a voluminous gown of russet brocade which seemed to emphasise her girth. When Francis left to join in the dancing she placed her hand on Mary's arm. 'I was so pleased when I heard.' She spoke in French, a wistful look in her eyes. 'I once dreamed of marrying for love.'

Mary glanced across at Francis and saw he was dancing with her fourteen-year-old lady-in-waiting, Mistress Anne Boleyn. Vivacious and accomplished, Anne made it her business to attract the eye of the king yet Mary hoped she would never become his mistress. She turned to Claude, who seemed unconcerned at her husband's blatant flirting.

'King Francis has been so generous with his support.' She glanced back at the king and saw he was now whispering in the ear of Lady Anne, who laughed at some witty remark.

Queen Claude also noticed and turned to Mary with a hint of sadness in her eyes. 'I understand you've incurred King Henry's displeasure.'

Mary glanced at Brandon, deep in conversation with the king's brother-in-law. 'He planned to use my marriage to secure another alliance, yet I pray he'll accept my choice soon enough.'

Claude's face suggested she doubted it. She stroked her hand over her bulging midriff and leaned closer, a conspiratorial tone to her voice. 'You must have a child, Mary, the sooner the better.'

She smiled at the queen's frank advice. 'And I must congratulate you. Do you think it is a boy or a girl?'

'Francis says it will be a boy and shall be named after him.' She frowned. 'He told his mother if it is a girl she will be named after her.'

Mary looked around and realised Duchess Louise had not attended their celebratory banquet. 'I shall miss you, Claude, now I am returning to England – but I most certainly will not miss your mother-in-law.'

Queen Claude brightened. 'We must correspond, Mary. I have few enough friends I can trust and will look forward to your letters.'

Mary took Claude's hand in hers. 'I am honoured to be your friend and must thank you for your kindness when I arrived here.' She smiled. 'I will pray your child is more like you than its father – or grandmother!'

They laughed together at the thought and Mary saw King Francis turn his head at the sound and fix them with a questioning look. His sharp eyes missed little and she guessed he wondered what his wife was up to. She would not miss him either, despite his support for her marriage.

Another letter finally arrived from Thomas Wolsey setting out in detail the cost of their return. He proposed payment of the money by instalments of two thousand pounds a year, and for Mary to sign all her property over to Henry.

Brandon cursed. 'He knows that's beyond our means. The de la Pole estates Henry gifted with my title are worthless until they transfer – and your French incomes are at the whim of King Francis.'

Mary was unsurprised, both at Wolsey's demands or Brandon's outburst. The whole business had been playing on his mind, causing him restless days and sleepless nights. It also revealed a darker side to his character. His aggression clouded his judgement under such stress.

'Thomas Wolsey needs to silence our critics with a substantial sum.' She saw understanding dawn in his eyes. 'We must play his game. Agree in good faith, then we'll negotiate a smaller annual charge if we find we can't afford the payments.'

Brandon nodded and stroked his thick beard, deep in thought. 'I could sell my wardship of Lady Elizabeth Lisle. She's ten years old now and her wardship must be worth a goodly sum.'

Mary glowered at him. 'I assumed you already had. I trust you're not still betrothed to the girl?'

He grinned at her jealousy, his mood already improving. 'In truth, I never was properly betrothed to her. I began to use the title in presumption of marriage and no one ever challenged it.'

'I shall be Duchess of Suffolk,' she smiled at the thought, 'but I will use my title of Dowager Queen of France when it suits me.'

'You will find it strange without an army of servants to take care of your every need, my lady.'

Mary laughed. 'Well. I have you, sir, to take care of every need.'

He gave her a wry look and kissed her as Mistress Anne Jerningham arrived to tell them their escort was ready to take them to Calais. Mary took one last look up at the high ceilings and gilded opulence of the French palace, then turned her back on it all to begin her new life.

King Francis surprised them one last time by riding with them the seven miles to Saint Denis on the outskirts of Paris, with fifty mounted knights. He embraced Brandon, wishing him a prosperous future, then kissed Mary's hand and promised to ensure she would receive the income from her dower lands.

They finally left for Calais, riding three abreast and followed by servants, the few ladies returning with them and two covered wagons laden with baggage. Dean West looked back over his shoulder. 'The king still watches.' He managed a rare smile. 'One could think he doesn't trust us to leave.'

Mary resisted the temptation to look. 'I can't help wondering if he made the point about my dower lands to remind me of the hold he still has over us.'

'Do you think he'll keep his word after we're in England?' Brandon's tone sounded doubtful.

'We must make certain of it. The income is worth several thousand marks.' Mary glanced across at Brandon. 'I shall write to Queen Claude as often as I can. We can never be free of the French court, so it will be useful to have at least one friend there we can rely on.'

Brandon agreed. 'Once we've been accepted back at court I'll arrange a joust in honour of King Francis and persuade Henry to meet him in France – without an invading army. If Francis sees we support his interests he'll be less likely to withhold your income.'

Mary smiled to herself, relieved to hear him talking of the future with optimism once more. Before they left Paris she'd prayed for Henry's forgiveness for them both. She drew hope from his promise to let her choose her own husband, and suspected Wolsey exaggerated her brother's anger.

It took five days of riding on deeply rutted French roads, stopping overnight in modest inns, before the welcome sight of Calais appeared on the horizon. Mary was pleased by their reception, as most of the town seemed to have turned out to greet them, including the mayor and the merchant aldermen in full livery, despite the late hour.

Sir Richard Wingfield, Lord Deputy of Calais, raised a gloved hand in greeting. 'Welcome to Calais, my lord,' he bowed his head to Mary, 'my lady.'

Brandon slid from his saddle and embraced his old friend. 'Good to see you again, Sir Richard. Is there news of our passage to England?'

'I sent Sir William Sidney with a message to the king, as you requested. We should have his reply any day now.'

Mary recalled Brandon's cousin, who distinguished himself in the jousts at her wedding to King Louis. He had crossed the Channel several times at Brandon's request carrying their letters to Henry, although too often he'd returned with no reply.

Sir Richard looked back at the wagons. 'Please allow me to escort you to your apartments.'

As they followed him through cobbled streets lined with the people of Calais, Mary realised this might be the last time she would be such a figure of interest. She felt tired after their long ride and was relieved when Sir Richard announced he'd arranged a private supper as he had important news to share with them.

He waited until they were alone then turned to Brandon. 'I must ask you to keep to my apartments while we wait for your passage to be approved.'

'Why is that?' Brandon gave him a puzzled look.

'I postponed a delegation to England, which has caused a little bad feeling among the merchants of the Staple.' He frowned. 'I wished a good welcome for you but instead it seems I've stirred up resentment.'

Brandon was dismissive. 'I'll take care of myself, although I'll keep my head down, if that's what you wish.'

Sir Richard looked relieved. 'You are no doubt wondering how the treaty discussions progressed in your absence?' He tore a chunk from his bread and used it to mop the rich sauce from his plate.

'I trust you found it easier once the king wasn't distracted by my endless haggling over my wife's jewellery?' Brandon refilled his goblet from the jug of red wine as he spoke.

Mary heard the note of irony in his voice. She'd known how difficult it must have been to swallow his pride and humble himself to appease her brother. At the same time, she felt a frisson of pleasure at the hint of pride when he'd spoken of her as his wife.

Sir Richard smiled. 'The peace treaty is agreed in principle, which is not unexpected,' he looked from Brandon to Mary, 'and I have good news, my lady. King Francis has agreed to repay your dowry.'

'The full two hundred thousand?' Brandon sounded surprised.

'It took some persuasion, and of course you'll see little enough of it, but King Henry might feel better disposed towards you now.'

Mary said a silent prayer of thanks for their good fortune. 'We are most grateful to you, Sir Richard.'

'I had a modest part in the negotiations, my lady. It seems Dean West spoke frankly to King Francis and persuaded him to understand your circumstances.'

'He rode with us all the way from Paris and didn't mention it once.' Brandon gave Sir Richard a questioning look.

'We received confirmation after you left Paris. All the same, he's the one who deserves your thanks.'

Mary's wine warmed her throat and left a delicious after-taste. Sir Richard had served his best and she'd devoured the well-cooked venison, realising how hungry she'd been. For the first time in weeks her mood began to lift.

After they retired to bed Mary lay wide awake, her head full of questions. 'Sir Richard's messenger has had time to bring news from England, yet Henry has still not consented to our return.'

Brandon put his arm around her. 'Yet he hasn't refused.' He kissed her, his voice sounding sleepy.

Mary kissed him back but her mind was still on their immediate situation. 'Do you think our punishment is to languish here in Calais?'

'I can think of worse things. I could be banished from court, lose all my titles, be locked up in a dungeon at the Tower of London, executed at Tower Hill...'

'Don't jest about such things.' She gave him a stern look. 'We will both write to Henry in the morning, advising him of the dowry settlement and that I've signed over my jewels. You can take some credit for the treaty, as you won over Francis before they even started the negotiations.'

He pulled her close. 'Sir Richard confided they are saying I conceded Tournai in return for Louis supporting our marriage. In truth, the only time I mentioned Tournai was to promote Wolsey's ambition to become bishop there.'

'You must tell Henry the truth.'

'In good time.' His voice sounded tired.

Mary frowned. 'If he believes these stories it will count against us.' He didn't reply and she realised he'd fallen asleep after too much good wine.

Mary took a deep breath of the fresh sea air and held tight to the ship's wooden rail. Their stay in Calais was pleasant enough but they'd both grown impatient waiting for Henry's consent for their return. When his letter finally arrived it triggered a flurry of packing and goodbyes, as Brandon secured a passage on a merchant ship leaving with the early tide the next morning.

A sea mist hung over the water, reducing visibility, but their captain assured them the winds were fair for the crossing. Mary stayed on deck with Brandon to watch as they manoeuvred from the crowded harbour of Calais and cleared the high Rysbank Tower.

The undulating coast of France melted into the grey mist and she did a quick calculation on her fingers. 'It has been seven months since I last saw England, although it feels like a lifetime.'

'You'll find England much the same as when you left — although you've changed.' He smiled at her. 'You left as a girl and return as a woman.'

'You are right.' She pulled him closer. 'I was innocent of the world outside London, let alone the French court.'

'It's good you've lived a little.' Brandon looked into her eyes. 'You know it will be a struggle, until Henry shows his forgiveness?'

'Where will we live?' Mary hadn't given it a moment's thought.

Brandon put his warm cloak over her shoulders as a chill sea breeze blew across the deck. 'I have a house by the Thames, close to Greenwich and Westminster. It will need work, but if I can raise the money it could be made fit for a queen.'

'I've never had my own house. Richmond belongs to Henry and I never felt at home in France.'

Brandon put his arm around Mary to steady her as the ship heeled a little in the wind. 'We shall name it Suffolk Place, and once we are established I'll build us another house in the country, somewhere we can escape to when London becomes too oppressive.'

At last Mary pointed as the faint shadow of Dover loomed in the distance. She'd been looking forward to this moment since they'd set out from Paris, yet now England was in sight her old misgivings returned.

Thomas Wolsey's letters warned there would be consequences for their actions and Mary had lain awake at night wondering what they might be. She'd seen Henry's displeasure in the past and she knew he was not a man to cross. Now she worried, not for herself, but for Brandon.

She looked up at him and saw him frown as he studied the distant white cliffs of Dover, topped by the dark outline of the castle. Their crossing had been uneventful yet Mary feared they were sailing into troubled waters.

13

MAY 1515

Nobles from the royal court rode to greet them, banners flying in the breeze. Twenty mounted yeomen of the guard rode behind them in the king's colourful livery. Mary's heart began to race. She wondered if they'd come to take Brandon to the Tower of London.

She brought her horse to a halt and looked across at him. 'You can't let them arrest you.'

He stopped at her side, shading his eyes from the early sunshine with his hand as he studied the approaching men, trying to judge their mood. 'I shall have to take my chances, as do we both. I know your brother as well as anyone and trust he will allow me the chance to explain.'

'What will we do if he locks you up in the Tower?' She frowned as she remembered horrific stories she'd heard of men driven to madness in their cells.

'Then you will have to speak on my behalf.' He turned to her, concern in his eyes. 'Have faith. Henry gave his word you could marry of your own choosing. He can't have forgotten – you've reminded him often enough.'

Mary felt her courage slipping away as she watched the

guards ride closer. Armed with swords and halberds, they would easily overtake her heavily laden wagons on the long straight road. Brandon was right, they would have to pray they found her brother in a benevolent mood.

'That's Thomas Howard, Duke of Norfolk, riding at the front with his sons.' Brandon scowled. 'My ancestors served his family and he's never let me forget it. I don't doubt he's been looking forward to this moment.'

'Sir Thomas escorted me to France. Perhaps he's here to greet me on my return.' Mary recognised a familiar, stout figure, dressed in long black robes. A crucifix flashed on his chest as it caught the sunlight. 'Thomas Wolsey rides behind them. Do you think it's a good omen that he's come in person?'

Brandon continued to study the approaching riders. 'We are about to find out.' He turned to look at her. 'If they arrest me, I want you to know I regret nothing. I would gladly do it all again.'

A stern-faced Thomas Wolsey remained in his saddle as he bowed his head to Mary. 'We thank God to see you safe back in England, my lady.' He gave a curt nod of acknowledgement to Brandon. 'The king waits to greet you at Sir George Neville's manor of Birling.'

'How is my brother the king?' Mary studied Wolsey's face, hoping to read the truth of their situation.

'The king is in good spirits, my lady.' Wolsey urged his horse closer and lowered his voice. 'He wishes you to wed the duke at Greenwich without undue delay.'

Mary was about to point out that they had already been married twice in France when she saw Brandon's signal. Henry was right. Thomas Wolsey was right. They had no record of either wedding and no bans had been read. Although there were witnesses, including the King of France, they risked their marriage being contested. Any child would be in the line of succession, so their legitimacy must be beyond question.

Their long procession caused quite a stir as it passed through Kentish towns and villages on the fifty-mile journey to Birling. The orchards were in full blossom and it felt good to be back in the warmth of an English spring after what had seemed an endless French winter.

A skylark sang high overhead as they followed the old drovers' roads through the undulating grassland of the Kent Downs. Dotted with peaceful, grazing sheep, the English countryside looked idyllic and Paris, with its gossiping court and stinking streets, already seemed a long way off, a different life.

When they stopped to rest the horses Mary took the opportunity to speak with Wolsey, conscious she must learn as much as she could while there was time. 'Is the king, my brother, still angry with me, Master Wolsey?'

'He is, Your Grace.' Wolsey gave her a stern look. 'It was a grave mistake to marry without the king's consent.' His tone softened a little. 'It was not the principle of the marriage, but the means by which it was achieved.'

'King Francis left me no choice.' Mary decided her best defence was to blame the French. 'He would have had me marry to suit his own purpose if I'd delayed any longer.'

Wolsey looked at her as if making a judgement. 'Did you leave King Francis on good terms?'

Mary nodded. 'He blessed our union and promised to honour my dower lands.'

Wolsey glanced back at Brandon, deep in conversation with Norfolk's younger son. 'The king has decreed that the French marriage is to remain a secret. I caution you to speak no more of it.'

Mary felt indignant at his sharp reprimand yet remained silent. This was not the time to cross Thomas Wolsey. His

power extended through church and state and Henr
to his counsel. Then her curiosity got the better of her.

'How do you propose to keep secret the fact v
married in France?'

'Sir William Sidney has been sent to persuade King Francis
that it will be in his best interests.'

'King Francis will enjoy extracting a price for his silence,
although I don't see how we stop the gossipers in the French
court.' She saw Wolsey's frown of disapproval. 'I shall write to
Queen Claude and ask her to support Sir William's mission.'

Henry had grown a well-trimmed beard and was dressed for
hunting, with fine leather riding boots and cape, and a gold-
handled dagger at his belt. His sharp eyes studied Mary's face,
as if seeing her for the first time, then he reached out with both
arms to embrace her.

'Dearest sister, you have returned to us!'

Mary stepped forward and embraced him, then spoke
softly in his ear. 'Forgive me, dear brother.'

She pulled back, reassured by the smile lighting up his face.
'I served you to the best of my ability in France – and learned
a great deal of their ways.'

Henry gave her a shrewd look. 'We will talk later.' He
looked behind her. 'Brandon, you rascal, you would defy the
wishes of your king?' His tone was bluff yet there was an
amused edge to his voice.

Brandon bowed. 'I am guilty of obeying your sister's
wishes, Your Grace.'

'With no thought for yourself?' Henry laughed and slapped
him on the back. 'Has my errant sister tired you out – or will
you come hunting with us?'

Brandon's face brightened at the prospect. 'I've missed our

hunting expeditions, Your Grace. Let's see what hides in the woods.'

'Good man.' Henry glanced back once at Mary then headed for the door, followed by Brandon and several younger nobles of the court.

Mary felt a great weight lifted from her as she watched them go. It seemed Thomas Wolsey exaggerated Henry's anger. She looked around for Catherine, then turned to Wolsey, who had watched her welcome in silence.

'Where might I find Queen Catherine?' Her tone was a little more confident now, yet she knew she must keep Wolsey close.

He hesitated, as if deliberating how much to reveal. 'The queen is indisposed, my lady.'

'Is she here, in Birling?'

He shook his head. 'The queen chose to remain at Greenwich.'

Mary sensed he withheld some important information but there would be time to find out what it was. He still treated her as an innocent young girl, rather than the Dowager Queen of France. She decided it suited her to encourage his mistake – for now.

Mary understood why the Church of the Observant Friars in the grounds of Greenwich Palace was chosen for their third wedding. A short walk from the palace, it was where Henry had been christened as a child and where he'd married Catherine. The limited space within the ancient church also suited their purposes.

King Henry, Queen Catherine and the entire royal court attended as witnesses, filling every seat. The ambassadors of France and Spain were conspicuous by their absence, although they would usually witness a royal marriage.

Mary wore the same silk gown she'd used for the ceremony with King Francis in France. The sum to be repaid each month had been halved, after some negotiation with her brother and Wolsey. It would be a struggle to repay even twenty-four thousand pounds and she'd already begun making economies.

She took some comfort that their union was blessed by her old friend John Fisher, Bishop of Rochester, Lady Margaret Beaufort's confessor. Mary remembered how Bishop Fisher had shown kindness to her grandmother at the end, as he had with her father.

She spoke her vows clearly, her voice echoing in the high-vaulted church so all could hear. Mary smiled as Brandon brought a note of sincerity to his well-rehearsed words. He took one of her hands in his and looked into her eyes as he repeated his promise to love and cherish her. She'd never heard of any couple being married so many times, but at least now there was no secrecy or contrivance.

They returned to the palace after the ceremony and she sought out Catherine, whom she'd not been able to speak to since her return. Catherine seemed to have aged during Mary's time in France. She wore an old-fashioned brocade gown which did little for her figure. A pomander scented with cloves hung from her belt and her face looked pale under an ornate gable hood.

Mary didn't care about raising eyebrows by wearing the fashionable, lighter French hood, which showed more of her reddish-gold hair. She wanted to bring something of the sparkle of the French court and her low-cut gowns were already making the English ladies take note.

Catherine embraced her. 'I thank God for your safe return, Mary. I was concerned for you.'

'You must tell me everything that has happened since I left – and I shall tell you stories of my adventures in France.'

Catherine nodded but didn't smile. Instead she placed her

hand on Mary's arm and glanced at Henry, already surrounded by young nobles. 'Will you come to my private rooms? I could do with someone to talk to, other than my confessor.'

Mary followed Catherine, who dismissed her ladies and closed the door on her servants. 'You've heard the rumours, no doubt?' Her voice had a note of sadness, mixed with resignation.

'No. I've hardly spoken to anyone since my return.' It was the truth, although she guessed what the rumours might be. She'd rarely seen Henry looking more pleased with himself or Catherine looking so sad. 'Is it Henry?'

Catherine nodded. 'He's taken a mistress. One of my maids of honour, Elizabeth Blount.' The bitterness in her voice as she said the name was unmistakable.

Mary remembered Bessie Blount. Young and full of fun, she was one of Catherine's most attractive ladies. 'Can you not dismiss her from your service?'

'It's too late. He's obsessed with her.' Her sharp tone revealed how deeply she'd been hurt.

'Does he still visit you?'

Catherine nodded. 'I pray each day that I will give him a son.' She frowned. 'I know the consequences if I fail.'

Mary took her hand, as if making a pact. 'Let us both pray we can give our husbands strong and healthy sons.'

Catherine's eyes went to her narrow waist in surprise. 'You are with child?'

Mary smiled. 'Not yet – but it's not for lack of trying.'

Catherine laughed at her frank admission. 'You must come and visit me often, Mary. I've missed you.'

'I shall, Catherine.' She saw something replace the sadness in Catherine's eyes and realised she still clung to the hope of a son. 'Have faith, and remember Henry loves you.'

The setting sun cast a golden glow over the River Thames as Mary left Greenwich Palace. Like Henry's court, the glittering surface perfectly disguised the dark, murky waters beneath. It angered her that Henry turned his back on Catherine for a pretty seventeen-year-old girl but now she understood this was the way of kings.

There were no celebrations to mark their marriage and they'd not been invited to stay on at Greenwich. They had no money and all her remaining possessions fitted in two wagons, yet Mary felt at peace with the world, happier than she could ever remember.

Brandon's riverside mansion at Suffolk Place needed a woman's touch. More like an abandoned soldiers' barracks than a home, the wood-panelled walls were decorated with the antlers of long-dead stags, ancient weapons, and faded tapestries of hunting scenes.

The rambling property was inherited from Brandon's family and enclosed a large courtyard. As well as formal gardens leading to a private jetty, there were some eighty acres of established oak woodland to the south, a potential source of useful income if money ran short, as Mary knew it would.

Brandon had grand plans for their home, despite their lack of funds. Inspired by what he'd seen in Paris, he commissioned an imposing new entrance and the courtyard soon rang to the clink of masons' chisels on stone and carpenters sawing wood.

The work had hardly begun when he had to travel north to oversee the transfer of his estates. There were over forty manor houses in different ownership and tenancies to resolve. It was work Brandon needed to do in person but Mary would have travelled with him if she'd known he'd be away so long.

Instead, she remained at Suffolk Place and filled her days

by making their house fit for a family. Mary explored the rooms before choosing one with the best view out over the River Thames. She set to work, directing servants to sweep away cobwebs, whitewash the walls and lay fresh rushes on the floors.

She smoothed her hand over the bulge, hardly visible under her gown, yet growing larger each week. She'd been loosening the lacing of her kirtle a little each week but now more drastic work was needed. Mary examined the new panel her seamstress had sewn into her gown. The material was a good enough match but the dress, one of her favourites, would never be quite the same.

She smiled as she remembered telling Catherine her news and hearing that they would both be having babies before Eastertide. She'd prayed they would have sons and they'd laughed together as they realised the obvious choice of name would be Henry.

After the baby was born she planned to send for Brandon's daughters by his first wife, Anne Browne, to complete their family. Little Anne, now eight years old, had been sent to the court of Margaret of Austria the year before. Despite Brandon's protests, Mary still wondered if it was because he'd planned to marry the archduchess. Little Mary, only five years old, remained in the care of her mother's relatives.

Upstairs in her new chamber she found the servants had left the painted wooden casket containing her personal belongings. She'd not opened it since their hasty packing in Paris and she had to try several keys before finding the right one. Mary opened the lid and took out the contents, placing them on the polished wooden top of her dressing table.

The little portrait of pale-faced Prince Charles seemed from another, more innocent age. She wasn't sure why she'd kept it but couldn't bring herself to throw it away. Next she took out a book of poetry in French which she'd read to King

Louis in his last days. Another memory that seemed to belong to another time.

She opened the little book at a random page and with a little effort translated the old French as she read: I die of grief a hundred times a day, and a hundred times revive with joy. She remembered the twinkle of adoration in Louis' eyes and wondered if she'd ever see quite the same in Brandon's.

Finally, Mary unwrapped the royal seal of the Queen of France. The symbol of the power she'd once had felt cold and heavy in her hand. The only time she'd used it for anything important was to sign over her dowry and all her property to Henry. A high price had been paid but she had no regrets, other than the way they'd been kept away from court.

Apart from occasional visits to Catherine at Greenwich, neither of them had been made welcome at the royal court since their wedding. She soon realised Catherine chose times when Henry was away, although that was hardly going to hasten their return to favour.

When the first invitation came it was delivered by the king's messenger. Mary broke the seal and studied the contents. Thomas Wolsey had finally achieved his ambition to be made a cardinal and Brandon was chosen as one of the lords to escort him to a celebratory banquet. She showed the letter to Brandon as soon as he returned from the north. He read it and grinned at her.

'He's done us few enough favours – but now he'll enjoy even greater influence. Whatever you think of him, Wolsey is our only true supporter at council,' Brandon reread the invitation, 'and look – it's signed in Wolsey's own hand.'

'This is the forgiveness we've been waiting for.' Mary smiled. 'Henry had to show our critics he'd not been too easy on us, although I was beginning to wonder...'

Brandon produced a second invitation with a flourish from a pocket in his doublet. 'There's more. We are also invited to the launch of the king's latest warship and to voyage with him down the Thames. A good omen,' Brandon contrived to look serious, 'although her name might cause you some embarrassment.'

Mary took the invitation from him and studied it, then looked up and smiled. 'The *Virgin Mary*? I hardly think my brother named her after me.'

'I've heard they are already referring to her as the *Princess Mary*.' He grinned. 'She's a full-bodied ship, you see, broad at the waterline.' He placed his hands on her hips as if she might not understand.

Mary laughed and gave him a playful jab in the ribs. 'I shall take it as a great compliment from my brother the king. I know he loves his ships more than anything he owns.'

The *Virgin Mary* towered over the buildings on the banks of the Thames, the latest symbol of Henry's power. With four great masts and over two hundred guns she was a floating fortress, and like the Venetian galleys, the massive sails were supplemented by sixty pairs of long oars.

The gathered crowds cheered as King Henry waved from the deck. Dressed in cloth of gold, he wore a diamond-studded sailor's whistle on a chain around his neck and called to Mary and Brandon as he spotted them.

'Dear sister!' Henry beckoned them to join him on the deck. 'Is she not the most beautiful ship?'

Mary lifted the hem of her gown as she made her way up the steep walkway on to the deck, then curtseyed as she approached her brother. 'Your ships are the envy of the world, dearest brother.'

She saw his nod of approval and smiled at Queen Catherine standing at his side. 'You look well, Your Grace.'

It was true. Catherine seemed transformed by the child developing inside her. Her eyes sparkled with happiness and she wore a magnificent gown of burgundy with gold brocade. Her lost children had tested her faith yet she remained confident that this time she would provide Henry with the heir he so desperately wished for.

Even the chill October wind did nothing to spoil the cheery mood as Queen Catherine had the honour of naming the ship, and gave a meaningful look to Mary as she did so. A choir sang a Mass of dedication and an army of servants carried tables and chairs on deck for a banquet of fish and seafood, with a sugar centrepiece of King Neptune holding a silver trident.

Brandon stood next to Henry as the king personally steered the *Virgin Mary* through the myriad small craft come to escort her down the Thames. Henry placed his whistle to his lips and blew a deafening blast, laughing loudly at the startled ladies.

Mary raised a gloved hand to acknowledge the cheering crowds jostling dangerously close to the water's edge for a view. She placed the other hand on her bulging middle. Her new life had begun and soon she would have new responsibilities.

A dark cloud of premonition made her look across again at Queen Catherine. She remembered the anguished sound of a mother who'd lost a newborn child and said a silent prayer. If all did not go well Mary doubted her friend would have another chance.

14

FEBRUARY 1516

High-pitched shrieks of delight brought Mary to the open window. She shivered and pulled her fur-lined cloak closer around her as she peered out into the misty morning. Children were playing on the frozen River Thames. This winter was the coldest she could remember yet the people of London made the best of it, as they always did.

She gasped in concern as she watched small boys speeding across dangerously thin ice on wooden sledges, their shouts of excitement carrying in the still air. For a moment she envied their freedom. Brandon had taken to riding to Greenwich early each day, leaving her at Suffolk Place with only her ladies for company.

A few, including Lady Elizabeth Grey and Jane Popincourt, had been with her in France. The others were daughters of nobles looking for influence at court. Their gossiping amused her while she sewed silk nightdresses for the baby, and helped keep her informed about what was going on at Henry's court.

The low winter sun gave way to a shadowy dusk before Brandon returned. He kissed Mary then pulled off his heavy riding boots to warm his feet in front of the roaring fire before sharing his news. 'Catherine's child is a girl.' His eyes twinkled with amusement as he watched her face to see her reaction, knowing she'd been waiting for word to arrive.

Mary hardly dared to ask but was unable to guess from his expression. 'Are they both well?' Her hand instinctively went to the growing shape of her own child as it gave a little kick. Her physician assured her it would be a boy, as it lay to the right.

'With God's grace.' Brandon grinned. 'Henry named her Mary, in your honour. First his ship and now a daughter.'

Mary sat back in her comfortable chair, one gold-ringed hand resting on the gently moving shape within her. She'd prayed for Catherine to have the son she longed for, yet it was a great honour Henry paid her.

'I'm pleased for Catherine – yet I fear for her future.' She frowned as she counted on her fingers. 'Three lost sons and two daughters we know of.'

Brandon agreed. 'It's little wonder Henry grows more impatient each time, although now King Ferdinand is dead we no longer need to worry about where her loyalty lies.'

'It's been difficult for her,' Mary heard the defensive note in her voice, 'but despite her father's scheming she's always been loyal. Catherine might fall from favour again – but a healthy child will encourage Henry, even if it is a girl.'

Brandon yawned and took off his black velvet cap, straight-ening the gold badge before running his fingers through his auburn hair, grown longer since their return from Paris. 'I've been invited to the christening. Henry plans to make quite an event of it. He's sent men to bring the silver font from Canterbury.'

Mary smiled. Since Brandon had been restored to the lists it was as if he'd never been out of favour. After the last joust Henry gave him a present of a fine black destrier, complete with a new jousting saddle. He spent long hours with Henry and, as his brother-in-law, was more influential at court than ever.

They were sinking deeper into a bottomless pit of debt but it seemed of little concern to Brandon. He'd sent more of Mary's remaining jewels to Thomas Wolsey. His note explained they could not make the payment due to delays with her dowager income from France. Then he'd promptly borrowed another thousand more from a Venetian merchant.

At least the craftsmen's work was done at last and Suffolk Place had become their home. She looked up at the dozen white candles glowing in an ornate gilded candelabra, one of many furnishings sent from France. Her ladies confessed that her choice of decoration inspired by her time in Paris was a talking point in London society.

'I wish I could see her.' Mary gave him a wistful look. Her visits to Catherine had ended, as she would soon be entering her confinement. Wolsey offered his own mansion for the purpose and she'd felt obliged to accept. It was yet another reminder of how he exerted a subtle control over their lives.

Since becoming a cardinal he'd been even more full of himself, if such a thing were possible. He'd replaced Bishop Warham as Henry's Lord Chancellor on Christmas Eve, and had taken to sitting on a cushion of cloth of gold, like a king. Brandon told her Wolsey's wide-brimmed scarlet cardinal's hat remained on display at Westminster Abbey like some revered holy relic. It was good to have his support yet, as always, there was a price to be paid.

~

Wolsey's mansion at Bath Place near Temple Bar smelled musty, despite the bunches of dried lavender, and reminded Mary of her time at Cluny in Paris. This time it was for the good of her unborn child yet she felt just as cut off from the world. Although the harsh winter was finally turning to spring her room had no view of the courtyard outside. The walls and windows were draped with heavy hangings according to her grandmother's ordinances for royal births. The tall beeswax candles had to be kept burning all day to lighten the gloom and Mary lost track of time.

At least she had Elizabeth Grey and Jane Popincourt for company. Jane revealed to her a secret letter bound with a thin blue silk ribbon and written in an elegant French hand. The Duke of Longueville begged her to return to him in France, with promises of a grand new life. Mary looked up at Jane and saw her eyes sparkling with excitement at her news.

She smiled. The scandal of Jane's affair still hung over her like a cloud but the duke seemed a decent man, handsome, influential and wealthy. 'He's still married?'

Jane nodded. 'I will stay with you until the baby is born, my lady, then I must go to Provence. He is the governor there now.'

'Anyone else would tell you to find a good marriage, Jane, but a love match is a rare enough thing, so you have my blessing.'

'Truly?' Jane's eyes widened.

Mary felt touched by her gratitude. 'You shall have a hundred pounds for your loyalty, Jane – and I expect you to write to me with all the news from France.'

'Of course. I'd be honoured, my lady.'

'I'm concerned about my dowager income, which has still not been paid,' Mary admitted, 'and am also worried about Queen Claude. She wrote to me after her daughter was born but there has been nothing since.'

Jane Popincourt frowned. 'I can ask Duke Louis to enquire about the money due to you, although Provence is a long way from Paris, so it might not be so easy to see the queen.'

'Claude should remember you but I shall write you a letter

of introduction. The last time I saw her she told me she has few enough friends she can trust.'

The holy girdle of Our Lady, assured to bring a safe and successful delivery, had been sent by Queen Catherine and lay across the small altar on one side of Mary's room. She kneeled at it now with some effort, as her time was close. Clasping her hands together Mary prayed, until her knees went numb, for the life of her unborn baby. She knew the risks. Her own mother died a week after giving birth to her eighth child.

Mary lit a candle in memory of her mother and tried to remember her kindly face. Taking the taper, she lit a second candle for the little sister she'd never had the chance to know. Women in childbirth were supposed to be surrounded by their relatives. She had no one other than her sister Margaret, last heard of fleeing the dangers of Scotland. Mary had no idea where she was.

It began as a dull ache that grew stronger in waves, with the relentless power of the tide advancing on a rocky shore. Her ladies had retired for the night, so Mary gripped the hard wooden bedpost until the worst passed. She called out to her midwife, sleeping on a pallet bed at the far side of the room.

'Quick! I think it's coming!'

The midwife, a stout matron who'd served Queen Catherine, looked doubtful. 'We have a little time yet, my lady.' She dampened a white linen cloth with cold water and held it to Mary's forehead. The coolness helped but now a new fear gripped her.

'We must have a priest ready, in case...'

The midwife smoothed Mary's long hair from her face.

'There are many priests close by, my lady, but if I'm any judge we'll not be needing to wake one in the middle of the night.'

Mary watched as the midwife rang a bell to rouse servants to build the fire and boil water. They'd talked about what would happen when the time came but now she struggled to remember the midwife's advice. Whatever the outcome, she sensed her life would never be quite the same again.

The door opened and Jane Popincourt appeared, a dark woolen shawl wrapped around her shoulders and a white linen coif covering her hair. 'I asked to be woken if the baby started coming in the night.' She saw the midwife's nod and carried a chair to Mary's bedside, taking her hand.

Mary tried to smile but gritted her teeth as another powerful wave passed through her. As it subsided she gave Jane's hand a firm squeeze. 'I'm glad to have you here. I must admit I'm scared.'

A look of concern crossed Jane's face. 'Is something wrong with the baby?'

Mary shook her head. 'The discomfort is hard to bear.' She glanced at the midwife, making her preparations with the servants at the far end of her chamber. 'Talk to me, Jane. Take my mind off this—' She gasped again and closed her eyes for a moment as another wave struck.

'We could talk of the christening.' Jane Popincourt smiled. 'The king and queen will both wish to attend, so there is much to do.'

Mary bit her lip as she tried to concentrate on the christening instead of the contractions. 'I'd like it to be at Suffolk Place, in the great hall.'

Jane agreed. 'There's more room there than at the church in Greenwich. At little Princess Mary's christening many of the guests had to wait outside in the snow.' She smiled at the memory.

'Bishop John Fisher should perform the service. He was my grandmother's confessor.'

'The king will be godfather,' Jane glanced back at the midwife and a look passed between them, 'and Queen Catherine of course will be godmother.'

Mary cried out at another contraction. She crumpled the silk coverlet with her hand and tried to focus on their plans. 'I'll have to ask Cardinal Wolsey to be godfather as well,' her voice sounded strained, 'and my Aunt Catherine as second godmother. I think my mother would have liked that.' Mary lay back in her bed and stared up at Jane Popincourt, unable to speak for a moment.

'The great hall must be decorated with red and white roses.' Jane still held Mary's hand, despite the way she squeezed with all her strength until her fingers ached.

'Would they be able to find roses this time of year?'

Before Jane could answer a new agony coursed through Mary's lower body, causing her to scream out in anguish. The sound reverberated around the chamber like the wail of a ghost.

The midwife came to her bedside and placed another cool cloth on Mary's forehead. 'I know it's not easy, my lady, but get what rest you can. You'll need all your strength soon enough.'

'Rest?' The idea seemed impossible. 'Do you have anything for the pain?' A note of desperation made her voice sound harsher than she intended.

The midwife frowned. 'There are potions of herbs, but I don't abide by them.' She gave Mary a knowing look. 'Nature knows best, that's my watchword. How often are the pains now?'

'All the time – but the worst are coming more often.'

'A good sign, my lady.' The midwife smiled. 'The child is on its way.'

Exhausted but happy, Mary held her baby and stared into his large eyes with the special love only a mother can feel. Her prayers had been answered with a fine healthy boy, as her physicians predicted. 'He's perfect.'

The midwife waited to bind him in linen swaddling and hand him over to the wet nurse. 'What name have you chosen for him, my lady?'

'Henry.' Mary smiled. 'My little Henry Brandon.'

Jane Popincourt leaned closer and let the baby grasp her finger with his tiny pink hand. 'It seems strange to think he could one day be King of England.'

'Take care who hears you say that, Jane,' Mary's eyes narrowed, 'even though it's the truth.'

Jane blushed at the mild reprimand. 'Shall I find Duke Charles and tell him the news, my lady?'

Mary nodded. 'Please do. He must be beside himself with worry.'

~

The years had not been kind to Mary's sister Margaret. Her waist had suffered the consequences of seven children and her teeth were discoloured and uneven, reminding Mary of her father. Her defiant eyes stared out from a pockmarked face and her fine new gown was a gift from her brother Henry.

Although they'd exchanged letters, Mary last saw Margaret thirteen years ago. She'd been seven at the time but remembered the look of anguish on her fourteen-year-old sister's face as she left to marry the rakish King James IV of Scotland.

Now Margaret had returned and was lodged at Baynard's Castle, once their grandmother's London home. Like Mary, she was running out of money and caused a scandal by marrying for love. Her new husband, the Earl of Angus, was the same age as her and on the wrong side of the civil war in

Scotland. She'd also given him a daughter named Margaret the previous autumn.

Henry invited them both to a state dinner at Lambeth Palace, the first time the three of them had been together since they were children. An awkward silence descended as Mary stood staring at her sister. She'd somehow imagined that their age difference would appear less now, but the contrast between them was stark.

Margaret stepped forward and embraced her with unexpected warmth. 'Dearest Mary,' her voice had the soft accent of the Scots, 'I've prayed for this day so long.'

'As have I.' It was true. Mary always remembered her sister in her prayers although she'd not expected they would meet again.

Margaret still held her by both arms, as if reluctant to let her go. 'I must congratulate you on the birth of little Henry.' There was an odd note to her voice and Mary saw her sister's sly glance at Queen Catherine, who watched their reunion surrounded by the ladies of the court.

The two of them had been on opposing sides while she'd been in France. Catherine had celebrated the slaughter of King James after his disastrous border raid. Reconciliation would take time and Mary realised it would fall to her to become the peacemaker.

She forced a smile. 'You must see him, and I can't wait to see your little daughter, Margaret.'

Margaret returned Mary's smile, forgetting to conceal her bad teeth. 'We have so much catching up to do.'

Henry joked he had three queens to contend with, each with a baby. The novelty drew every noble in the land and crowds of the curious to the tournament at Greenwich, as he knew it would. Queen Catherine sat in the centre of the royal grandstand with Mary to her left and Margaret to her right as Henry led the competitors in a colourful procession.

Mary felt a surge of pride as Brandon rode past on his huge black destrier at the king's side. He wore his best armour with a blue ostrich plume on his helmet, matching the king's. No one watching could doubt he'd become the most important of all Henry's companions.

They watched and cheered as, one by one, Brandon defeated thirty-four knights with apparent ease. As the last threw up both hands in surrender Catherine turned to Mary with a frown. 'You know what this means?'

Mary did. 'Only my brother remains, so they must ride against each other?'

'It troubles me. Henry is so competitive, yet your Charles is not one to surrender without a fight.' Catherine shook her head at the thought.

Until then Mary had imagined it was like watching a mummers' play where no one could come to real harm. Now she saw Catherine's point. If Brandon unhorsed the king it could undo the progress they'd made since returning from France. If he dropped his guard to let Henry win he could be injured.

Trumpets blasted a fanfare and the Master of the Joust announced the final tournament of the day. The two champions would meet in a grand finale. Mary held her breath as she watched them line up at each end of the tiltyard. Henry raised a hand to a cheer from the watching crowd then lowered the visor of his helmet.

Brandon took his lance and did the same. Then, at the sign that both were ready, they charged. Mary wanted to look away but had to watch as they closed with a violent crack of shattering lances. The air seemed tense as the Master of the Joust declared the first pass for Brandon.

On the second run she gasped as Henry's lance crashed

into Brandon's breastplate, forcing him back in the saddle. The crowd cheered and called out 'Long live the king!' This time the points were awarded to Henry, so the winner would be decided by a final joust.

Mary tried to catch Brandon's eye but he was too far away to see. He raised and lowered his new lance then charged with a rumble of hooves on the hard-packed ground. They closed again with a deafening clash and she saw both lances shatter.

It looked a draw, then Brandon's seconds rushed to his aid. He dropped the broken lance and grimaced as he pulled off his right gauntlet. It seemed he'd injured his hand. Mary hoped this was a ploy and not a serious wound. Her brother must always win but not at any cost.

Brandon cursed his luck. 'It hurt like hell, Mary.' He held up his bandaged hand for her to see, like a badge of honour. 'I'm told it will heal well enough – but I won't be riding at the joust for a few months.'

Mary threw back the brocade bedcovers, inviting him to join her. 'That might not be such a bad thing. I might see more of you – and it could have been worse for us if my brother were injured.'

Brandon gave her a wry grin as he struggled to undress with his good hand. 'You think I meant it to happen?'

Mary smiled. 'You fought well. I was proud of you.'

He climbed into their bed and pulled her into his arms. 'And I was proud of you, Mary.' He kissed her. 'Your sister looks old enough to be your mother. You'd never guess she's only seven years older.'

'Margaret's been through a lot.'

Brandon stroked Mary's long hair, freed from its restraining plaits and brushed until it shone in her nightly ritual. 'Margaret seems determined to exploit the possibilities of her visit to her brother's court.' A note of disapproval sounded in his voice.

'She confided to me that she plans to stay at least a year.'

'Henry will tire of her before then, mark my words.'

Mary gently took his injured hand in hers. 'This is an omen. You will have to take a rest from tournaments for a while, so take me to your home in Suffolk. You could spend more time with your son and daughters, learn to be a father to them.'

Brandon agreed. 'It's time we lived together as a family, not as the former Queen of France and the king's stable boy,' he grinned, 'but as the Duke and Duchess of Suffolk, lord and lady of the manor.'

15

SPRING 1517

T he rolling Suffolk countryside continued to the hazy horizon, uninterrupted by any sign of a town or village. It reminded Mary of rural France, with narrow, twisting roads and green pastures. Although London was some seventy-five miles distant, the ride had taken five long days, so it seemed much further.

Her horse stumbled on the potholed road and with a jolt Mary realised she'd drifted off to sleep in the saddle. Her back ached as she turned to look at the straggling line of servants and packhorses following them, loaded with all her possessions.

Little Henry travelled in one of the covered wagons they called a char with his two nursemaids. Mary worried about how pale he'd looked last time she checked on him, despite her physician's assurances. She felt a twinge of anguish at the thought he might be ill, then forced it from her mind.

Brandon saw her look of concern. 'Not far now.' He raised his arm and gave her a grin of encouragement as he pointed a gloved hand. 'That's Westhorpe Hall ahead.'

She peered into the distance and sighed with relief as she saw brick towers rising above the trees. Brandon told her the old manor was in such a state of disrepair he'd decided to rebuild it, despite their rising debts. He was keen for her to make it their family home but Mary had mixed feelings about living so far from court. They'd argued about it, as she'd been happy at Suffolk Place and suspected she was being moved out of the way.

'Out of sight will mean out of mind, at least as far as my brother is concerned.' The note of bitterness in her words had been unintended, as they had no choice, yet she'd noticed her husband's frown of annoyance. He knew she was right.

Mary understood they could no longer afford the lifestyle she'd been used to. The last payment from France failed to arrive and her supply of precious jewels dwindled. Despite her brother's patience, she worried about their growing debts. Cardinal Wolsey was not a man she wished to owe favours to.

They crossed a stone bridge over a wide green moat and Mary had her first view of her new home. A freshly painted red-and-white Tudor rose decorated an imposing three-storey gatehouse. She smiled when she saw the rose, then realised it must have replaced the crest of the previous owners, the ill-fated de la Pole family.

Through the open gates she could see the house was built around an open square courtyard with a wooden dovecote in the centre. High towers at each corner, topped with turrets and pinnacles, reminded her of those built by her father at Richmond Palace. Two-storey ranges linked the towers to the gatehouse on each side, with new mullioned windows which must have cost a small fortune.

A line of servants waited to greet them and bowed or curtseyed as she passed. A few Mary recognised from Suffolk Place but most were strangers to her. She felt their eyes making a judgement but smiled back. She counted forty-seven men and seven maidservants and wondered how they would afford so large a household.

A young groom offered a hand to help Mary dismount and Brandon led her through heavy oak doors into the great hall. Despite the money he'd spent her first impression was one of disappointment.

It looked unfinished, with one wall of bare stonework not yet rendered in whitewashed plaster. Lack of funds meant rushes on the floor instead of the patterned French tiles she loved, and the tang of soot and smoke suggested the new chimneys weren't drawing properly.

She saw he waited for her opinion and stared up to the high, vaulted ceiling before turning to him. 'We shall make this one of the finest houses in Suffolk.'

He frowned at her tone. 'I hoped you would like it—'

'I do.' She placed her hand on his arm. 'I'm just a little tired after the journey.' She saw no point in upsetting him now.

He nodded in understanding and led her into the dining chamber, where a dark oak table was set for a meal with silver candelabras. Mary counted a dozen place settings and noted the two high-backed chairs, side by side, like thrones.

She smiled at Brandon. 'We're expecting guests?'

'We must always be ready for a visit from the king.' He grinned at the thought. 'I've suggested a royal progress of the north, and I look forward to entertaining our neighbours.'

She noticed a mischievous twinkle in his eye. 'There's something else you want to tell me?'

Brandon made a sign to the waiting servant, who opened a side door. Two young ladies entered, dressed in flowing satin gowns and headdresses in the latest French fashion. It was only when the eldest curtseyed and flashed her a confident smile that Mary realised who they were.

'Good day, Lady Mary. Welcome to Westhorpe Hall.'

Mary looked at Brandon's daughters in astonishment. 'Anne. You've grown into a beautiful young lady. It seems you have learned much at the court of Margaret of Austria. How old are you now?'

'I am ten, my lady.'

Brandon grinned and nodded to his youngest daughter, Mary, who took one step forward and bobbed a curtsey with less confidence than Anne, her eyes to the ground.

'My lady.'

Mary smiled. 'How old are you now, Mary?'

Brandon's daughter looked up at her with his same grey-blue eyes. 'I shall be seven this year, my lady.' Her well-educated young voice echoed in the chamber.

'Well, I welcome you both to our new home. I'll be glad of your company, as I expect your father will be away at court often.' Again, she heard the note of unintended criticism, although she knew their future depended on retaining his influence at her brother's court. 'You must meet little Henry. He will be tired from travelling but it's good to have our growing family together at last.'

They continued the tour of the house, visiting the newly lime-washed kitchens, where he showed her an enormous range with storerooms, a well-stocked pantry and cavernous cellars lined with barrels of wine. Mary wondered how much of it was paid for by their loans. Brandon had been evasive when she'd asked him how much he'd spent but he'd admitted it must be over twelve thousand pounds.

He led her out through a door and across the open cobble-stoned courtyard, with its white painted dovecote. White doves fluttered into the air as they crossed to the arched doorway of the private chapel. The iron-studded door swung open. Mary gasped at the sight of the magnificent stained-glass windows, a final surprise he'd been saving for her. The spring sunlight cast the bright colours of blue, red and gold on to the chapel floor, giving the room an ethereal quality.

In the centre glowed a magnificent Madonna and Child, while the window to the left had a Tudor rose with Mary's fleur-de-lis and crown as Queen of France. To the right shone Brandon's gold-crowned coat of arms and Order of the Garter.

'They are so beautiful.' She took his hand.

Brandon looked pleased with himself. 'I brought a craftsman over from Paris.' He smiled. 'You must be tired. Let me show you our apartments. There's a view of the deer park from the new windows – we might even see a stag.'

She followed him along a gallery to a winding stone staircase which led to the upper floor. Mary saw he'd made an effort to recreate their chambers at Suffolk Place but the floorboards creaked like an old warship and the unfashionable furniture was probably left behind by the de la Pole family.

At least the great carved bed was new, with burgundy velvet hangings trimmed with gold tassels and a finely woven brocade coverlet. Mary lay back on it and gestured for him to join her. The ropes supporting the mattress creaked as they tensioned under their weight.

She felt an overwhelming desire to close her eyes and sleep but too many questions troubled her. She turned to Brandon. 'We came here to make economies but I can see you've already spent a fortune and there is still much to do.'

He turned and studied her face for a moment before replying. 'You are a Tudor princess, Queen of France. I could not have you live like a commoner.'

'What will happen if King Francis withholds my dower payments?'

'Then I shall sell some of my estates in the south and make the most of our holdings in the north.'

She smiled. 'You make it sound so easy…'

Brandon grinned. 'I've been in debt all my lif is in no hurry to be repaid.'

'What of Wolsey? We must owe him a small fortur.

He nodded. 'We should give him some of your je keep him from demanding what is owed.'

'I shall write to him. I don't wish to make an enemy of Cardinal Wolsey.' Mary stroked Brandon's thick beard, a trick she knew disarmed him. 'Your daughters have grown into beautiful young ladies. Anne is much like her mother but little Mary has your eyes.'

Brandon smiled at the thought. 'It's a comfort to me that you welcome them. They will be good company for you when I'm away.'

'You mean to return to court without me?'

'There will be times when I have to. I also need to be seen by my tenants or we will never have the income due to us from our estates.' He reached out an arm to pull her close. 'You are safe here, and is it not good to be rid of the stench of the London streets?'

Mary relaxed back on the soft bed. He was right. 'The country air will be good for young Henry's health.'

'And the new baby.' His hand slid to the growing bulge in her emerald-green silk gown. 'A girl this time?'

Mary smiled. 'God willing. I shall be happy if it's a girl or another boy, so long as the child is healthy.'

The summons came sooner than expected, but not from the king. The letter, delivered by a royal herald, was from Queen Catherine, recalling Mary to court as her sister Margaret was soon to return to Scotland.

Brandon gave her a look of concern. 'I've heard talk of rioting in London. I'd prefer you to remain safe here with the girls and little Henry.'

Mary nodded. 'I know, but this might be the last time I will see my sister.'

'You could write to her suggesting she breaks her journey here?'

Mary frowned. She'd been glad of the excuse to return to court. 'It's most unusual for Catherine to summon me like this.' Her hand fell unconsciously to her bulging middle. 'She is also with child again. I hope this doesn't mean there is a problem.'

The king's armed guards patrolled the grounds of Richmond Palace, halberds at the ready, making it feel to Mary as if they were under siege. Henry's court had moved from Greenwich after the rumours of plague and rioting in the city. Brandon was right. The streets of London had become a dangerous place. As usual, Queen Catherine seemed well informed.

'The people blame foreign merchants for their troubles. They are looting the properties of the Flemish and the French and rioting in the streets.'

Mary frowned. Anything which endangered her fragile dower income from France could plunge them deeper into debt. 'Something must be done, and soon.'

Catherine nodded. 'We tried to keep the peace but Norfolk's men have hanged so many that London has been called a city of gibbets.'

Mary had heard the stories. The aging Thomas Howard, Duke of Norfolk, who'd escorted her to France and her marriage to King Louis, had been heavy-handed with the rioters. Many, including women and young boys, had been condemned without trial.

Catherine shook her head as she continued. 'They've arrested the ringleaders and will bring them for sentence before Henry. He must make an example of them.'

Margaret looked thoughtful. 'I've seen the same in Scotland. It will cause greater unrest and make them martyrs if they have a traitor's death. Could they not be punished in some other way?'

Catherine hesitated before replying. 'It is within the king's power to pardon them. Henry has little affection for foreign merchants who profit at the expense of the English.'

Mary glanced up at the note of resentment in Catherine's voice. She was proudly Spanish at heart but something about the way she spoke sounded as if she was critical of Henry's handling of the situation. Her eyes went to the bulge in Catherine's gown. She turned to Catherine.

'A show of clemency would make him popular with the people but the French ambassadors would protest.'

'Let them protest.' Margaret sounded unconcerned. 'The three of us should propose this to Henry. Even a king cannot ignore the pleading of three queens.'

Brandon held her close in the darkness. He'd returned after dark to Richmond Palace, where Mary had chosen to stay in her childhood apartments. She guessed he'd had a long day in Westminster but seemed in good spirits as he told her about the king's show of mercy. 'The people love you, Mary.'

'I can't take the credit for his pardon.' She pulled him closer. 'The idea was Margaret's and Henry didn't have to agree to our plea.'

He kissed her. 'You offered him a clever way out of a difficult situation. I happen to know he was grateful.'

'It is humbling to think we saved people's lives. What happened in the courtroom?'

'I've never seen such a crowd at a trial. There was a rousing cheer when Henry announced his pardon. Wolsey tried to take the credit, of course, but Henry said it was the queen and his sisters who'd pleaded for clemency.'

Mary lay back in her bed, deep in thought. She turned to Brandon. 'You were right when you warned me of the dangers of London.' She smiled in the darkness. 'Catherine seems well enough with her child and now my sister has left it's time we returned to our family home.'

'It warms my heart to hear that.' He smiled at her in the moonlight from the window. 'I love you, Mary Tudor.'

She kissed him. 'I've seen how my sister overstayed her welcome and don't wish to do the same. Henry has been generous with her, but I suspect he'll not be so willing next time.'

The hooves of a hundred horses clattered on the cobblestones and cheering crowds greeted the Burgundian delegation as it made its way to Greenwich Palace. Brandon led the escort of the senior nobles of court, riding his fine black destrier at the side of the grim-faced Duke of Norfolk.

Mary's decision to return to Westhorpe Hall in the spring proved timely, as London had been in the grip of the sweating sickness for most of the summer. Now it seemed to have passed they were invited, along with every noble family in England, to Henry's extravagant reception for his devious Burgundian allies.

Queen Catherine and Mary both dressed in cloth of gold and wore coronets glittering with diamonds as a mark of their status. Henry managed to outshine them all with a heavy golden collar studded with the largest rubies Mary had ever seen.

After days of banqueting and a grand tournament in a specially built tiltyard, Mary felt weary. She also worried that

Henry's Burgundian treaties could alienate King Francis and further endanger his promise to ensure her French revenues were paid on time.

As usual, the jousting culminated in a battle between her brother and her husband which lasted for over four hours. Her hand went to her mouth each time their lances clashed, sending shattered splinters high into the air. She turned her head at the sound of a shrill laugh and saw it came from one of the ambassadors, already drunk on Henry's best wine.

She whispered to Catherine. 'Would it be disloyal to wonder if the Burgundians warrant such expense?'

Catherine agreed. 'Henry is determined to impress them, although I worry he tempts fate with such ... determined jousting.'

Mary smiled. 'Brandon is the same, refusing to leave such sports to younger men. I believe they encourage each other.'

Catherine looked thoughtful. 'Will you be returning to your home in Suffolk when the delegation leaves?'

'I would like the child to be born at Westhorpe.' Mary lowered her voice to a whisper only Catherine could hear. 'I will not have Wolsey take control and closet me at Bath Place, as he did when little Henry was born.'

Catherine nodded in understanding. 'I was wondering if I might ask a great favour?'

'Of course.' Mary studied Catherine's face, wondering what it could be.

'I wished to make a pilgrimage to the priory at Walsingham to pray for a son but Henry will not permit it. Walsingham Priory is not such a great distance from Suffolk, so I must ask you to visit the shrine on my behalf.'

Mary hesitated. She was close to the time for her confinement and knew what Brandon would say when he heard. Walsingham was some fifty miles north of Westhorpe, yet she found herself agreeing. God willing, Catherine's child would be the healthy boy needed to save her marriage.

The memory of her little Henry's difficult birth was still fresh in her mind. As well as travelling to Walsingham to pray for Catherine she would also say a prayer for the child she felt moving inside her.

Mary's small pilgrimage of servants and escorts had hardly completed twenty miles on the Great North Road from Richmond before the pains began. Although she rode in a covered wagon, the summer heat left Mary feeling faint and she decided to rest at the nearby manor house of her old friend Nicholas West, now Bishop of Ely.

Fortunately, Bishop West was at home and bowed to Mary as he smiled in greeting. 'Welcome to Hatfield, Your Grace.' His eyes went to her hands which cradled her middle.

Mary glanced back at her small retinue. 'It's good to see you again, Bishop West.' She fought back a sudden stab of pain. 'We need your help, as it seems God's plan is for my child to be born earlier than expected.'

Bishop West gave her a look of concern. 'Please come in, Your Grace. I will send for a midwife right away. You must rest while a room is prepared for your confinement.' He led her through to a large hall with religious tapestries on the walls and left to make the arrangements.

Mary felt another wave of pain, stronger than before, and was glad to sit in a comfortable chair. She looked around at the gleaming silver candlesticks and rich tapestries of biblical scenes. The furniture was of carved oak and there were more servants than she had at Westhorpe. Nicholas West seemed to be making a good living for himself since their time together in France.

The midwife, a kindly, middle-aged woman, soon arrived and took charge of Mary's confinement. 'Do you think you can manage the stairs, my lady?'

Mary smiled. 'With your help, mistress. I think the baby will not be so long coming now.'

The midwife gave her a knowing look and supported her as she made her way up the winding stairs to a bedchamber where the fire had already been lit to boil water, despite the summer heat.

Mary lay back on the bed and prayed for the pain to stop. She turned to the midwife. 'Please send one of the girls to summon the bishop.'

Nicholas West must have been waiting close by, as he appeared in a moment and sat in the high-backed chair at the side of her bed. 'My lady?'

'I need your blessing, bishop.' She spoke with some effort now, the pain threatening to overcome her.

Bishop West thought for a moment, then clasped his hands in prayer and bowed his head. 'Dear Lord, have mercy on this good lady, for her hour has come, and when her infant is delivered, let her think only of the joy that man is born into the world.' He looked into Mary's anguished eyes. 'Amen.'

Eighty men holding burning torches lined the route of the christening procession from the bishop's house to Hatfield parish church. The king and queen were absent, as was Brandon, although Catherine sent two of her ladies to represent herself and her daughter Mary as godmothers.

Mary looked up as she entered the church and gave thanks to the figure of Christ on the cross for the life of her child. Born on St Francis' day, she named her Frances Brandon.

16

MARCH 1518

While the sweating sickness ravaged London, life at Westhorpe Hall settled into a routine for Mary. Brandon was in good spirits since he'd secured agreement with Wolsey to repay their debts, and their children thrived in the fresh country air.

Rising early to bright spring sunshine, Mary busied herself with managing her household, reduced now to less than fifty staff and two ladies-in-waiting, Elizabeth and Anne Grey, who'd been with her since she first left for France.

Now the long winter was over she'd been creating formal gardens like those she'd seen in the royal palaces in Paris. Her gardeners planted borders of sweet-scented lavender, already in bloom, around orderly herb gardens. Freshly cut English roses would soon brighten her rooms with their delicate perfume and fresh herbs would be used every day in the bustling kitchens.

Little Henry, now two, grew stronger and had the red-gold hair of the Tudors. Baby Frances was proving to be a lively child and a challenge to her nursemaid, a buxom local woman called Anne Kyng, known to everyone as Mistress Annie.

In the evenings Mary taught Brandon's daughters to play the lute and clavichord, and together they sang tuneful French and English songs. Mary still missed the intrigue and excitement of Henry's court but the girls were good company, particularly when Brandon stayed away on estate business.

Anne was almost tall enough to fit into Mary's beautiful French silk gowns and they would sit late into the evenings talking together as they made alterations. Mary took it on herself to complete their education and found they were full of questions, particularly about life at Henry's court.

'I saw the king once, in a joust against Father.' Anne pulled a face. 'He seemed quite terrifying. He made his horse rear up and jump into the air more times than I could count!'

Mary laughed. 'I shall arrange for you to be introduced to Henry when the time is right.'

'I would be honoured,' Anne's nimble fingers made fine stitches with her needle as she spoke, 'although I wouldn't know what to say to him.'

'He loves music. You could play the lute and sing at one of his banquets.'

Anne stopped her sewing and looked up at Mary with questioning eyes. 'Do you think I'm good enough to play for the king?'

'We will practise until you feel confident.'

Anne nodded. 'Thank you.' She looked at Mary as if trying to make a judgement. 'Has my father said anything to you about finding me a husband?'

'He has not,' Mary frowned at the thought, 'but I know he only wishes the best for you, Anne.'

'I pray he doesn't choose someone who is too old.' She spoke softly, as if to herself. 'I couldn't bear it.'

Mary put her hand on Anne's arm. 'We must follow our destiny and trust in the Lord.' As she said the words she recalled the adoration she'd seen in King Louis' eyes. 'My first husband was much older but showed me great kindness.'

Later that night, Mary remembered Louis in her prayers. She knew Brandon's idea of an ideal husband for his daughter would take little account of the difference in age. His main concerns in choosing a suitor would of course be power, influence and wealth. She resolved to do what she could to influence his choice, for young Anne's sake.

The royal herald arrived at Westhorpe late in the afternoon with a summons from the king. Henry wished Brandon and Mary to join the court at Abingdon for Easter. Mary helped Brandon word a reply confirming they would be honoured to attend and read it back to him before he signed it.

Brandon nodded in approval. 'I'm surprised we're invited. The accommodation at Abingdon Palace is so limited less than half the court will be staying there.'

'It's good news,' Mary smiled, 'and we must count our blessings. I was beginning to fear my brother had forgotten us.'

'I expect he'll feel more at ease away from the daily count of deaths in London.'

'The sweating sickness?'

He nodded. 'Henry's right to stay away from the city. I heard that Lord Grey and several servants in the royal kitchens have succumbed. They say this is the worst ever, with few lasting more than a day. It seems only Thomas Wolsey is immune and continues to live in London, ruling like a king in Henry's absence.'

'His reward for leading a devout life.' She gave him a wry look. 'Are the physicians any closer to finding a cure?'

'All the victims can do is pray for God's mercy.'

Westhorpe Hall became a buzz of preparation as everyone packed for the journey. Mary asked Anne to accompany her as one of her ladies-in-waiting. It would be her first time at court and much time was spent trying on different gowns, head-dresses and jewellery.

Such excitement over Easter reminded her of when she was a girl at her father's court, so many years ago. She'd learned to appreciate the peace of rural Suffolk but worried about being forgotten. The summons was the first letter from her brother in months.

Brandon kept busy with his estates but she knew he'd also been concerned about the length of time they'd been away. Norfolk and Wolsey would take advantage of his absence to promote their own interests and even plot against him.

Mary found the court at Abingdon strangely subdued. Henry gave them a warm welcome and showed great pride in his infant daughter Mary, now two years old and already dressed in cloth of gold. Catherine looked tired and wore a brocade gown with a gable hood trimmed with pearls that made her look older.

They were guests of honour at the banquet on their first evening yet there was no music, and the overlong grace by the aging Archbishop Warham took Christ's suffering as a theme. Mary thought Henry seemed preoccupied and was unsurprised when Catherine retired early.

Once they were in the privacy of their chambers Mary dismissed her servants and turned to Brandon. 'What has become of my brother's court? Where are his young compan-ions? It seems so quiet here without them.'

Brandon pulled off his boots and lay back on the bed, watching as she unpinned her French headdress and began to unplait her long hair. Although usually the work of her chambermaid, Mary didn't want anyone overhearing her questions – or Brandon's answers.

He stared at her for a moment. 'I can't tell you much. They keep the details even from me,' he frowned, 'but there's been talk of a plot to overthrow the king.'

Mary's eyes widened at the news. 'Who would be behind such a thing? You should have told me.'

'Better you don't know, Mary. It seems no one is above the king's suspicion.'

'Does it have to do with his young revellers?'

Brandon shook his head. 'No, but the council has taken the king to task about their bawdy behaviour. He's banished them from court, although I'm sure it's only temporary.' He smiled at her. 'As you well know, he was often the worst offender.'

'You encouraged him on more than one occasion.'

'Well, I'm still not in the clear. It seems our benefactor Thomas Wolsey conspires against me again.'

'I thought you'd reached a settlement with him?'

'Hardly a settlement. We repay him more than we can afford,' he scowled at the thought, 'yet now he's back to accusing me of offering Tournai to the French.'

She looked at him in surprise. 'Wolsey will never be Bishop of Tournai. Surely he accepts that ship has sailed?'

Brandon nodded. 'He's using it to reduce my influence. They're saying I promised King Francis Tournai, in return for supporting our marriage. You know we did no deal with Francis, but I can never prove it.'

Mary sat on the edge of the bed and began running her comb through her hair as she tried to think. 'Perhaps … this business with Cardinal Wolsey can be turned to our advantage.'

Brandon propped himself up on the thick pillows and gave her a questioning look. 'What do you mean?'

She stroked the silver comb through her hair again. 'King Francis would pay for Tournai if the price was fair. My brother could broker a new peace accord with France and my dowager payments would be secured once more.'

He looked at her in surprise. 'Henry has no need for Tournai – in fact it costs him dearly to keep the garrison there.' Brandon stroked his beard as he thought. 'He could come out of this with a good profit, as well as being seen as a peace-maker, but we risk making an enemy of Thomas Wolsey.'

'My father's old advisor, Archbishop Richard Foxe, is here at court. He could broach the idea to Wolsey, who will be quick enough to take the credit – and could negotiate a pension from the French for his troubles.'

'You are your father's daughter, Mary Tudor.' He laughed. 'He would have been proud of you.'

Mary offered to play the lute for Henry's entertainment at the banquet the following evening. Fine wine flowed freely and the entire court packed into the great hall. She was pleased to see Brandon seated at the king's right hand and Queen Catherine back in her place on his left.

Feeling a little nervous, she checked the tuning then played one of her brother's favourites, to rapturous applause when she finished. Next, she sang an old French song about unrequited love, to her own accompaniment. Satisfied the moment was right, Mary made a sign and Anne entered, carrying a lute. She waited until she was in place, then spoke directly to Henry.

'Your Grace, I wish to introduce my student, Mistress Anne Brandon.'

'You are welcome, my lady,' Henry grinned at Anne, 'and you have an excellent teacher in my dear sister.'

His words were met by more applause as Mary began a delicate introduction on her lute and the room fell silent with anticipation. Then with a nod to Anne they launched into the spirited version of Henry's own composition which they had rehearsed for this moment at Westhorpe Hall.

Past time with good company
I love, and shall until I die
Grutch who lust, but none deny
So God be pleased, thus live will I
For my pastance
Hunt, sing and dance
My heart is set;
All goodly sport
For my comfort
Who shall me let?

When they reached the end of the last chorus Henry led the applause then leaned over and said something to Brandon, who nodded and looked pleased. Mary saw Anne's blush but knew their long hours of practice had been time well spent. Her family were now truly accepted back into the king's good grace.

Mary woke with a pain that throbbed like someone beating a drum deep inside her head. The heat was unbearable, although it had been a cooler spring than usual. She threw back the thick coverlet and looked across to the hearth to see if a fire had been lit. The iron fire basket was cold and empty, as was the bed at her side.

She put a hand to her forehead and a shudder of fear ran through her as she felt the damp heat of perspiration. A woven silk cord hung down at the side of her bed canopy and she pulled it to summon her maidservant. She lay back on her bed, her body now aching with cold as she struggled to gather her thoughts.

The timing could not be worse. The court was due to return to London after the St George's Day celebrations. With an effort, Mary propped herself up on her pillows as the door opened. Anne looked excited and wore one of her best gowns with a new French headdress.

'Stop, Anne. Don't come any closer.' Her voice sounded sharper than she intended and Anne froze in the doorway.

'What's wrong?'

'I'm unwell.' Tears formed in her eyes. 'I fear it might be the sweating sickness—'

'No!' Anne gripped the half-open door to steady herself. 'It can't be.'

'Have you seen your father this morning?'

Anne nodded, her eyes wide with concern. 'Should I fetch him?'

Mary thought for a moment. 'Tell him I must see him urgently – and please be discreet, Anne. I don't want anyone else to know I'm unwell.'

Anne slipped back through the door and was gone. As she waited, Mary tried to recall what she'd heard about the signs of the sweating sickness. The victims began to shiver as if cold, despite complaining of the heat. She knew the shivering was followed by a dreadful sweating from which few recovered.

Mary lay on her back and clasped her hands in prayer. She prayed for her children and wept at the thought of never seeing them grow up. She focused on the love in little Henry's eyes whenever she entered the nursery. A sudden coldness replaced the heat and she ground her teeth in an effort not to shiver, as if to do so would be to surrender to the sickness.

A deep melancholy swept over her as she realised how easily life could go on without her. Brandon would find a wealthy, younger wife. Even little Frances would forget her soon enough. She'd been seven years old when her own mother died, yet now she struggled to recall her face.

The door burst open and Brandon entered but stopped when Mary held up her hand. 'The queen's physician has been sent for.' He sounded breathless as if he'd been running, and took a hesitant step forward.

'Please stay back,' Mary pleaded. 'It could be the sweating sickness.'

'Have you been shivering?' His voice wavered with concern.

'No, but one moment I feel hot, then so cold I can hardly think...'

'There are no reports of the sweating sickness here. I would have heard if there were, so let us pray you are mistaken, Mary.'

She pulled herself up a little straighter in bed. 'I cannot be the one to bring the sweating sickness to court. Henry would never forgive us.'

It was mid-morning by the time the physician arrived but Mary remained in her bed, too weakened by the fever to rise. He wore the black robes of a cleric and tried his best to reassure her. 'I have seen cases of the sweating sickness in the city, my lady. None seemed as well as you do now.'

Mary studied his face. He had a neatly trimmed white beard and seemed to know his business. 'My head spins and I feel hot, then feverish and cold. Is there something you can give me for this pain in my head?'

The physician crossed to the window and opened it, taking a deep breath of the fresh country air before turning to face her. 'You suffer from an ague, my lady. You should not travel until you are well again.'

Mary frowned. 'Is there a cure?'

'Rest, my lady. My advice is to remain in bed and let this fever run its course.'

'But is there some potion that might speed my recovery?'

'I have used a tincture of sage of virtue, with the herb grace and a little elder. With white wine and ginger it is tolerable to take as a medicine.'

Mary nodded. 'If you could…'

The physician's tone softened a little. 'I shall prepare a draught, but have faith in the Lord, my lady.'

The magnificent procession of over six hundred horses and wagons clattered through the narrow London streets, with the senior noblemen riding at the front, their colourful banners flowing in the autumn breeze.

Queen Catherine frowned as they waited to greet their guests. 'They look more like an invading army than a visit from the ambassadors of France.'

Mary smiled at the thought. Wolsey led the negotiations and claimed the idea as his own, so Catherine would never know the ambassadors were in London thanks to her husband's influence behind the scenes. They would take delivery of Tournai for six hundred thousand gold crowns and sign a new peace agreement.

Henry loved Mary as a sister and forgave her transgressions, yet valued her as an ornament to brighten his court and entertain his guests. He used her courtesy title of Queen Dowager of France when it suited him but would never see that her true worth was so much more. She believed her father would have been proud of how she'd turned a disaster to peaceful advantage.

'I wish Queen Claude had been able to attend her son's

betrothal. I promised to write but it has been more than a year since her last reply.'

Catherine nodded. 'She has my sympathy. I understand King Francis is not the easiest of husbands. My ladies tell me he openly cavorts with his mistresses.' Her tone was scathing and her face creased in a frown at the thought.

Mary wondered if this was a reference to Henry's indiscretions but a sharp fanfare of trumpeters interrupted her reply and the moment passed. She felt angry at her brother for his treatment of Catherine but was powerless to do anything about it.

Since her strange fever broke she still felt weakened but had learned to hide it. She had little choice as Catherine, now close to full term, asked for her support with entertaining the French delegation, while Brandon was to support Henry with the peace treaty.

As well as the formal handover of Tournai and agreement of the new treaty at St Paul's, Catherine's little daughter Mary would be betrothed to the dauphin at Greenwich Palace. Guillaume Gouffier, Seigneur de Bonnivet, was to stand proxy for the son of King Francis and Queen Claude, who was not yet one year old.

The banquet was one of the finest Mary had ever seen and seemed extravagant after her forced economies in Suffolk. Henry was determined to make a good impression on the ambassadors, despite the absence of the King of France.

Gilded suckling pigs were followed by dishes of swan and venison from the royal parks. Mary had little appetite since her illness and picked at her food. She found herself seated next to Admiral Bonnivet, who had grown up with King Francis and was the most senior French nobleman present.

With his piercing blue eyes and flirtatious smile, Mary could see why he'd become the right-hand man to the king and Admiral of the French fleet while so young. He'd shown her kindness after the death of King Louis and she sensed an unspoken bond between them even now.

'Tell me, Admiral Bonnivet, how is my good friend Queen Claude?'

His smile faltered for a fleeting second. 'The queen was ... distressed after the tragic loss of her daughter but I'm pleased to tell you Queen Claude is with child again.' He placed his hand on hers. 'King Francis is certain it will be a boy and says he will name him Henry.'

Mary felt an unexpected frisson of arousal at the warmth of his touch. She remembered how he'd offered to take care of her after Louis' death and thought how different her life could have been if she'd remained in Paris. Then she realised he was being indiscreet. The charming young admiral undoubtedly had a beautiful wife waiting for him in Paris, just as she had waited for Brandon's return.

Withdrawing her hand from his, she took a sip of the rich red wine to calm her thoughts before replying. 'Please tell Queen Claude I wish her well and look forward to hearing from her when she is able to write.'

'Of course, my lady.' Bonnivet raised his own goblet, a twinkle in his eye. '*Ma magnifique reine*, you should have stayed in France, where we would truly have appreciated you.'

Mary felt her face blush at his compliment, the wine now warming her throat and improving her mood.

She'd been glad to help make the French visit a success for the sake of her dower payments but had not expected to enjoy it, weakened as she was by her recent illness. Sometimes she wished her husband was as attentive as the handsome Admiral Bonnivet.

The moment passed as cheering and a ripple of applause greeted the men carrying the heavy centrepiece. Mary saw it was a perfectly scaled sugar model of St Paul's Cathedral, complete with stained-glass windows through which the yellow light of candles glowed.

Later she joined Brandon in a masked dance and felt an irrational jealousy when she saw Admiral Bonnivet had already turned his attentions to one of Catherine's ladies-in-waiting. As the dancers turned she saw it was Lady Mary Boleyn laughing at his joke. They would have known each other in Paris, before the advances of King Francis caused her to return to England.

Only once the dancing ended and they removed their masks did she see that one of her fellow performers was her brother's not-so-secret mistress, twenty-year-old Elizabeth Blount, known to everyone as Bessie. As Mary watched her catch Henry's eye and be rewarded by a smile she felt a pang of sympathy for Catherine, who deserved better in return for her faithful loyalty.

Two days after the banquet the entire court sailed down the Thames on a fleet of barges to Greenwich Palace. Mary sat at Catherine's side in the gilded royal barge and watched as the oarsmen strained against the incoming tide. The sun emerged from behind a cloud, turning the murky waters to sparkling silver as crowds of onlookers cheered on both banks.

As everyone gathered in Queen Catherine's richly decorated chambers, little Princess Mary seemed bewildered by her betrothal ceremony and looked up wide-eyed as Admiral Bonnivet spoke for the infant Francis.

Cardinal Wolsey, officiating, frowned as they realised the jewelled wedding ring was far too large. With a grin, Bonnivet slipped it over her tiny finger anyway. Mary watched as the royal families of England and France, Tudor and Valois, were once more united in marriage.

17

APRIL 1519

A hush fell over the waiting congregation as Mary made her way to their pew, the hem of her satin gown swishing on the tiled floor. Behind her followed Anne and little Mary Brandon, carrying their prayer books, with her ladies-in-waiting, Lady Anne and Lady Elizabeth Grey, all in their best Sunday gowns.

Mary enjoyed her role as lady of the manor and her regular attendances at the parish church were her most visible commitment. A short walk from Westhorpe Hall, these services and the summer fairs provided her main contact with real people, the merchants and farmers of her adopted county of Suffolk.

Her royal pew was one of Brandon's more astute investments of their limited funds. He'd ordered it to be made from local oak, finely carved with red-and-white painted Tudor roses and Mary's gilded fleur-de-lis of France. It was good to see and be seen by the people of the village, and helped pass the weeks when Brandon was away at court and on estate business, as he was much of the time. Mary missed him but knew her duty was to raise the children as well as she could.

The village priest, a portly man with a rich local accent, waited until they were seated then led them all in a prayer of thanks to God, his deep voice echoing from the vaulted roof.

'Gloria in excelsis Deo et in terra pax hominibus bonae voluntatis. Laudamus te. Benedicimus te. Adoramus te. Glorificamus te. Gratias agimus tibi propter magnam gloriam tuam...'

Mary clasped her hands together and bowed her head. She had much to give thanks for. Little Harry, now three years old, grew stronger and was learning to ride a pony, with patient tuition from his father. Frances had the red-gold hair of the Tudors and delighted visitors as she tottered around in her blue silk gown, trimmed with gold lace, like a miniature version of Mary.

Her mind wandered as the priest continued with his sermon. She prayed for Queen Catherine, who had not been so fortunate. The nation mourned when the queen lost her infant daughter the previous November, the baby so weak she died before she could be christened.

Brandon told her the king's pregnant mistress had been moved to the Priory of St Lawrence near Ingatestone and Henry prayed for a son. Little her brother did surprised Mary. She'd said how unbearable the news must be for Catherine, particularly as Bessie Blount had been her maid of honour, but had been shocked at Brandon's reply.

'Queen Catherine is not getting any younger.' He made it sound like an accusation.

Mary found herself springing to her friend's defence. 'She could hardly have done more to provide my brother with an heir—'

Brandon interrupted her with a knowing look. 'There's talk at court of an annulment.' His words had hung in the air like a threat.

'Henry would never do such a thing to Catherine.' She gave him a scornful look.

Brandon shrugged. 'All I can tell you is w.

She suspected there was more he'd chosen ,
her, for fear she would feel obliged to share it with
Catherine. In her heart, Mary knew her friend was doomed
angered her but Brandon was right. Catherine was in her mid-
thirties. With every passing year her chances of a healthy son
were reduced, which meant her own little Henry could one day
become king.

Mary heard the clump of Brandon's riding boots on the
wooden stairs. The household had retired for the night but she
was expecting his return, her tall candles, imported from Paris,
burning low. The door of her chamber swung open. Brandon
pulled off his cap and ran his fingers through his long hair. He
looked tired and dusty from his long ride but pleased to see she
was still awake.

She climbed from her warm bed, pulling her long nightgown around her as she crossed the room to welcome him
home. He smelled of ale and horse sweat as he held her close
and kissed her, then stared into her eyes.

'Has something happened?' He gave her a questioning
look, his head tilted slightly to one side as he did when curious.
'I know you too well, Mary Tudor.'

She smiled, glad to be able to tell him at last. 'I'm with
child again, Charles. We're going to have another little
Brandon in this growing family.'

He grinned at the unexpected news. 'Let us pray it is
another boy.' He looked thoughtful. 'We shall name him
William Brandon, to honour my father.' He unbuckled his
sword, placing it with care in the corner of their chamber,
then sat on the bed and pulled off his boots, grunting with
the effort. 'This time you must take more care. No pilgrim-
ages to Walsingham when the baby is due.' His voice

sounded stern and he wagged a finger at her in mock seriousness.

'Of course, my lord.' She curtseyed for him, like a servant, her head bowed.

He poured water from the heavy earthenware jug into the bowl they kept in their bedchamber. 'How long have you known?' He splashed the cold water on his face and dried his hands with a linen cloth. 'When is the child due?'

'So many questions.' She laughed. 'I wanted to be certain.' She made a quick calculation, counting on her fingers. 'Our baby will be born in December, before Christmas.'

He embraced her again, with more care this time. 'I've missed you, Mary, and the children. How have you all been while I was away?'

'Little Harry is learning French. I teach him a few words each day and he's doing well. Anne has fashioned a new gown from the blue silk I'd been keeping for a special occasion. You must ask to see her in it in the morning.' She stroked his beard playfully. 'Have you found your eldest daughter a suitable husband?'

He gave her a wry look. 'There are plenty of candidates but none worthy of her. How is little Mary?'

'She takes after her father, which I expect you think to be a good thing.' Mary laughed at his frown. 'She's adopted all the doves in the dovecot and tends to them every day as if they were your thoroughbred mares. She's given them names and says she can tell one from another. The oldest, which can hardly fly, is called the Duke of Norfolk.'

He laughed at the thought. 'Does she know they are destined for the kitchens?'

Mary shook her head. 'I should not like to be the one to tell her.'

'The king has a son?' Although Mary knew a child was on the way, the news could change everything. Her hand went unconsciously to the swelling at her own middle as she felt pity bordering on grief for Queen Catherine.

Brandon nodded as he wolfed down his meal of roast venison, dipping his trencher of bread into the rich gravy. He'd been out hunting when the messenger arrived and still wore his leather riding doublet and boots.

He took a deep drink from his tankard of ale then hacked another slice of the tender meat with his knife. 'It seems he's chosen not to keep the boy a secret. They will no doubt use it as an excuse for celebration in the taverns of London – but the child is a bastard and will never inherit.'

Mary glanced at the girls, who looked shocked at their father's tone. 'Please, Charles...'

He looked up at them and then at little Henry, who ate in silence but was listening to every word. 'The children must understand the ways of the world, Mary.'

Brandon returned from London with more unexpected news. 'Charles of Castile has been appointed as emperor and plans to visit in the new year to discuss a treaty.'

Mary recalled how she'd stared at the little gold-framed portrait of Charles so long ago, wondering if he would make her Empress of Rome. 'Do you think my brother will invite us?'

'He will, as we are to accompany the entire court to a meeting in France with King Francis in the spring.'

Mary looked at him in amazement. 'The entire court? It will cost Henry a fortune!'

'Well, he is determined to outdo the French – you know how competitive they both are.'

She laughed as she remembered the last time Henry and

Francis met. 'I was beginning to wonder if I would ever return to France.' She looked down at her fading gown. 'For once we will not make economies, Charles. I must have a new wardrobe.'

Brandon grinned. 'We shall show your Emperor Charles what he has missed out on!'

~

Mary kneeled with some difficulty on the cold stones of the floor of her private chapel and said a prayer for the child within her. She'd told no one she suffered from a strange pain in her side, which worsened as her pregnancy progressed.

She should have told her physicians but the thought of watching their leeches swell with her blood made her feel sick. Worse still would be their foul-tasting potions, which she feared could harm her child. Instead she'd decided to trust in the divine grace of the Lord.

Mary struggled to recall what her father had told her about her mother's death. He'd rarely spoken of it, and when he did his face was always anguished. She knew her mother died on her thirty-seventh birthday in the queen's apartments of the Tower of London. It seemed she never recovered from giving birth to her seventh child.

Tears formed in her eyes as she prayed for her mother and father, and her little sister, christened Katherine Tudor, who lived for barely a week. Her father had never been the same again. On his deathbed, he'd told her his faith had been tested and he could never understand why a merciful God should allow such a cruel fate for her mother.

Queen Catherine had still not replied to the letter Mary sent when the pains began as a dull ache. Even when she did, Mary knew she would advise another pilgrimage to the shrine of Our Lady of Walsingham, which she had promised not to do. Although she spent long hours praying in the silent chapel the pain in her side steadily worsened. She would have to do something, for the sake of her baby.

As she prayed, the words of Saint Augustine, taught to her as a child in Eltham Palace, drifted into her mind. *He who created us without our help will not save us without our consent.* She'd been asking for divine guidance and this was a good omen. She resolved to travel to the closest Augustinian priory.

Hidden deep in the sandy heathlands some thirty miles ride east of Westhorpe, Butley Abbey was named after the nearby river. A stone wall enclosed twenty acres of land, barns and cottages, as well as the grand abbey, built in the reign of King Henry II. With some seventy-five staff, including servants and farm workers, as well as the prior and twelve canons, it was more like a small village than a priory.

Prior Augustine Rivers was a shrewd, grey-bearded man who walked out to meet Mary as she arrived with her small coterie of servants. He wore the black-hooded habit of the Augustinian order with a wide belt, the shining silver crucifix around his neck the only sign of his rank.

'We are blessed by your visit, my lady.' He bowed his head briefly then leaned on his staff for support while he studied her with bright blue eyes, as if trying to read her intentions.

'Good day, Prior Rivers. Did you receive my message?'

The prior nodded. 'You are always welcome, my lady. Apartments adjoining the priory have been made ready for your use, and you may remain as long as you wish.'

'That is most gracious of you. There are matters I would like to discuss once I have rested.'

Mary rose early the next morning and met the prior in his

study, a simply furnished room with whitewashed walls. Late autumn sunlight streamed through the small windows on to an illuminated book of hours, open on the prior's desk with a pile of letters, his inkpot and quill.

'Good morning, my lady.' He bowed his grey head. 'What can I do for you?'

'I wish to be received into the Augustinian order, so the brothers might pray for me.'

The prior looked up in surprise. 'We pray for whoever needs our help, my lady.' His voice sounded softer than before. 'A donation to our funds would be most welcome but I confess to being intrigued. Why do you wish to follow the teachings of Saint Augustine, my lady?'

Mary hesitated, then took a deep breath. 'I heard a voice, telling me to do so.'

'A voice?' He leaned forward in his chair with new interest.

Mary nodded. 'The words of Saint Augustine came into my head when I was praying for my mother, who died after the birth of my sister Katherine.' She saw his nod of understanding. 'I am now carrying my third child and saw it as a sign.'

He studied her for a moment. 'I too have heard the words of the saint when praying.' He smiled at her for the first time, revealing perfect white teeth. 'You were right to come to us, my lady.'

An early fall of snow dusted the courtyard of Westhorpe before the baby began to make its way into the world. Mary was well used to the signs. She gave thanks that the pain in her side had eased since her stay at Butley Abbey. Now she looked forward to the birth with renewed faith that all would be well.

She'd woken in the middle of the night and lay awake until dawn, thinking about her brother and Catherine. Henry made no secret of his illegitimate child, proudly naming him Henry Fitzroy, son of the king. Now Brandon told her Henry had a new mistress, Lady Mary Boleyn. She found it impossible to understand how Mary Boleyn had learned so little from her affair with King Francis.

The midwife placed a dampened linen cloth on Mary's forehead. The soothing coolness helped her think. She called out to her waiting chambermaid. 'Please will you send for my stepdaughter Anne?'

'Yes, my lady.' The maid bobbed a curtsey and disappeared through the doorway.

Mary was glad to have chosen Westhorpe for her confinement. It was traditional at such times to be surrounded by female relatives, but she was unsurprised there had been no reply from her sister Margaret in Scotland. Mary preferred the company of Anne, who played her lute to help pass the long hours and told Mary fanciful stories of her time at the court of Margaret, Duchess of Savoy.

'The duchess told me a secret once,' Anne confided. 'She said after the Duke of Savoy died she decided to end her life. She jumped from a high window but called out to the Virgin Mary. It was a miracle, as she survived the fall.'

Mary smiled at Anne's wide-eyed innocence. 'I heard that story, Anne, it is not such a secret.'

'But did you know she had the duke's heart cut out and carried it with her all the time in a silk purse?'

'She must have loved him very much.'

Anne nodded. 'She took a vow never to marry again.'

Now Anne sat in the chair at the side of Mary's bed and dismissed the midwife with a nod. Not yet thirteen, Anne was already as tall as Mary. A French hood which showed her dark hair, and one of Mary's altered gowns with a diamond necklace helped to make her look older.

'How are you feeling this morning?'

Mary took the folded linen cloth from her forehead. 'I didn't sleep well but the baby is due soon.' She studied Anne's face and wondered what the future held for her young step-daughter. 'I wanted to thank you for being such good company while your father's been away.'

Anne smiled. 'He is due back tomorrow – and has promised to bring more silks from London. I am to help you sew new gowns for your visit to France.'

'I'm grateful, Anne, I will be glad of your help.' She smiled. 'Let us hope he doesn't forget again. Last time all he brought back was that dangerous dagger for Harry. I don't know what he was thinking of.'

'Will I be allowed to go with you to greet the new Emperor Charles?'

Mary shrugged. 'If your father agrees, although I think he will wish you to help look after the rest of the family here while I'm away.' A new pain swept through Mary and she knew what it meant. 'There is something I wanted to tell you.'

'What is it?' Anne looked at her with concern in her eyes.

'All my remaining jewels have been promised to the king when I die – but I've told your father that you and Mary are to have your pick of them before they are handed over.' She flinched as another pain came. 'Some given to me by King Louis are worth a great deal.'

Anne looked confused. 'Will the king not miss them?'

'We've been giving jewels to Cardinal Wolsey in payment for his loans, so the king has no idea what remains.'

Anne frowned as a thought occurred to her. 'Are you telling me this now because you think you might die?'

Mary shook her head. 'Call for the midwife, Anne, the baby is on the way.' As she watched Anne rush from the room she said a silent prayer that all would be well. She had a lot to live for.

Brandon loosened the tight swaddling which bound his new daughter's arms and watched in wonder as her tiny fingers grasped his thumb. He grinned at Mary. 'What shall we name her?'

Mary, propped up in bed on silk cushions, still felt tired and weak but was relieved he didn't show disappointment the child wasn't the boy they'd wished for. 'I named our last daughter Frances, so this time it must be your choice.'

Brandon looked thoughtful for a moment. 'I've always liked the name Eleanor.'

'Lady Eleanor Brandon.' Mary smiled at the sight of the two of them together. 'A good name.'

18

MAY 1520

'You've never looked more beautiful.' Brandon beamed with pride as Mary took her place at his side. His ceremonial sword with its gold hilt gleamed at his belt and he wore the heavy gold chain of the Order of the Garter, with a bright ruby shining in the badge on his black hat.

She smiled at his compliment. Her gown of ermine-edged cloth of silver glittered with diamonds and her French head-dress was ringed with the purest white pearls. Even her velvet slippers, hidden under her gown, were embroidered in silver and gold. She had no idea how Brandon met the cost of her new wardrobe but, for once, she didn't care.

They waited in Canterbury to greet Henry and his guest, Emperor Charles, King of Castile and Aragon and now King of the Romans, who rode from Dover Castle. His fleet of some sixty ships was blown off course by a savage storm and he'd arrived late, the day before Henry planned to depart for France.

The dull ache in Mary's ribs on the left side had returned, despite her prayers. She'd decided she could keep it secret no

longer but a succession of physicians ha&
her. Some brewed potions of mandrake root w&
out of desperation she permitted them to try b&
Prescribed rest, she'd remained in bed for several wee&
found the lack of exercise and loss of blood left her in a wea&
ened state.

Brandon became increasingly concerned and wrote to Wolsey advising that she might be too unwell to travel with the king and queen to France. Although the pain was at its worst when riding, Mary remembered her motto, *La volenté de Dieu me suffit*. This was God's will, something she had to live with. Compared with her grandmother Margaret Beaufort's penitent hair shirt it seemed a small price to pay for her three healthy children.

A sharp fanfare of trumpets sounded outside and Mary tensed. She had been so taken by the idea of returning to France she'd not thought a great deal about finally meeting the man who'd been her fiancé for six years. Now she felt unexpected anxiety about how to address him and what she might say.

She saw him first, an unmistakable figure in a large hat with lank hair and a jutting chin. He looked a poor substitute for her rugged Charles Brandon. Four men carried a golden canopy emblazoned with the emblem of Rome, the double-headed black eagle. His narrowed eyes scanned the waiting nobles as he entered and he bowed to his aunt, Queen Catherine, waiting in the centre – but his eyes were on Mary.

She thought about that moment as Henry's grand new barque, the *Katherine Pleasaunce*, ploughed through the white-crested waves of the English Channel on the way to Calais. Ten more ships led her way, loaded with supplies and whinnying horses. She turned and looked behind to see more ships than she could

...g in their wake. Their flotilla looked more like an ...on than a peace mission.

She leaned on the wooden rail and thought back to her meeting with Emperor Charles in Canterbury. He'd embraced Queen Catherine, an awkward moment as she seemed surprised and flustered, with tears in her eyes, at such intimacy.

Keen to avoid the same, Mary waited until he stood opposite her then held out her hand. He placed a soft kiss on her gold-ringed fingers, never taking his eyes from her face.

'*Reine Marie, tu es le joyau de la cour du Roi Henri.*'

She stared into his intelligent brown eyes and saw an appraising look. '*Bienvenue en Angleterre, Votre Majesté.*'

As their ship plunged through a breaking wave, sending a shower of salty spray into the air, Mary wondered if he might regret the paths their lives had taken. At the grand banquet he'd been seated on the other side of Henry, but whenever she'd glanced in his direction he'd been looking at her. He declined to join in the dancing yet she'd been aware of his eyes following her with the intensity of a hawk watching a swinging lure.

Brandon joined her at the ship's rail and put his warm cloak around her shoulders. 'How is the pain in your side?'

'The motion of the ship makes the ache worse, but I pray I won't be ill once we reach France.' She looked up at him and managed a smile. 'You've spent too much on my gowns to miss the chance to show them off.'

He grinned. 'They've done their work, Mary. You must know you made quite an impression on young Charles.' The note of jealousy in his voice hung in the salty air like one of the white seabirds following in their wake.

'He hardly spoke to me.' Mary tried to sound dismissive. 'I think he had more important things on his mind.'

'Like his latest marriage proposal?'

'He's marrying?' She looked to see if he was joking.

'Henry's offered him the hand of his daughter, so Emperor Charles might marry Mary Tudor after all.'

'Little Princess Mary? She's already promised to the dauphin.' She heard the surprise in her voice. 'What will King Francis say when he hears?'

Brandon didn't reply but gave her a knowing look.

Calais harbour was a chaotic jumble of ships, moored in rafts five deep. Men and horses struggled to get ashore before the light failed. Barrels and crates were piled high on the quayside and the crisp evening air rang with shouted commands. Mary recalled the last time they'd been there, preparing to face an uncertain future in England.

She'd been fearful Henry might lock Brandon up in the Tower of London but instead he'd shown them both compassion. It cost almost everything they had and Mary doubted they would ever repay their debts but she'd been happy at Suffolk Place and then at Westhorpe Hall, which she now thought of as her home.

After a restless night as the guests of a wealthy merchant Mary rose early for the six-mile ride to the Val d'Or. Brandon rode behind King Henry, leading his royal escort of fifty mounted nobles. Mary, elevated by her status as Queen Dowager of France, rode at the side of Queen Catherine. Behind them followed their ladies-in-waiting, a seemingly endless line of grooms and servants and a hundred mounted yeomen.

As the towers of Guines Castle appeared in the distance the entire procession stopped to admire the impressive sight before them. The flat plain between the old castle and the town of Ardres had been transformed.

In front of the castle a circle of colourful marquees, each flying the standard of a different noble family, surrounded the grand central palace. Those of the king's household had the green and white stripes of the Tudor livery but others were pure cloth of gold and burgundy damask, depending on the courtier's rank and wealth.

Mary turned to Queen Catherine. 'I had no idea the encampment would be on such a scale.'

'It's taken an army of workmen weeks of preparation, with no expense spared.' Catherine didn't trouble to hide the note of criticism in her voice as she looked ahead to where Henry proudly surveyed the scene. 'Sir Thomas Boleyn told me King Francis has no more than four hundred tents at Ardres – but Wolsey has drained our coffers with seven times that number.'

Mary frowned at the mention of their ambitious ambassador, Thomas Boleyn. His daughter Mary rode with Catherine's ladies and she realised her friend must be unaware of her disloyalty. Even though she was with her new husband, William Carey, Mary Boleyn seemed a poor choice for a meeting with King Francis. Wolsey would not have chosen her without good reason.

'There must be at least five thousand staying here.' She changed the subject as they stared at the rows of colourful tents and bustling preparations.

'Let us pray this is a wise investment. We flatter the French king with our extravagance.'

As they rode closer Mary could see Catherine wasn't mistaken. Four impressive lions guarded the entrance to the palace of illusions like golden sentinels. With foundations of red brick and finely glazed windows, the temporary palace was over three hundred paces square with a high round tower at each corner and an open courtyard at the centre. Wolsey had taken Henry at his word and spared no expense.

A handsome bronze statue of the Roman god Bacchus stood next to fountains already gushing with red wine. Mary studied a sign next to silver cups, inviting visitors to help themselves at the king's pleasure. A grinning, gilded Cupid, suspended above their heads, caused Queen Catherine to raise an eyebrow.

'Henry might profess to love the King of France but he doesn't trust him.' She saw Mary's puzzled expression. 'There are rumours Francis has an army hiding close by, so we have a secret passage to escape to the real castle if we are betrayed.'

Mary looked up at the gold roses decorating the green silk ceiling of the royal chambers and wondered how much it had all cost. Hung with Henry's finest tapestries, her apartment was furnished with a gilded bed complete with a canopy of estate carried all the way by wagon and ship from Greenwich.

With her fine new silk and satin gowns, one for each day of her stay, she'd been left in no doubt of the importance of her role in France. She was there to dazzle King Francis and his nobles and ensure the secret escape passage would never be needed.

A salvo of cannons boomed with smoke and flame from the ramparts of Guines Castle, echoing across the plain as the kings of England and France set out for their first meeting. The acrid tang of gunpowder drifted across to Mary as she watched from a distance with Catherine. As the cannon fire died away a sweeter sound carried on the still air. A hundred golden bells sewn to the harness of Henry's warhorse jingled as he rode.

Discordant French trumpets announced the arrival of King Francis, dressed in cloth of gold and black and white, with his flamboyant Swiss guards. He seemed to have become grander over the five years since she'd seen him last. The sight of him brought back more repressed memories of his daily visits during her long days in the darkness of Cluny, where she'd prayed at her altar for salvation until her knees ached.

The two kings cantered ahead of their mounted escorts

and met in the middle of the plain. A cheer rang out as they clasped each other's arms.

'They embrace like brothers.' Catherine gave Mary a wry glance. 'Your father would have been proud of Henry today.'

The mention of her father jolted Mary from her daydreaming. Seeing the two kings embrace in the saddle reminded her of the first time she met King Louis. He'd leaned across and embraced her, without dismounting, placing a soft kiss on her lips. Jane Popincourt told her he was a lecherous old man without morals, yet she found him to be loving and kind, despite his illness.

She peered into the distance and saw Henry and Francis dismount and walk together towards the French pavilion. Henry's arm was clasped around the shoulder of King Francis, who could so easily have been his bitter enemy. The first step towards peace had been taken.

Mary turned to Catherine. 'I wonder if they will be quite so amicable after the joust?'

'I've asked Henry not to ride against King Francis, although I doubt he'll take notice.'

Mary nodded. 'Charles is taking charge of the jousting, with Admiral Bonnivet. They are to run the same number of courses, with special lances that break for show, not competition.'

'I pray you are right. Henry doesn't always listen to his advisors but your Charles knows how to persuade him.' She smiled. 'I think it will be some time before Henry returns. You should take this opportunity to pay our respects to Queen Claude. She has my sympathy if what we hear is true, that King Francis openly favours his mistress, Françoise de Foix, Comtesse de Châteaubriant.'

The French Queen's apartments near Ardres were lined with

azure-blue satin embroidered with fleurs-de-lis. The ceiling twinkled with a thousand golden stars and a crescent moon shone in the centre. Although simpler than the temporary English palace, it had Parisian style that appealed to Mary and evoked memories of the last time she'd been in France.

Queen Claude stood to greet Mary and her escort. She looked pale and needed the support of her ladies to return to her seat. Seven months pregnant, she carried extra weight and her left eye drooped, giving her an odd squint.

Mary bowed her head, then embraced her friend warmly. 'I've never forgotten your kindness to me, Queen Claude.'

'*Bonjour Marie*, you look just as I remember!'

Mary shook her head but laughed. 'You are too kind, Claude. I've had three children since we last met.'

Queen Claude's hand went to the front of her bulging gown. 'As have I. The same as you, two girls and a boy, and another on the way.'

A woman dressed in rich damask stepped from the shadows and gave the briefest curtsey. Mary stared into the calculating eyes of the king's mother, Duchess Louise of Savoy. Queen Claude had done everything in her power to support Mary when she was last in France but the king's mother schemed and plotted against her.

'Welcome, duchess.' Louise spoke in heavily accented English and looked at Mary with a mixture of curiosity and contempt. 'There was also a girl, named after me, but she lived for only two years.'

The use of her lesser title would have troubled Mary in the past but now her duty was to preserve the fragile peace. 'I was sorry to hear that, duchess. Your support must be a great comfort to the queen,' she smiled, 'as it was to me, after my husband King Louis died.'

Duchess Louise returned Mary's smile but her eyes remained cold. 'It was a difficult time for us all.'

In a flash of insight Mary realised how it must have been a worrying time for the duchess. If she had been pregnant with Louis' child, all their futures would have been quite different. Duchess Louise had been doing her best for her son, as any mother would. Mary resolved to forget her past hostility. Duchess Louise was an important ally, one of the few King Francis listened to.

Brandon looked unusually agitated as he returned from his work preparing the tournament, a white linen bandage wrapped around his hand. Mary embraced him and studied his blue-grey eyes. 'What's happened?'

He cursed and lowered his voice, aware they could be over-heard through the thin walls of the temporary palace. 'It's Henry. He challenged King Francis to a wrestling match.'

Mary frowned. 'We feared something like this. Dare I ask the outcome?'

'King Francis has kept himself fit with his Italian campaigns.' Brandon scowled. 'He threw Henry to the ground like a sack of corn.'

Mary smiled at the thought. 'Perhaps Henry let him win?'

Brandon looked at her for a moment before he realised she was joking. 'Sometimes I forget you are a Tudor.'

'And what of you?' She gave him a stern look. 'How did you injure your hand?'

He grinned and held up the bandage like a badge of honour. 'It seems I'm getting too old for this sport. A young Frenchman caught me off guard.'

Mary shook her head. 'The jousting doesn't start until tomorrow.'

He embraced her again. 'Would I dare to lie to the Dowager Queen of France?'

She studied his face. 'Out of loyalty to my brother the king,

I would say you are quite capable of anything, my lord of Suffolk.'

Four strong yeomen of the king's guard carried Mary in her litter to the impressive new tiltyard, specially built by the French. Covered with cloth of gold embroidered with fleurs-de-lis, her carriage featured the porcupine badge of the late king, to leave the crowd in no doubt of her status as Dowager Queen of France.

They applauded and cheered when they saw her take her place on the grandstand under her canopy of estate. A deep French voice called out '*C'est la Reine Blanche!*' and soon the tilt-yard echoed to more cheering and cries of '*Vive la Reine!*' and '*Vive la Reine Blanche!*'

Queen Claude, in cloth of silver, took her place to Mary's right, with Duchess Louise in a gown of black velvet. Queen Catherine, her long hair proudly displayed under a jewelled Spanish headdress, sat to Mary's left. All their ladies, dressed in scarlet trimmed with gold lace, surrounded them like a guard of honour.

Once the ladies were seated, the competitors, English and French, paraded on their fine warhorses, with Henry and Francis leading. The English wore gold and royal purple, with the French in gold and white. King Henry's destrier was dressed in russet damask decorated with golden waves to symbolise his command of the seas.

Queen Catherine pointed to Henry's armour. 'The king's craftsmen used two thousand ounces of gold. Henry complains it's made his armour too heavy.'

Mary nodded. 'It does look magnificent.' She had a sudden recollection of her father, hunched over his ledgers as he personally checked each entry. It was up to her brother how he used his inherited wealth but she imagined her father would have been unimpressed.

As they passed, the shields and crowns of both kings were placed at an equal height on a great gilded tree, with green damask foliage, in the centre of the tiltyard. The shields of the other competitors were added below until the tree shone with the colourful badges of every noble family of note in England and France.

Mary felt a frisson of pride as Brandon cantered back to the royal grandstand. In his element, he wore his shining, burnished armour with white ostrich plumes on his helm and a flowing purple cape over his shoulders. He rode up to Mary to seek her favour, as he'd done when they were both young.

Raising his lance high in the air then lowering it, he called out in a confident voice so that everyone could hear. 'My lady, I would be honoured to ride as your champion.'

Mary stood and reached out with the favour she pulled from a pocket in her gown. The crowd applauded as he tied her purple ribbon to his harness and grinned at her, raising a gauntleted hand in salute before lowering the visor of his helmet.

A trumpet blast signified the start of the tournament and a herald announced that King Francis would ride against Sir Henry Courtenay, the Earl of Devonshire, one of Henry's most skilled jousters. Both riders charged, riding low in the saddle. Their lances were blunted at the ends and Brandon had promised her it was only for show, yet the violence of the clash as King Francis shattered his lance against the earl's buckler made Mary gasp.

The crowd cheered and applauded as Francis waved in acknowledgement. It reminded Mary of one of Henry's masked charades, with each playing his part, until the final pass, when the earl's lance struck the French king's helmet with a juddering crash of metal.

A cry of alarm erupted from the French crowd as King Francis dropped his lance and reeled in his saddle. He was helped to dismount and his supporters led him to his tent. After a few anxious moments the king emerged, without his helmet, holding a cloth to his bloodied nose, the first casualty of the tournament.

At last it was Brandon's turn to ride against the Count of St Pol, who dressed in gleaming silver armour decorated with gold fleurs-de-lis, his warhorse caparisoned in flowing white silk. Mary doubted if anyone other than herself noticed her husband rode with such care to ensure both broke an equal number of lances. He should have had an easy victory against the less-skilled French count.

The jousting continued all day, with food and wine being served by a procession of liveried maids. Mary's side ached and she was glad of the endless cups of rich red wine which helped to deaden the pain. This was only the first of twelve days of tourneying, with archery and contests of arms, but she knew she must keep her smile as she waved to the cheering crowds.

When the weather turned for the worse the tourney was agreed as a draw. Although King Francis sustained a broken nose and a black eye, only one of the three hundred contestants had died. Henry grumbled when he'd accidentally killed one of his favourite warhorses, yet Brandon and Admiral Bonnivet were congratulated for presiding over a successful tournament.

A temporary chapel was built in the tiltyard and decorated with relics and tapestries of the Holy Virgin. Cardinal Wolsey presided over a grand Mass, wearing his scarlet robes and wide-brimmed cardinal's hat.

For once, Mary found herself standing at Brandon's side as both Henry and King Francis took turns to sing the refrains. Familiar with her brother's fine tenor voice, she was surprised to hear Francis even took this as a competition and sang louder.

He had another surprise waiting for them once they'd retired with their retinues of nobles and ladies to an open banqueting gallery beside the chapel. King Francis stood and proposed a toast to lasting peace and friendship, then raised his eyes to the heavens as if seeking divine inspiration.

With perfect timing, a giant rocket made its thunderous way like a mythical dragon across the cloudless June sky above them and exploded in a shower of bright sparks. The noise startled several horses, which bolted, but drew cheers and applause from the surprised English.

Brandon leaned across to Mary. 'Once again the French have outdone us!'

Mary smiled as she watched the trail of white smoke drifting overhead. 'And at significantly less expense.'

'Emperor Charles is here?' Mary struggled to understand the summons from Henry to attend the meeting. 'I thought I might never see him again.'

Queen Catherine shook her head. 'Not here. We must travel to Gravelines, a day's ride north-east, to welcome the emperor's delegation.'

'What about the French?' The ache in her side seemed worse than ever now and she heard the frustration in her voice. 'Is Henry prepared to risk everything we've done?'

Catherine looked uncertain. 'I encouraged him to meet with my nephew the emperor, Mary. Surely you see we cannot rely only on our alliance with the French?'

Mary felt in no mood for the long ride but realised she had no choice. 'Could the emperor not come here? We could entertain him in style.' She didn't try to hide her disapproval.

'This meeting is to confirm the betrothal of Mary to Charles instead of the dauphin.' Catherine shook her head. 'Not something we would wish to discuss within the hearing of the French.'

'I've already heard, so the French will soon enough.' Mary suspected Catherine had been behind the idea, which would unite the thrones of England, Castile and Aragon. As she watched her maidservants packing her gowns for the journey she knew her father would turn in his grave if Catherine's plan succeeded.

19

MARCH 1522

Mary's carriage wound its way through the Suffolk countryside. She'd been summoned yet again to attend Henry's court in London to welcome Emperor Charles and his delegation of Spanish ambassadors, and could guess the reason.

Mary thought back to the meeting in Gravelines, almost two years ago. She had been intrigued to finally meet the mysterious Archduchess Margaret of Savoy. The archduchess could have become her stepmother, if she'd not rejected her father's advances. Attending the meeting in Gravelines as Regent of Austria and to support her nephew, Emperor Charles, Margaret had seemed keen to promote her own interests to Henry.

Mary knew a great deal about Margaret from Anne's stories and saw why Brandon had once been attracted to her. More than a match for either Henry or Charles, she'd been shrewd and persuasive. Mary suspected the archduchess planned to benefit from turning England away from the new alliance with France.

The last time Brandon returned from court he'd been in a

furious mood. 'Your brother seems to have forgotten his promises.' He cursed as he wolfed down the venison pie she'd had the servants keep warm. 'It places me in an impossible position – and you too, Mary.'

'He plans to invade France?' She studied his frowning face. Brandon's grim expression was her answer. They'd both known war with King Francis was inevitable, yet it would mean the loss of her dower estates and the income they now relied on. It also saddened her to think she would no longer be permitted to write to Queen Claude. Henry dreamed of being a warrior king and winning an empire of his own.

At Greenwich Palace, Brandon and Henry hunted in the deer park with Emperor Charles and jousted against his knights, while at York Place Mary rehearsed a pageant. Devised by Henry, it was to be performed on the evening of Shrove Tuesday for the entertainment of their guests.

The great hall of Cardinal Wolsey's palace had been transformed into an enchanted forest, complete with an impressive emerald-green castle. The smell of newly sawn timber and fresh paint hung in the air as Mary inspected the craftsmen's work with Anne Boleyn.

Now twenty-one, Anne had been recalled to England from Queen Claude's court to serve as one of Queen Catherine's ladies-in-waiting. Anne had been chosen as one of the masked virtues for the pageant, together with her sister Mary and another five others of Catherine's ladies.

Mary remembered Anne as a cheerful young girl in her service in Paris seven years before and saw her standing behind Queen Claude at the Field of the Cloth of Gold. Keen to hear the latest news from France, Mary had contrived to have this moment alone with her.

The walls of the darkened chamber were hung with beautiful Flemish tapestries of hunting scenes, and branches of trees created the illusion of the mysterious forest. A cloth of gold canopy of estate covered the gilded throne where the emperor would watch the pageant, surrounded by his Spanish ambassadors. Tiers of benches had been provided for other courtiers and it seemed they would have quite an audience.

The wooden castle reached almost to the roof beams, with a working drawbridge and battlements on a central tower flanked by two smaller towers. Each tower was hung with colourful embroidered banners and metal cressets on brackets, filled with scented oil. Mary frowned as she looked up at the central image of a bleeding, scarlet heart being torn in two. On the smaller left tower, another heart was held in what looked like a lady's hand and on the right a lady's hand turned a heart around.

'The emperor seems a dour man, my lady.' Anne pointed to the garish banners. 'Do you think he'll understand our pageant?'

'The message of it seems clear enough, although we learned from the last meeting with Emperor Charles that he's not impressed by extravagance.'

Anne gave Mary a conspiratorial look. 'I heard the king's cloth of gold tent at Gravelines blew down in the wind.' She smiled at the thought. 'Were you all inside it at the time?'

'It did blow down,' Mary tested the walls of the wooden castle but they seemed firm enough, 'but fortunately it happened in the middle of the night. I don't think the emperor even knew about it.' She turned to look at Anne. Although plain, she brought something of the style of the French court to London and still seemed cheerful, despite her circumstances.

'I heard you are to marry James Butler, the Earl of Ormond?'

'That's my father's plan – and he has the support of Cardinal Wolsey.' Anne grimaced. 'All they talk about is settling

the inheritance but it's m*
she'd already said enough.

'You intend to object?'

'I must obey my father, my la

Mary saw the glint of stee.
doubted it. Brandon had mentioneo
rose gardens at Greenwich with anoth
household, young Henry Percy. Heir
Northumberland and of similar age to An   d
better match.

'How is Queen Claude? It's been some tin.   .nce I last
heard from her.'

'You know she had a daughter, Madeleine, named after the
king's sister?'

'Yes – and in her last letter Queen Claude wrote that she
was already with child again.'

Anne nodded. 'It was another boy, named Charles – after
your husband or the emperor, my lady?'

Mary smiled at the thought. 'Neither. I imagine the boy is
named after the king's father, Charles, Count of Angoulême.'

'King Francis wasted little time, although I fear so many
children have taken a toll on Queen Claude's health.'

'I pray for her, Anne. There is little else we can do, particularly now...'

Mary didn't wish to say how she feared they would all be
caught up in a war she wasn't confident they could win. The
French would be fighting on their own territory, with battle-
hardened soldiers. The English had few experienced commanders and had not fought a battle for many years. It would be
determined by the outcome of her brother's talks and the will
of God.

Candles fixed in the tree branches and scented oils in the metal up the enchanted forest with a warm, ne king's musicians played a melodic tune as paraded past the Spanish ambassadors, each stopping to curtsey before the emperor. All wearing masks and dressed in identical, flowing white satin gowns, they announced their pageant names, embroidered in gold on their jewelled headdresses.

Mary was the first and did her best to disguise her voice, although she was sure the emperor knew it was her. 'Je suis la Beauté, votre Grâce.' She curtseyed and was pleased to see a rare smile on the young emperor's face before she realised it was a look of embarrassment.

Lady Mary followed as the virtue of Kindness, with her sister Anne making an elegant curtsey and catching the emperor's eye as she told him her name was Perseverance. The other ladies curtseyed in turn and said they were the virtues of Honour and Constancy, Bounty, Mercy and Pity.

Less fortunate were the unlucky bare-footed maids with soot-blackened faces, dressed in black rags, chosen to play the parts of Danger and Disdain, Jealousy, Gossip and Unkindness, Scorn and Strangeness. Their role was to skulk around the darkened forest and prevent the lords from reaching the green castle.

Stirring music and a drum roll sounded to announce the dramatic entrance of the masked lords, dressed in cloth of gold with cloaks of azure-blue satin. Their leader, swathed in shimmering crimson satin decorated with golden flames, bowed and announced himself as the Lord of Ardent Desire.

The other masked lords each stepped forward in turn and bowed to the audience, announcing themselves as Amorousness and Nobleness, Youth and Attendance, Loyalty and Pleasure, Gentleness and Liberty. Mary recognised Brandon and suspected her brother chose the role of the Lord of Ardent

Desire for himself, although she found it difficult to be certain as he played his part so well.

On the thumping boom of a bass drum, meant to represent cannon fire, she called out to her ladies. 'Follow me, graces and virtues, to the safety of the castle!'

Once they were all inside she pulled on a rope to raise the wooden drawbridge, which creaked as it lifted and banged into place, securing the door. The lords roared as they besieged the castle, while the maids dressed in black did their best to defend it by throwing cups of rose water and sugar-coated comfits.

The leader of the lords called out to them in a commanding voice. 'As Ardent Desire, I order you to surrender the virtues!'

One of the black-garbed women replied in a shrill shout. 'As Scorn, I refuse.' Another called out. 'As Disdain, I have no fear of you.'

The lords threw oranges, brought as gifts by the Spanish ambassadors, some striking the green wooden castle with solid thumps, making Mary and the ladies inside shriek and call out for mercy. The siege seemed to be getting out of hand when the king's musicians struck up a lively dance, the signal for the ladies to surrender.

The blackened maids made good their escape and the wooden drawbridge lowered, allowing the ladies to emerge from the confinement of the castle. The lords each took one of them by the hand and they danced Henry's favourite pavane, changing partners in the formal pattern of steps until each had danced with them all. At last when the dance was over, the lords and ladies pulled off their masks, to applause and cheers from the ambassadors.

At the lavish banquet which followed, the emperor seemed in good spirits and made a short speech. He thanked King Henry for the hand of his daughter and raised his goblet, proposing a toast to a new future for England and Spain. It was only at this point that Mary looked around the cheery faces and realised Queen Catherine was nowhere to be seen.

～

Harry seemed taller each day, growing out of his clothes faster than Anne could keep up with her skilful alterations. His latest outfit, a jerkin of forest green, made him look more like a verderer than the heir to the dukedom of Suffolk, in direct line of succession to the throne of England.

Mary laughed as he strutted around the great hall at Westhorpe with his overlong sword slung low on his belt, in an amusing impression of his father, still away at court. The dangerous sword was yet another attempt by Brandon to win his son's affection. He could not be prouder of his son but didn't seem to realise all the boy wanted was his attention.

His daughter Anne, now a tall fifteen-year-old, had become Mary's constant companion and together they ran the household and estate. Money was as tight as ever yet they'd grown used to finding economies, making the most of the gardens and sewing their own gowns.

Anne's sister Mary, now twelve, helped to look after Frances and little Eleanor, who were also growing fast. She took a great interest in the horses and, like Harry, complained that she missed their father. The prospect of an invasion meant he spent far more time at Suffolk Place to be close to Henry when needed.

Mary had remained at Westhorpe since the emperor's visit, relying on her husband to keep her informed of matters at court. Never much of a letter writer, he'd become increasingly reticent about the impending war with France, although she knew the prospect troubled him.

Mary worked in the room she called her study, checking the estate accounts, initialling each entry as she'd watched her father doing at Richmond Palace. When she was a girl she hadn't understood his personal attention to such details, yet now she did. It was important to keep a firm hand on the reins if they were to live within their means, particularly now her dower income was at risk.

The windows were open to let fresh air into the room and she could hear a commotion in the courtyard. It was hard to tell, because of the thick walls, but Harry seemed to be annoying his half-sister Mary again. She made a mental note to have a word with them both. Harry had developed a forceful personality, not unlike her brother. He was easily bored and had taken to finding new ways to annoy his sisters.

She frowned as she saw how much they'd spent on the upkeep of Brandon's horses. He'd been keen to breed them and swore the income would far outweigh the cost. If he troubled himself to look at the accounts he would see they needed to sell the foals before the winter.

Mary came bursting in from the courtyard, her face red. 'Harry is shooting arrows at my doves.' She raised her hands in despair. 'He says he's hunting them, just like Father does.'

'I told Harry he is not to use his bow in the house.' Mary frowned. 'Please send him to me, it's time I had a talk with him.'

She turned back to the accounts and picked up her quill, dipping it in her silver inkpot when she heard a sharp yell from outside. Her mother's instinct told her there was something wrong. The cry had been followed by an unnatural silence. Laying down her quill she rushed down the corridor and into the courtyard.

Harry lay on his back on the cobblestones, making a strange whimpering sound and holding his head with both hands. Mary kneeled at Harry's side and saw blood on the cobbles. She turned to her stepdaughter, who seemed to be in shock.

'What happened?'

'When I came to fetch Harry he was climbing up the dovecot to recover his arrows, then...' She wiped a tear from her eye. 'He was nearly at the top when a dove flew out and I saw him fall.'

'Fetch Anne, as fast as you can – and tell her to bring clean linen for a bandage.'

While she waited she cradled her son in her arms. His eyes opened and he groaned, 'I'm sorry, Mother.'

The family followed Mary's habit of rising early but Harry was the one exception. He liked to remain in his pallet bed for as long as possible, so Mary didn't miss him until mid-morning. She sat at her desk writing a letter to Queen Catherine when one of her maids from the nursery approached.

'It's Master Harry, my lady.' She bobbed a curtsey. 'He refuses to rise from his bed.'

She turned to look at the maid. Known as Mistress Radford, she was a well-meaning woman but with little initiative, which meant everything had to be explained to her, often more than once. It was annoying to be distracted from her letter, as she was struggling to find the right words. If the rumours Brandon hinted at were true, Catherine must be going through a difficult time.

Mary sighed as she set down her quill and climbed the narrow staircase to Harry's bedchamber, followed by the maid. The wound on his head had soon stopped bleeding, although she told him to keep it bandaged and hoped he'd learned an important lesson. Harry looked up as she entered and groaned, holding his hand to his bandaged head.

'I have a thirst, Mother, and my head aches.'

Mary held her hand to his forehead. It felt cool, with no sign of a fever. She removed the linen bandage and examined the wound where he'd hit his head. It was healing well, so she turned to the maid, waiting in the doorway. 'Bring a cup of sweet mead, Mistress Radford. I shall sit with him for a while.'

She frowned as she turned back to Harry and saw he'd closed his eyes. There was something wrong. Harry was a lively boy and had gone to bed early, so he shouldn't be tired. Mistress Radford returned with Harry's mead, a trencher of freshly baked bread and a slice of cured ham.

'The cook thought Master Harry might be hungry, my lady.'

Mary thanked her and gave Harry a gentle shake to wake him. 'Please sit up, Harry. Cook has sent you some fine ham and bread.'

Harry pulled himself up and waited while Mary put a pillow behind him to support his head. He sipped his mead and nodded in approval, copying his father, then tasted a little of the bread and ham.

Mary crossed to the window and opened it to let in the fresh air. 'It's a lovely day, Harry, would you like to ride to the village?'

He shook his head. 'I feel too tired today, Mother.'

Mary thought he looked pale. She had little confidence in physicians, who had failed to help reduce the ache in her side. At the same time, if his condition worsened she would have to seek a professional opinion, if only to put her mind at rest.

When she went to check on Harry later she found him still sleeping. She felt his forehead. It was much the same as before, so she pulled a chair to his bedside and sat with him, watching the gentle rise and fall of his chest as she tried to decide what to do. At times like this she wished her husband wasn't so far away.

Mary asked Anne to sit with Harry while she returned to

writing her unfinished letter. Catherine had shown no inclination to invite her to court since the visit by Emperor Charles in March. In the meantime, Brandon seemed to think the king had found a new mistress, although her identity was a closely guarded secret he didn't wish to share.

She decided to suggest that Catherine make the pilgrimage to the shrine at Walsingham Abbey and stay at Westhorpe, which would be on her route, overnight. Although it would mean additional expense, it would be good to see her again.

The house would be filled with the queen's entourage, which would be good for the girls and a welcome break from the daily routine of Westhorpe. She thought she might arrange a concert and play the lute with Anne to entertain them. Mary finished her letter, satisfied with her proposal, and placed her seal in the molten sealing wax.

She was arranging for a groom to ride with her letter to Greenwich Palace when Anne appeared in the doorway, a troubled look in her eyes.

'You need to come and see Harry – I think we need to send for a physician.'

The physician was a thin, dour-faced man with a grey beard. He'd ridden all the way from Bury St Edmunds and spent some time examining her son before asking to see Mary.

'Do you think his condition is serious?' Mary studied his deep-set eyes for any clue to the truth.

The physician looked grave. 'How old is the boy, my lady?'

'He was six in March – why do you ask?'

'He seems to have taken quite a fall.' He shook his head. 'I fear there may be internal bleeding or damage to his brain, my lady. I shall prescribe a potion to be made up by the apothecary and taken each morning and night.' His matter-of-fact tone was that of a man who saw such things every day.

Mary felt an ominous premonition. 'Yet he will recover?'

The physician hesitated before replying. 'Some children with such an injury will heal in time, but I must tell you in my experience they are the exception.'

'He seemed to be recovering well.'

'My lady, the difficulty with young children is it takes longer for the consequences of such injuries to be observable.' The physician softened his tone. 'A child of your son's age might remain conscious, so injuries might not be thought serious, even though they may well be.'

Mary put her hand to her mouth. 'Do you think I should summon his father from London?'

He nodded. 'It would be a wise precaution, my lady.'

She sat at Harry's bedside through the night, lighting a new candle from the stub of the previous one as each burned down. Unable to sleep, she began to blame herself for her son's accident. She'd been quick to criticise her husband for the lack of attention he gave to his son, yet at least he had good reason.

She could have ridden with him to the village but instead had left him to play with his bow while she studied her accounts. She'd intended to help him learn to read and write, yet for no good reason had not found the time. She consoled herself with the knowledge it was an accident and the physician had said he could make a full recovery, in time.

As she watched over her sleeping son she recalled his christening at Suffolk Place. She'd been in her confinement but ordered the great hall to be decorated with hundreds of red and white roses. The king and queen attended with the senior nobles of the court, because Harry was in the direct line of succession. Poor Catherine had failed to provide Henry with an heir, although it seemed her new plan might work. There could one day be an Empress Mary Tudor on the throne of England.

Mary made her way to their private chapel. The stone floor felt cold, as there was no fireplace and the stained-glass window filtered the early morning sun. She kneeled alone before the statue of the Virgin, clasped her hands together and wept.

She cried for little Harry, who had woken briefly at dawn, and opened his eyes and looked into hers. Grey-blue and expressive, they seemed to be asking her a question. She'd taken his hand and felt his fingers grip hers for a moment, long enough to give her false hope.

She wept for the life he would never now have, taken from him too soon. Everything which had seemed important now seemed futile and pointless. She would have to be strong for the girls. No mother should ever have to bury her child. Now she must arrange his funeral. First, she would have to tell her husband and knew it would break his heart.

20

MARCH 1523

Mary supported her middle with both hands as her carriage rattled over another deep rut in the narrow road. The decision to make a pilgrimage to Butley Priory was not an easy one, as the aching in her side now made riding painful and the roads worsened with each mile she travelled east.

God willing, her child would be a boy, a Brandon heir to inherit the Suffolk title and estates. She knew her husband believed so. He'd said her pregnancy gave him hope and helped him deal with his grief. At the same time, she knew no child could replace little Harry. They would mourn his loss for the rest of their lives.

The tragedy changed them both and brought them closer as a family. Brandon spent less time at court, returning from London whenever he could, often riding through the night to be with them. He took back control of the household, and new income granted by Henry meant he could begin improving Westhorpe to better suit their growing family.

Their good fortune had come at the expense of Edward Stafford, Duke of Buckingham, who'd been executed for treason, his children disinherited. Although it eased their debts, Brandon had attended his trial and confessed to Mary that it was a sham. He'd known and respected Buckingham all his life and had been troubled by the way his enemies celebrated his downfall.

He tried to be a better husband to Mary, supporting her when all she wanted was to descend into despair. He also became a better father to the girls, buying much-needed new gowns and promising to see they all married well. He seemed to know another child would give Mary the renewed purpose she needed, and now she wanted to rebuild her life.

Prior Rivers bowed his tonsured head as he greeted Mary. 'Welcome, my lady.' He made the sign of the cross in the air and blessed her. Once they were in the privacy of the cloisters he looked at her with sympathy in his eyes. 'I was sorry to hear of your loss, my lady.'

'Thank you, prior. I confess my faith has been tested.'

He nodded in understanding. 'Saint Augustine taught us faith is to believe what you do not see.'

'And the reward is to see what you believe.'

The elderly prior smiled. 'You remember our teaching, my lady.'

'Could I ask the Lord to grant me another son?' Mary blurted out the question that had been in her head all the way to the priory.

'Who can know what miracles our future has in store, my lady?' He studied her face for a moment. 'We shall pray for you, and your unborn child. Each birth is a new beginning.'

Mary found comfort in the simple routine of the old priory. She dressed in a plain, undyed habit and read the psalms and prayers four times each day. She soon became used to rising with the bell for prime at dawn and watching the sun appearing over the sea on the eastern horizon.

She joined the canons for the two simple meals a day, served with small loaves and eaten in silence in the refectory. She learned to tolerate the malty taste of the weak ale, brewed in the abbey grounds, taken both at dinner and supper. Talking was not allowed but there would always be reading at meal-times and Mary took her turn, reciting aloud in Latin from the psalms.

She passed the long hours learning the psalter by heart, as required by the order, and in prayer, alone in the privacy of the shrine of the Virgin. The excess, intrigue and infidelity of her brother's court seemed a distant memory. She thanked the Lord that the tragedy of her son's accident helped her see what was truly important.

The child within her kicked, reminding her life must go on. When she'd first arrived at the priory she'd prayed each day for a boy, for Brandon's sake. Now she prayed only for a healthy baby. Mary's condition limited her usefulness to the close community until the prior suggested she might assist in the infirmary.

Set apart from the other buildings, the infirmary was a tranquil sanctuary of peace and rest. The long room was scented with burned incense and had six pallet beds, of which only one was occupied. An elderly, white-bearded canon named Joseph waited for his time with dignity, despite being in great pain.

He seemed glad of Mary's company and after prayers she would sit at his bedside and share stories of their lives. Well-educated, the old canon could converse in Latin and French and had once made a pilgrimage to the Holy City of Jerusalem.

'My lady,' his frail voice rasped. 'I have been praying for you…'

'I came here to pray for the child I carry yet my mind was full of doubt.' Mary looked into his rheumy eyes. 'I believe the will of God is sufficient for me, yet each time I have suffered a loss, my faith is tested.'

Canon Joseph nodded. 'God knows what is needful for us … but we are not always ready to receive it.' His words seemed to take great effort.

'My time here has reminded me to be thankful for the short time I had with my son.'

Canon Joseph managed a weak smile. 'Return to your family, my lady. We serve the Lord through our acts, as well as our prayers, and your family has need of you.'

'Thank you, Canon Joseph.' She smiled. 'I shall pray for you and will carry your words in my heart.'

~

The midwife brought the baby swaddled in fresh white linen. 'Your prayers have been answered, my lady.' She handed the tiny bundle to Mary, propped up on pillows in her bed. 'A strong and healthy boy.'

A single tear ran down Mary's cheek as she studied the face of the tiny child in her arms. She'd promised herself not to be disappointed if it was another girl, yet she knew what this would mean.

'Will you send for my husband.' She looked up at the kindly midwife. 'He has waited long enough.'

Brandon seemed to sense the good news from her face before she even spoke. 'A boy?' He grinned and kissed her. 'We shall name him Henry.'

'I hoped to call him Joseph…'

'Joseph?' Brandon shook his head. 'It must be Henry. He

might one day be King of England.'

Mary looked up at her husband and remembered grateful for what she had. She brushed the tear from h cheek and forced a smile. 'Welcome to my world, Henry Brandon.'

The routine of Westhorpe changed after her return from the priory. Instead of leaving her children to the care of nurse-maids and servants, Mary knew she must treasure every moment spent with them. This made it difficult for her when the queen's herald arrived with an invitation from Catherine.

Mary reread the letter she'd once longed to receive. The occasion requiring her attendance was to entertain Queen Catherine's niece, the emperor's sister, Isabella, visiting with her husband Christian, King of Denmark. Her first thought was to plead exhaustion after the birth of her child, something Catherine would understand.

She'd found a closer bond with little Henry than she'd expected and now spent every waking moment with him. It would be impractical to take him on the long journey to London. She would have to leave him with his wet nurse for weeks and would miss him too much.

She asked Brandon's opinion after they'd retired for the night. He pulled her close and ran his fingers through her long hair. 'It will be good for you to return to court, and right that you do so, my Dowager Queen of France.'

'It's a long journey by carriage. I could be away for weeks.' She gave him a questioning stare. 'Would you not miss me, my lord of Suffolk?'

'I shall ride to London with you.' He grinned. 'I've heard the Queen of Denmark is quite a beauty.'

She gave him a playful slap. 'What about the children?'

'We have servants enough to care for them. It will be good

Mary to have the responsibility. She's thirteen now and we must not treat her as a child.'

'Anne will travel with us?'

'Of course, as your lady-in-waiting. Perhaps this is an opportunity for you to propose her as a lady-in-waiting to the queen?' He watched for her reaction.

Mary lay back and stared up at the velvet canopy over their bed. Now turned sixteen, Anne had grown into a dark-eyed beauty. It made her shudder to think what could happen to her innocent stepdaughter at Henry's court.

'Perhaps when she is eighteen. I'm not ready to part with Anne yet and I value her company here at Westhorpe. You won't forget your promise to find her a suitable husband?'

'I'm working on a plan to make Anne a baroness but I don't want her to know until I'm sure.'

'Or me, evidently? You keep too many secrets from me, Charles. You've said nothing about my brother's latest mistress. If I'm to see Queen Catherine I need to know what he's up to behind her back. Has my brother sworn you to secrecy?' She stroked his greying beard.

He reached out and took her hand to stop her. 'You must promise not to speak of this to anyone. Henry still sees Mary Boleyn – or Mary Carey, as she is now. They've kept it secret from all but his closest circle.'

'I guessed as much, so I'm sure Catherine knows.' Mary leaned over and kissed him. 'I owe it to Catherine as a friend to support her. Is there nothing you can do to influence my brother?'

'It seems I can't even influence my wife.' He pulled her close to him again and stroked her hair. 'For the sake of our family we must take care not to cross the king.' His voice sounded serious. 'Remember what happened to Buckingham.'

~

It took over a week to make the hundred-mile journey south to Greenwich. London seemed noisier, dirtier and a little dangerous after the tranquil Suffolk countryside. As they passed through the city gates they were welcomed by a skeletal corpse hanging on a gibbet. The River Thames stank of sewage and a row of grisly severed heads adorned London Bridge, their empty eyes pecked out by crows.

Mary noted the vigilance of the armed guards at the entrance to Greenwich Palace, a sign the country still simmered with unrest. Brandon told her that, as in her father's day, there was opposition to new taxes to fund an army. The people didn't share Henry's ambition to make war on France if it meant they had to pay.

As she entered the queen's apartments with Anne, Mary sensed the tension in the air. The queen's ladies-in-waiting, who'd been at their needlework, stood and bobbed a curtsey yet seemed unusually silent and Mary guessed the likely reason. She recognised Anne Boleyn but noticed her sister was absent.

They were led into Queen Catherine's private chambers, where she waited to receive them. She wore her formal Spanish headdress and a dark, brocade gown, her only jewellery a crucifix of dark-red rubies, with three large pearls. At her side was Princess Mary, now seven years old. The red-gold hair of the Tudors showed at the front of her French headdress and her sharp eyes held Mary's with a confidence beyond her years.

Catherine smiled at them as they curtseyed. 'Welcome, Mary – and Anne, how you've grown since I saw you last. I trust you had a good journey?'

'Each time it seems longer, Your Grace.' The ache in Mary's side felt worse after the long carriage ride.

Catherine studied Anne appraisingly. 'I remember you played for us, most beautifully.'

Anne nodded. 'It is an honour to return to court, Your Grace.'

Catherine turned to her daughter. 'Mary is being tutored by Sir Thomas Moore. She is fluent in French and Latin and has a talent for singing.' Her pride was evident as she looked down at her daughter. 'She is learning the spinet as well as the lute. Would you take Anne to hear you play, Mary?'

They watched as Anne left with Princess Mary. After the doors closed behind them, Catherine put her hand on Mary's arm. 'I was sorry to hear of the loss of your son.'

'Thank you, Catherine. It was a difficult time for us all.'

'I heard you have been graced with another son.' There the faintest trace of envy in her voice.

Mary nodded. 'I wish I could have brought little Henry for you to see him.'

'Next time.' Catherine forced a smile. 'Now we must greet other new members of our family – my niece Isabella and her husband, the King of Denmark, Norway and Sweden.'

'I am intrigued to meet the sister of Emperor Charles,' Mary admitted. 'They say she had her husband's lover poisoned.'

Catherine shook her head. 'My niece could not do such a thing – and it can never be proven.' There was a note of reproof in her voice yet she gave Mary a meaningful look.

The great hall of Greenwich Palace had been improved by each successive owner. The alternating blue and gold fleurs-de-lis tiles were the legacy of Queen Margaret of Anjou. The high, arched windows were installed in the time of Mary's father and the oak banqueting tables, carved with Tudor roses, were her brother's contribution.

Mary looked out through her father's windows at the view of the River Thames as a tan-sailed barge floated silently past.

She was at the top table at the banquet to honour the Danish king and queen. A sallow-faced man with a pointed black beard and flamboyant hat, King Christian sat between Henry and Cardinal Wolsey. His reedy voice sounded strangely accented and Mary smiled when Brandon gave her his secret sign to show he didn't like him.

Queen Isabella sat between Catherine and Mary. She had a pale complexion and looked older than her twenty-two years. She wore a gown of white silk edged with gold lace, and a starched white coif over her hair which Mary guessed was in the Danish fashion.

Mary rinsed her fingers in a glass bowl of rose water as she listened to the grace from Cardinal Wolsey, who'd chosen to dress in his scarlet robes. He'd hoped to become pope yet Emperor Charles had failed to back him. Since that disappointment, his enthusiasm for the alliance against the French had been lukewarm.

Once the self-important cardinal was seated, green-and-white liveried servants appeared, to pour wine and set out a bewildering variety of dishes. One placed a glazed suckling pig on the table before Mary. Lying on a bed of fresh herbs, the pig had sugared plums for eyes and a gilded apple had been forced into its mouth, as if it was about to eat it.

'The poor thing looks too lifelike for my taste.' Mary shook her head when the servant offered to carve it. She took a sip of her wine and turned to the Danish queen. 'I understand you were at the court of Margaret of Savoy as a girl, Queen Isabella?'

'Please call me Elizabeth.' She smiled, revealing crooked teeth. 'I'm using the English for Isabella now.' She spoke softly in English with a Dutch accent. 'Archduchess Margaret was most kind to me.'

'My stepdaughter, Anne Brandon, was also tutored by the

archduchess.' She pointed out Anne, seated with Princess Mary.

'I owe the archduchess a great debt. She taught me how to ensure my place,' Elizabeth glanced across at her husband, 'as a woman in a world ruled by unscrupulous men.'

Mary raised an eyebrow at the queen's forthright tone and decided she was perfectly capable of removing King Christian's mistress. She could see why Brandon sent his daughter to Archduchess Margaret and had been reluctant to recall her. He'd somehow known she would also learn to survive at Henry's court and it was all part of his plan.

Brandon gathered the family together in the spacious new study he'd built at Westhorpe. He glanced at Mary, then turned to his daughters. 'I have to go to France and might be away until next year.'

Anne was the first to speak. 'Are you going to fight the French, Father?'

He nodded. 'I'm in command of fourteen thousand men, so it's a great responsibility.'

'But are the French not our friends, Father?' His daughter Mary frowned as she tried to understand.

Brandon nodded. 'They are, Mary. Our friends, our family and our neighbours.' He looked around at their shocked faces. 'The king has promised our allies, Emperor Charles and Archduchess Margaret, that England will support a revolt by the Duke of Bourbon against King Francis.' He glanced again at Mary. 'I have to help him keep that promise.'

Anne shook her head. 'There are others who can do that, Father. You haven't been to war for years...'

Brandon nodded. 'Ten years, Anne.' He softened his tone when he saw she was on the brink of tears. 'It's a great honour to be chosen by the king to lead his royal army. If I lead them to victory it will secure the future of our family.'

Once she was alone with him, Mary took him in her arms and wept. They both knew his mission carried enormous risks. The French were battle-hardened from their foreign wars. The English army were a poor mix of ageing veterans and novices, inexperienced men with no idea what lay ahead of them.

When the time came for him to leave, Brandon gave each of the girls one last embrace and took a long look at little Henry. He kissed Mary and forced a smile, then whispered, so only she could hear. 'I love you, Mary. Pray for me.'

She struggled to remain composed as she watched him fasten his gleaming new silver breastplate over his tunic, the badge of his command, and mount his warhorse. A hundred local yeomen, all wearing the blue-and-yellow Suffolk livery, waited for him. Mary thought some looked too old to fight, while others seemed little more than boys.

Brandon turned to look back at Westhorpe Hall and his family one last time, as if trying to fix them in his memory, then raised a black-gloved hand in farewell. He shouted a gruff command and led his men over the old stone bridge and out of sight.

21

MARCH 1525

Mary shivered as she waited in the cold abbey church, the hard wooden pew and chill air making her more aware of the nagging pain in her side. She stared up at the blue-cloaked statue of the Virgin Mary and noticed a dusty cobweb in the flickering light of the tall candles.

She clasped her white-gloved hands together and prayed for her stepdaughter. Although she'd long since stopped praying for relief from the ache that tormented her, she believed in the mystical power of prayer. She'd prayed each day that her husband might return safe from the war in France. Even when the rumours of disaster drifted home Mary kept faith that a merciful God would listen to her.

She felt conscious of the empty pew at her side. Her husband had returned from the invasion of France a changed man, with greying hair, his spirit broken. It took over a year for him to lose the haunted look in his eyes. Once, he'd woken her with his shouting in the middle of the night and confessed to recurring bad dreams about those dreadful months.

He rarely spoke about what happened but told her the

rebellion by the turncoat Charles, Duke of Bourbon, proved a dismal failure. The French king's spies alerted Francis to their plans and he'd been ready for them, although they somehow allowed the treacherous duke to escape. After all his promises to Henry, the soldiers of Emperor Charles didn't meet up with them as agreed and those of Archduchess Margaret arrived too late.

Mary heard from her surly blacksmith, who served with Brandon in France as a yeoman, that the English army suffered one of the worst winters anyone could recall. She'd watched as he pounded the glowing red horseshoe, his hammer blows adding emphasis as he answered her questions.

'When the supplies ran out, my lady, we drank stagnant water from ditches.' He plunged the hot iron shoe into his trough with a hiss of steam and stopped his work to mop his brow with a rag as the memory returned. He'd squinted at her with dark, deep-set eyes. 'In truth, we survived by eating our horses. Men lost fingers and toes through frostbite. Some died of the bloody flux. Others froze to death while they slept.'

Mary knew he told the truth. Her brother's ambitious campaign ended in disaster when the English army mutinied. Many deserted, to make their own way back to Calais. Henry might have thrown Brandon in the Tower for returning home without permission. Instead, he forgave him. He knew Brandon was a man of his word and that he'd suffered in the freezing fields of France.

Even after the jousting accident last year, a worrying time for them all, her brother refused to blame Brandon. His lance struck Henry's brow at such an angle his visor was raised, allowing sharp splinters of wood to enter his helmet. Brandon said Henry was lucky to survive the blow and had suffered with headaches since that day, yet rewarded him with the office of Earl Marshal.

The choir broke through Mary's thoughts with the *Te Deum*,

their pure tenor voices in perfect harmony, sounding ethereal in the old abbey church. She turned and looked back towards the half-open doors at the entrance. Their daughters waited, silhouetted in the doorway, all in matching bridesmaids' dresses, the result of much discussion and work.

Her stepdaughter Mary had become a beautiful and confident young woman. She would be fifteen next month and might one day become a lady-in-waiting to the queen. She loved to hear the stories of the French and English courts and longed for the day when she would be presented to Queen Catherine.

Next to Mary Brandon stood their daughters Frances, now eight, and Eleanor, aged six, in their shimmering satin gowns. Both had the same Tudor red-gold tresses as Mary, although Eleanor had the ways of her father. They beamed with anticipation as they waited for the wedding couple to arrive.

Mary searched for little Henry and spotted him with his nursemaid at the rear of the abbey church, ready to be taken outside when he became bored, as he inevitably would. He was already taking after his father and seemed much stronger than poor Harry, although Mary never took a single day with him for granted.

Applause from the waiting villagers and the clatter of hooves on cobbles announced the arrival of the carriage, pulled by a team of white horses. Mary watched as Brandon, wearing his heavy coat with thick collar of black fur, helped Anne step down.

Anne looked radiant in her wedding gown, the result of almost a year of embroidering precious gold thread on fine silks. She wore the same French headdress Mary had worn for her wedding in France and the twenty diamonds, set in the filigree border of gold, flashed in the early spring sunlight as she moved.

Mary saw the pride in Brandon's eyes and felt an irrational

jealousy. She'd not forgotten how he'd once said Anne looked more like her mother each day. Watching her effortless charm, it was easy to understand why he'd chosen Anne Browne as his mistress, then caused a scandal by making her his wife.

All heads turned as he escorted Anne to the waiting Edward, Baron Grey of Powys. Brandon had kept his word as, only four years older than Anne, the baron was handsome and courteous, with significant estates in Wales. He'd served with Brandon on the disastrous mission to France and been knighted on his return.

The choir fell silent and the elderly Bishop Foxe blessed them and began the formal ceremony. With typical stubbornness, her father's loyal friend refused Henry's suggestion he should accept retirement. He officiated at the wedding as a special favour to Mary, despite his failing eyesight. She guessed he must be close to eighty years old yet his voice carried well in the still air of the abbey church.

As she watched, Mary found herself recalling her first marriage to King Louis, so many years ago, in the Church of Notre-Dame. She'd been eighteen, the same age Anne was now, when the Bishop of Bayeux conducted the Nuptial Mass in his strange mixture of old French and Latin. She remembered repeating her wedding vows in a daze before the bishop blessed their union and King Louis gave her an overlong kiss. It seemed endearing now but at the time she'd felt her life was over.

Mary decided she would have been pleased enough if she'd known what the future would hold. She felt a stab of grief as she thought of little Harry but thanked the Lord for Henry, heir to Brandon's Suffolk estates. She was proud of her daughters and stepdaughters and had prepared them as well as any duchess of Savoy.

Brandon frowned as he tried to fasten the silver buckle on his sword belt. His waist had grown by another notch. Wolsey's messenger brought orders for him to disperse rioters in nearby Lavenham with the Duke of Norfolk, in the name of the king. He'd shown the terse note to Mary. In Wolsey's own hand, it looked hastily scratched.

'Have you not done enough?' There was an edge to her voice and she felt an instinctive foreboding.

Wolsey's request seemed fitting work for Sir Thomas Howard, who'd inherited his father's title after the old Duke of Norfolk passed away the previous year. Norfolk's private army of yeomen were notorious thugs, little more than mercenaries employed to do his bidding. Brandon could barely muster a hundred local men, poorly armed and of questionable commitment.

Brandon pulled on his riding cape. 'Wolsey gives me no choice. I'm damned if I go – and damned if I don't.' He cursed under his breath. 'Henry's been dreaming of his new invasion of France since King Francis was captured in Italy. Now Wolsey seeks to win his favour by raising the money he needs, regardless of the cost.'

A worrying thought occurred to Mary. 'Cardinal Wolsey knows it's an impossible task.' She frowned. 'While he sits drinking good wine in Hampton Court Palace, you risk your life to enforce his unfair tax.'

He paused his preparations for a moment and looked at her with a raised eyebrow. 'You sound like one of the rebels, Mary, but you are right. Parliament never approved Wolsey's amicable grants, so it's little wonder people are refusing to pay.'

'I'm concerned for you, Charles.' She embraced him. 'There's no telling what these rioters might do and you don't have an army, just your retainers.'

'Norfolk will bring his yeomen – and is bound to be too heavy-handed if I'm not there to see people are treated fairly.'

He kissed her on the cheek. 'I'll be fine. We'll round up ringleaders and the rest will soon disperse.'

'Then you'll speak to Henry?'

He gave her a farewell kiss on the cheek. 'This time I will.'

Mary found herself once again on her knees in their cold private chapel, praying for her husband. Two long weeks passed before he returned, looking tired from his journey but thankfully unharmed. Mary waited until he'd washed off the dirt of the road and changed out of his riding clothes. She poured him a tankard of strong ale from a jug.

'What happened?'

He took a drink of ale before answering. 'I had to wait for Norfolk and his men. By the time we reached Lavenham many thousands had gathered there. They outnumbered us so greatly my men looked ready to desert, but the rioters proved to be ordinary men and women trying to make an honest living.' Brandon rubbed his eyes. 'Norfolk saw his chance to give Wolsey a kick up his scheming backside, so we agreed to put the rebels' case to the king. They dispersed soon enough after that.'

'What did Henry say?' Mary held her breath as he took another deep drink and wiped his mouth on his sleeve.

Brandon gave her a wry look. 'He agreed with us – and is angry with Wolsey.'

She placed her hand on his arm. 'If he doesn't raise the money for an invasion, you might not have to go to war again.'

'I hope you're right, Mary, but preserving the peace has come at a price.'

'Wolsey?'

Brandon nodded. 'Let's pray I've not made us a dangerous enemy.'

～

Bridewell Palace, on the banks of the River Fleet, was built by Henry at considerable cost to replace their father's old palace at Westminster, destroyed by fire. Like Wolsey's Hampton Court, the rambling, red-brick palace had high chimneys and surrounded three spacious courtyards.

As the palace had no great hall the banqueting room filled with the entire court to witness the investiture ceremony. Mary felt a frisson of pride as her bewildered little Henry was confirmed as the new Earl of Lincoln. As well as securing his place in the nobility, his title completed Brandon's control of the former de la Pole legacy.

It would have been the talk of London but for the investiture which followed. Queen Catherine looked stony-faced as Henry Fitzroy, now aged nine, was made the Earl of Nottingham and Duke of Richmond and Somerset. Henry knew what he was doing. His son now took precedence over his legitimate daughter.

After the ceremony, in the privacy of the queen's chambers, Mary found Catherine weeping. She placed her hand on her friend's arm to console her. 'You must rise above this. I thought Henry could never surprise me, yet now he has.'

'He says my lack of sons is God's punishment on him for marrying his brother's wife. I know he is secretly working to have our marriage declared invalid, which would make Princess Mary illegitimate.' Catherine dried her eyes. 'I wish I had your strength, to overlook my husband's failings as easily as you do yours.'

'Brandon is far from perfect yet he's a loyal husband and a good father to his children.'

'Henry sat his bastard son at his right hand, for everyone to see.' Catherine spat the words in a bitter voice. 'At least

Brandon shows discretion about the consequences of his affair.'

Mary felt the cold shock of realisation. 'Charles is having an affair?' Her voice was little more than a whisper, her mind numbed by the thought.

Catherine put her hand to her mouth. 'I should never have spoken of it.'

Mary braced herself. 'Please tell me what you know.'

'I'm afraid it has been common knowledge at court for a long time. You know how my ladies-in-waiting gossip. I understand he also has a bastard son.'

Mary looked at her wide-eyed in disbelief. 'Who with?'

'I've said enough. You must ask your husband, Mary.'

Brandon seemed pleased with himself at the dinner which followed the investiture. Mary found herself thinking about things she'd accepted as a necessary part of his work. His profligate spending, his long absences, staying at Suffolk Place, encouraging her to remain at Westhorpe – all now took on a deeper significance.

The worst thing was imagining Catherine's ladies talking about her behind her back. It seemed a cruel world where her reward for absolute loyalty had been such betrayal. The enormous, overwhelming sense of loss felt like a bereavement but she had to carry on. She'd told Catherine she must rise above Henry's manner. Now Mary knew it was her turn.

She didn't confront him until they were alone at home, preparing for bed. The servants had retired for the night and all the children were sleeping. Her words, so carefully rehearsed, tumbled out as a single question.

'Is it true you have a son with another woman?'

His reaction told her all she needed to know. He looked away from her unblinking stare and cursed, his hand forming a fist. He took a moment to compose himself then turned back to face her with a steady gaze.

'It was a long time ago, Mary. I'm not even certain the child is mine.'

'Who is she?'

'No one of importance, then or now. I can imagine what you must think. It was a mistake.' He shook his head. 'A poor judgement on my part, not an affair.'

'Poor judgement?' Her voice sounded shrill, louder than she'd intended.

Brandon held up a hand to silence her. 'Please, Mary, for the sake of the children.'

She tried to calm herself but found his tone infuriating. A mixture of anger and despair made it hard to think, but she needed to know. Mary dug sharp fingernails into the palms of her hands as she tried to calm herself, although she could feel her heart racing in her chest.

'When was this?'

'Four years ago. After we returned from France.' His voice sounded flat and matter-of-fact, as if he was giving evidence in court. 'I'm sorry, Mary. I should have told you at the time but I didn't think you'd understand.'

'You were right. I don't understand. In fact, I wonder if I know you at all.'

Mary's life settled back into the routine of managing her household at Westhorpe. She had no choice but to carry on, for the sake of her children. Part of her felt scarred by Catherine's revelation but she decided it was better to know such things than to live in blissful ignorance.

Brandon refused to discuss the child, as if that would help her forget. Even when she asked him to, he would not tell her the mystery woman's name or where she lived, although he swore to her it was over. Mary believed it was, although she would always wonder whether Brandon's illegitimate son would one day emerge into the public gaze, as Henry Fitzroy had done.

One casualty of the disastrous invasion of France had been Mary's dower income. At the time, there was nothing to be done about it but now she needed the comfort of her own income. As far as she knew, King Francis remained a prisoner of Emperor Charles. Henry might be willing to recover her dower income but could use the money to fund another war.

There was one man who might help her. Mary took a fresh sheet of her best parchment and dipped her sharpened quill into the black, ox-gall ink before writing:

To my Lord Cardinal,

My Lord in my most hearty wise I commend me unto you so it is divers of my rights and duties concerning my dues in France have been of late time stayed and restrained in such ways as I nor my officers there may not have me receive the same as they have done in times past.

She paused as she thought of the charming Guillaume Gouffier, Admiral Bonnivet, chosen to oversee her dowager income as her agent in France. News of what happened trickled back to England through visiting ambassadors and Henry's spies.

The handsome admiral had been as close to King Francis as Brandon was to Henry, his right-hand man and loyal friend. After the French victory in Milan, it seemed the admiral encouraged Francis to pursue their retreating enemy south into Italy. The French king's horse was killed and he was captured at the Battle of Pavia, along with most of his army and commanders.

Henry celebrated the death of Richard de la Pole, the last

Yorkist pretender to his throne, killed fighting for the French, but Mary grieved the loss of her friend, Guillaume Gouffier. Brandon told her he'd died a heroic death, but she suspected he spared her the details.

Reading her letter to Wolsey she decided it was best to appeal to his vanity and encourage him to use such influence as he still had with her brother.

My Lord in this and in all others I evermore have and do put my only trust and confidence in you for the redress of the same. Entirely desiring you therefore that I may have the king's grace my dearest brother letters and yours into France as such my said servant shall desire and by the same I trust my said causes shall be brought to such order and good conclusion.

Cardinal Wolsey had been her saviour in the past and would be so again if he saw advantage in it for himself. She dipped her quill in her silver inkpot and continued, aware her fortune might depend on this one page of parchment.

I am evermore bold to put you to pains without any recompense unless my good mind and hearty prayer wherof you shall be assured during my life to the best of my power as knoweth our Lord who have you in his blessed tuition.

Mary checked her words one last time and made a few alterations before signing her letter, *Yours assured, Mary the French Queen.*

22

___

APRIL 1527

The plague ravaging the people of London kept King Henry from the capital for over a year. Horrific stories travelled north of entire families wiped out in a week, their bodies burned on pyres or buried with little ceremony in mass graves.

Mary remained at home while Brandon travelled the country on a progress with the king. He rarely returned and never wrote. She missed him, but at least felt more secure now she no longer depended on his income. Cardinal Wolsey had saved her once again, successfully negotiating the resumption of her dower payments from France and securing a generous back payment of all the money due to her.

There was plenty to keep her occupied at Westhorpe as she prepared for the wedding of her stepdaughter Mary who, like her sister Anne, was to become a baroness. She would miss Mary, who'd stepped into the shoes of her sister Anne as her main companion and confidante.

At sixteen, Mary Brandon had many of her father's engaging qualities. Despite her youth, she'd taken over the running of Westhorpe, which would be good preparation for her future married life. She also learned much from Mary's recollections of life in her brother's court and her time in France, and asked many questions.

When the long-awaited summons arrived from the queen it felt like a turning point, a new start, after so long away from court. Mary was commanded to travel to Greenwich to attend a visit by French ambassadors. She called her stepdaughter and showed her the letter.

'This means London is free of the plague at last, Mary. I would like you to travel with me, as my lady-in-waiting.'

'It would be an honour.' She read the short letter again, as if it might hold some hidden clue. 'Will I meet the queen?'

'With luck, you might even meet my brother the king. He can't hide in hunting lodges forever with your father.'

Her stepdaughter smiled. 'I long to see Father again.'

Mary felt the strange sense of loss that haunted her since she'd seen him last. They'd not parted on good terms after she asked him to try to restore Catherine's place in her brother's affections. Her instinct told her he was keeping secrets again. He'd shouted at her and ridden off without even a farewell kiss.

Henry's court had changed almost out of recognition, reminding Mary that she'd remained away too long. Greenwich Palace looked bigger and brighter than she remembered. Colourful new tapestries of huntsmen chasing stags replaced her father's faded biblical scenes. The windows had been enlarged and the room glowed with the light from hanging candelabras.

A group of musicians with lutes accompanied a man singing of courtly love in a soft tenor voice. Henry, dressed in dazzling cloth of gold with an ostrich plume in his cap, surrounded himself with a new coterie of handsome and athletic younger men, replacing the sober clerics and soldiers of her father's court. The old guard, except for Norfolk and her husband, were gone.

Brandon greeted her as she arrived. 'I'm sorry I've not been able to write.' He kissed her on the cheek but without affection. 'You know what it's like on Henry's progresses.'

She studied his face, not sure how to respond to his weak excuses. His greying beard needed trimming and he'd put on weight but she longed to have him back. Despite the company of her daughters and little Henry she'd been lonely at West-thorpe. She missed feeling his strong arms around her as they drifted off to sleep. She missed having a husband.

'You look well, Charles.' She flattered him like she had as a young girl, although she noted the gold embroidery on his doublet and wondered how much it had cost. 'It seems my brother has done some much-needed pruning since I was here last.'

He looked puzzled for a moment then grinned. 'There were far too many leeches at court, sucking his coffers dry. Wolsey saw the chance to remove those who opposed him – which is why there is hardly anyone left.'

Mary frowned. 'The cardinal saved my dower income, for which I'll always be grateful.'

'And forever in his debt?' There was a scornful edge to his voice but he was no longer interested in her answer, as he looked over her shoulder in surprise. 'Mary? I didn't expect to see you here.'

'Good day to you, Father.' She smiled. 'I am here by invitation as lady-in-waiting to the queen.'

He gave her a quizzical look. 'I wasn't aware...'

'To *La Reine Blanche*,' she smiled at Mary, 'the Queen of France.'

The French king's ambassador was a bear of a man, with piercing eyes that seemed to read Mary's thoughts. He bowed graciously as they were introduced and kissed the gold rings on her offered hand.

'Charles de Solier, Comte de Morette, at your service, Your Grace.'

She'd expected him to address her in French yet he spoke perfect English. Dressed in black and gold, he wore a heavy gold medallion on a thick chain around his neck, one hand resting on the hilt of a jewelled golden dagger. By any standard he was an impressive figure. Even his beard looked like burnished gold.

'I am most pleased to make your acquaintance, ambassador. I trust King Francis is well, after his adventures in Italy.'

The count smiled at her understatement and leaned a little closer, lowering his voice. 'The king asked me to tell you he was most touched to receive your letter on his release, Your Grace. Your loyalty is beyond value.'

'I was grieved to learn of the passing of Queen Claude. She showed me such kindness when I first arrived in Paris.'

'France is a poorer place without her, Your Grace, as it is without you.' His eyes held hers for a moment too long, full of warmth and illicit possibility.

Mary acknowledged his compliment with a modest smile but her heart raced. She'd forgotten how charming the French king's envoys could be. 'Your king is not a man to remain unmarried for long. Who has he chosen as the new Queen of France?'

Count Charles glanced over his shoulder to where Henry stood in discussion with the other ambassadors from France. 'That is, in part, what brings me to England, Your Grace, to arrange the betrothal of the Princess Mary, as well as a renewed treaty of peace between us.'

Mary glanced across the room to where Henry laughed

loudly at some joke the ambassadors had made. She'd not forgotten what Queen Claude confided the last time they were alone together. Her frail condition after childbirth was not helped by the fact her husband suffered with the pox, his reward for so many mistresses.

Her stepdaughter was still talking with Brandon. They had a great deal of catching up to do, particularly about her wedding plans. Perhaps at last he would realise how he's been neglecting his family. Mary decided this might be her only opportunity. She would have to speak to Queen Catherine without delay.

It was only then she realised Catherine was not present, although several of her ladies-in-waiting were entertaining the visiting ambassadors. Mary found her in her privy chamber with Maria de Salinas, Baroness Willoughby. Dona Maria, who'd arrived in England with Queen Catherine from Spain, was recently widowed. She was also a Suffolk neighbour, as she lived at Parham Hall, a day's ride east of Westhorpe. The elegant woman Mary remembered as a girl had grown matronly but greeted her with a curtsey.

'Your Grace.'

Mary placed her hand on Maria's arm. 'I was sorry to hear of your husband's passing. He was a good man.'

'Thank you, Your Grace. It is a great comfort to me that I am permitted to return to court.' Her voice still carried a trace of her Spanish accent despite having lived longer in England. 'I find I am lonely now my husband is gone.'

'Yet you have a daughter?'

'Yes, Your Grace. My daughter Catherine is eight years old now, and becoming a true English lady.' Her pride was unmistakable. 'I understand His Grace the king is to agree that your husband shall purchase her wardship.'

Mary hid her surprise at the news – yet another example of how far they had drifted apart, as he'd never mentioned it. She guessed he planned for their son to one day marry the wealthy heiress. Young Catherine Willoughby would be a good match but she would have liked to be consulted about her son's future.

'She is the same age as my Eleanor. They would be company for one another, Dona Maria.' She glanced at Catherine. 'If you will excuse us, I must speak with the queen, in private.'

'You may speak freely.' Catherine smiled at Dona Maria. 'We need have no secrets from one of my oldest friends.'

Mary took a deep breath. 'You must find some way to prevent Princess Mary becoming engaged to King Francis.'

Catherine shook her head. 'I must confide to you, Mary, that I proposed the match to Cardinal Wolsey, although I suspect he might soon regret his haste.'

Catherine's response was a surprise to Mary, although she saw the twinkle in her friend's eyes. 'Forgive me, I don't understand.'

'Henry sent an envoy to Rome, to see if a way could be found for my marriage to be annulled.' She looked saddened for a moment, then composed herself. 'I cannot allow him to make Princess Mary illegitimate, so must remind him of her value.'

'At what cost?' Mary shook her head. 'I don't need to remind you of the reputation of King Francis...'

'Nothing will come of it, Mary, you may be sure of that, although I took the precaution of forgetting to summon her, in case the French ambassadors encourage King Francis with their reports.'

'Where is the princess?'

'Safe in Ludlow, where she was sent to escape the plague.' Catherine nodded, sensing Mary's concern. 'I've not forgotten your brother, my Arthur. I visited Mary in Ludlow and it was most strange to return after all these years.'

Mary had been six years old when her brother died in

Ludlow, too young to understand. Her father had explained to her once, with tears in his eyes, how his life had never been the same since that fateful April day. Now, after little Harry, she understood all too well.

Mary's dull pains returned before the banquet. To ease the ache in her side she drank more of the rich red wine than she should, allowing the steward to keep refilling her goblet. Although the strong drink helped a little, she felt giddy and worried the wine had already begun to cloud her judgement.

A servant in green-and-white Tudor livery placed a steaming haunch of venison on a golden platter before them. It looked enough to feed their entire household at Westhorpe although she knew nothing at court was ever wasted. Unfinished platters would be shared by those who toiled unseen in the steaming palace kitchens.

The meat was tender, glazed with a honey sauce spiced with ginger, but Mary had little appetite. She picked at the brightly coloured marchpane fruits, made from sugar and ground almonds, meant for decoration, and tried to understand how her brother's court had changed.

Henry had given her the place of honour, seated at his right hand, as the Queen Dowager of France. Cardinal Wolsey sat to his left in his scarlet robes but Queen Catherine was again nowhere to be seen. Mary knew the message her brother sent would be clear to everyone in his court, as well as the visiting envoys – Catherine was no longer welcome at his table.

Similarly, Brandon should have been to her right but instead chose to sit with the French ambassadors, although he hadn't seen her for weeks. Their raucous laughter caused Henry to cast them a wistful look, as if he would rather be with them than with his sister. Mary saw her opportunity to keep in his favour.

'Dear brother, I was most grateful when you restored my dower income.' She raised her silver goblet. 'I am again indebted to you.'

Henry beamed. 'The credit is due to the good cardinal,' he glanced at Wolsey, 'whose adoration of the French is only outweighed by his contempt for the Spanish!' He laughed at his own joke.

Wolsey raised his own goblet in reply to Mary. 'My only wish is to prolong the peace your father worked so hard to achieve, Your Grace.'

Henry took his knife and hacked another slice from the roasted leg of venison, nodding as he used his bread to mop up the sweet-tasting sauce. 'Our father, may the Lord rest his soul, would have approved of your ambition, Cardinal Wolsey.'

Mary felt the pain beginning to return in her side and took another drink. She looked at the ambassadors then back at Henry. 'I understand you plan to bind us to the throne of France a second time through marriage?'

Henry studied her for a moment, as if surprised at her interest in matters of state. 'If not to the king, then to his second son, Henri, Duke of Orléans.' Henry leaned closer so he'd not be overheard. 'I doubt even our silver-tongued Cardinal Wolsey can persuade King Francis to wed a skinny eleven-year-old girl.'

Wolsey leaned forward. 'Prince Henri is eight years old and could one day inherit the throne from his father. Whatever the outcome, we are hopeful these discussions will result in a treaty of peace – and a dowry of two million gold crowns.'

'Let us pray you are right, cardinal.' Mary glanced at Henry and saw he'd been distracted.

She had a sudden memory of when they were in the nursery schoolroom at Eltham Palace together as children. Henry's tutors would despair at how easily he could be diverted from his studies. She followed his narrowed eyes and saw he

watched a lady talking with the handsome Frenc
Charles, Count of Morette.

It was no mystery why the woman held her brother s
tion. Dressed in what must be the latest French fashion, i.
shapely scarlet gown was cut lower at the front, revealing more
than Mary considered decent. She seemed to know the count
well. As Mary watched, she turned, calling out to a steward in
French and holding up Count Charles's silver goblet to be
served more wine. Mary recognised her as one of Queen
Catherine's ladies-in-waiting, Lady Anne Boleyn.

~

Suffolk Place looked like a palace. Mary was amazed at Brandon's improvements, made without her knowledge. He said it
was intended as a surprise, which it was. The great hall had
been converted for the service, with tiers of gilded seats with
red velvet cushions.

Mary sat in place of honour under a canopy of estate with
Queen Catherine and Princess Mary, who was now officially
engaged to Henri, Duke of Orléans. As well as her dowry,
Henry had been promised a pension of fifty thousand gold
crowns. Catherine had been right. Henry now appreciated the
value of his daughter, and danced with her at a banquet to
rapturous applause.

The remaining places were taken by familiar faces from
every noble family in England. Sir Thomas Howard, Duke of
Norfolk, sat alone, without his wife, Duchess Elizabeth, as he'd
caused a scandal by leaving her to live openly with the
daughter of his steward.

Also absent was Cardinal Wolsey, sent on a diplomatic
mission by Henry. Brandon told her he'd taken several chests
of gold to use as bribes. Although the purpose of his journey

was a mystery, Mary suspected it had something to do with her brother's plans to annul his marriage.

Mary remembered how they had increased their debts to import the decorative floor tiles at great expense from Paris, now almost covered with a sprinkling of red and white rose petals. Costly beeswax candles added their warm light and honeyed scent. Brandon wished to show off their wealth and success at the wedding of his daughter.

The bride, soon to be Duchess Monteagle, shone at her first visit to Henry's court but now looked magnificent in a shimmering gown of silk decorated with pearls. Mary's wedding present had been a precious sapphire pendant, once part of the crown jewels of France. It now sparkled on a silver chain around her stepdaughter's slender neck.

The groom, tall and handsome in his soldier's uniform, wore a gleaming silver sword on his belt, a present from the king. Mary smiled as she wondered what her grandmother, Lady Margaret Beaufort, would have said about Brandon's choice of husband for his daughter.

Young Thomas Stanley inherited his late father's title of Baron Monteagle and was named after his grandfather, Lady Margaret's fourth and last husband, Thomas Stanley, the Earl of Derby.

Mary missed Lady Margaret, who'd been like a mother to her, and prayed each day for her soul. She knew her grandmother would have approved of her choice of confessor, Bishop John Fisher, to officiate. Apart from the greying hair showing under his mitre, Bishop Fisher looked almost as he had when her father was alive, his sharp eyes missing nothing.

Mary watched as, once again, her husband took his daughter's hand and escorted her to where her future husband waited. She felt great pride in her own daughters, Frances and Eleanor, following in silk bridesmaids' gowns, with little Henry dressed like a miniature of his father, as Mary's page.

As she listened to her stepdaughter repeat her vows in a clear and confident voice Mary realised how fast the years were passing. It seemed only a moment ago when she'd first met little Mary Brandon at Westhorpe with her sister, yet both were now grown women, baronesses soon to have children of their own.

She glanced to her side and was surprised to see a tear run down Catherine's cheek. With a jolt she realised how difficult it must be for her. It was unlikely she would ever give Henry the legitimate heir he craved, and now it was public knowledge that he couldn't wait to be rid of his Spanish queen.

23

MAY 1530

Mary threw open the small leaded-glass window and breathed in the fresh spring air. The delicate scent of lavender drifted up from her herb garden below, the only sound the sweet song of a skylark hovering above her garden. She thanked the Lord she lived in the country, away from the noise and dirt of London.

Much had changed in the past year. Her aches and pains worsened, sometimes making her stay in her bed for most of the day. The girls would take it in turns to keep her company, improving their Latin and French, playing the lute and reading to her from one of her precious books.

Even on her better days Mary found riding too uncomfortable so rarely left Westhorpe and walked only as far as the village church. This wasn't the problem it might have been as she was no longer needed to ornament King Henry's court, her place at his side taken by Lady Anne Boleyn.

She wished she'd protested in the strongest terms against Queen Catherine's banishment, although with hindsight her silence might have been more effective. When she heard Anne Boleyn and her manipulative father suffered with the sweating sickness, she committed the sin of wishing them dead. She had mixed feelings when they both recovered, for a different outcome would have solved a lot of problems.

Queen Catherine told her she would trust in God that her husband would see sense, but Mary knew her brother too well. Even as their father lay dying, he'd been more interested in how soon he could marry Catherine. Now it seemed that same passion was directed at undoing the promises he'd made to her.

The door burst open and Frances entered, dressed in her best gown and wearing one of Mary's pearl-rimmed hoods. Now the same height as Mary, she would be thirteen in July. At Queen Catherine's suggestion, she'd been away for the first time, as company for Princess Mary, who was only a year older.

Although Mary missed her, the experience had been good for Frances. She was now a close friend of her cousin, Princess Mary, and she'd become fond of her aunt, although she was troubled by events at court. When Frances asked what would happen to the queen and Princess Mary, she'd been unable to answer.

She joined Mary at the window and peered out. 'They'll be here soon. Do you still feel well enough to make the journey, Mother?'

Mary forced a smile. 'Of course, Frances. I've never missed a May Fair.' In truth, she knew the sixteen-mile ride to Bury St Edmunds would be a trial for her but she had no choice. People travelled from all over the county to see their lady of the manor, the Queen Dowager of France, sister to the king.

A thought occurred to her. 'Will you find Eleanor and Catherine and make sure they are ready?'

Frances nodded and left Mary thinking about how easily Catherine Willoughby had become part of their family. Brandon admitted he'd agreed to pay Henry a substantial sum each year for five years for her wardship but considered it a good investment for their son's future. It helped that Catherine proved to be a likeable, well-mannered girl and soon became inseparable from Eleanor, who was the same age.

Mary fastened a carcanet of gold set with jewels around her neck and fixed her best headdress in place with silver pins. She checked it in her polished silver mirror, a present from King Louis. The surface had dulled over the years but she still used it every day.

The metallic jangle of a harness and the clip-clop of hooves sounded on the cobbles outside. As she went to greet them she heard little Henry's excited reply to Brandon's deeper voice. She'd played along with their secret for Henry's sake, although she'd known what they were up to with their mysterious whispering behind her back.

The carriage had been transformed to make the long ride easier. Brandon had his carpenter construct a portable set of steps and replace the unforgiving wooden bench-seats. Mary now had a comfortable chair with velvet cushions and a fringed canopy to keep off the rain. The wheels were also now painted bright red with the hubs finished in gold.

Henry seemed happy to take the credit. Now seven years old, he grew more like his father each day. 'What do you think of it, Mother?' He climbed up the steps and sat on the new cushions. 'Father says it is fit for a queen.'

Mary smiled at her husband, who stood watching their son with obvious pride. One good thing about the trouble at court was he spent less time in London, using her illness as an excuse to remain at Westhorpe. He'd put on weight and his thick beard had turned grey but he was still a striking figure.

The passage of time had mellowed him a little. They'd agreed to put their problems behind them for the sake of the children. He'd kept his promise to be a better father and spend more time with them. Now he took Mary by the hand and steadied her arm as she climbed the steps to join Henry in the carriage.

'The procession is ready and waiting, my lady.' He bowed to her, with a wink to amuse little Henry. Then he looked round and called to his daughters and Catherine. 'Come along, there's room enough for all of you.'

The girls climbed up into the carriage while Brandon placed the toe of his boot in the stirrup and mounted his magnificent black stallion, a gift from the king. Mary looked up at the sky as he rode to take his place at the front. Clouds obscured the sun but there was a gentle breeze and thankfully it didn't look like it would rain.

Even after all these years she felt a sense of anticipation for the May Fair. It was a chance to see and be seen by the people and it felt good to be reminded she was still a lady of importance. When they could, she and Brandon helped with small favours, such as writing letters and settling the occasional dispute.

Their groom called out to the horses and the traces creaked as they took up the weight of the carriage. He flicked the reins and they lurched forward to join the procession. Ahead rode Brandon with their escort, twenty of his mounted retainers in Suffolk livery. Behind followed the servants and staff in two wagons.

They heard the lively music before the fair came into view. The musicians and travelling mummers were paid for by the Bury St Edmunds guild of merchants. Brandon, as lord of the manor, provided a whole ox and several roasted hogs. The tang of woodsmoke carried in the air, along with the delicious aroma of sizzling meat and the shouts of vendors.

The May Fair was held on an open field which had always been known as Angel Hill, although it was quite flat, between the old abbey and the town. Little Henry stood up in the carriage and pointed excitedly at the rows of brightly painted booths and tents with banners and pennants.

People travelled great distances for the May Fair. As well as traders and drovers selling everything from jugs of ale to live-stock, the fair was renowned for the stalls of the foreign merchants selling bolts of brocade, precious silk, fine wines and rare delicacies.

An excited crowd jostled to welcome the royal procession. From experience Mary knew some were simply curious to see the king's sister, while others hoped to win influence and perhaps even be received at court. She wondered if they would be so eager now she was no longer in favour with the king.

Brandon made a short speech, thanking the guilds and the abbot for their generosity, before declaring the May Fair open. They took their places on raised seats with red velvet cushions, under a canopy of estate supported on four long wooden poles, topped with golden finials.

The girls knew they had to wait for the formal visits of all the minor nobles before they could explore the fair, but seemed to be enjoying the attention. Little Henry seemed less willing and tugged at his father's sleeve, asking for coins to spend at the stalls of sugared sweets.

The May Fair began with a fanfare of trumpets and the bringing of the tree of life, carried on the shoulders of four stout yeomen, led by a capering green man covered in leaves. He stopped to bow graciously to Mary and removed his cap to reveal his bald head, which was also a bright forest-green.

Next came the young girl chosen as the Queen of the May, garlanded with spring flowers and followed by her handmaid-ens. Brandon applauded a troupe of foreign jugglers with painted bodies who threw sharp swords and bright flaming torches high in the air and skilfully caught them before they fell.

Mary smiled, glad to see her husband enjoying himself. He'd been withdrawn since returning from London but the preparations for the fair had kept his mind off matters at her brother's court. He hated the idea of having to play Thomas

Boleyn's games at the expense of men like Thomas Wolsey but would soon have to – or pay the price.

Frances nudged her. 'They look pagan, don't you think, Mother?'

Mary nodded. 'I suppose they do, Frances. The May Fair goes back longer than anyone can remember. It's good to celebrate the coming of spring after such a cold winter, don't you think?'

Frances looked uncertain. 'Doesn't this trouble the monks from the abbey?'

Mary shook her head. 'This land belongs to the abbey but they would never stop it, even if they don't approve.'

Since her time with Princess Mary, Frances had become a more devout Catholic, even making little Henry attend Mass in their private chapel. Mary saw a lot of herself in her daughter. Of all her children, Frances was the one who seemed more Tudor than Brandon, so it would be a great shame if she chose to enter a convent. Mary resolved to make sure she married well.

Shouting voices interrupted her reverie as stewards cleared the space in front of them for the traditional mummers' play. A raised stage with simple wooden scenery was erected and iron braziers lit to keep the audience at bay. The crowd cheered as a giant grey-bearded man, swathed in white linen robes and wearing a laurel wreath, took to the stage and raised his painted wooden thunderbolt into the air.

'I am Zeus, supreme ruler of the gods, lord of the sky and rain, and bringer of the spring!' His deep voice carried well, drawing an even greater circle of onlookers. 'Listen to my cautionary tale – and learn from it!'

A second man, wearing robes dyed to represent the sea, stepped on to the stage carrying a long wooden trident which he brandished, alarming the small children sitting at the front.

'I am Poseidon, brother of Zeus, and have been led astray by a temptress named Medusa.'

The musicians began playing a lilting tune and the attractive girl playing the part of Medusa began to dance provocatively before the gods, flicking her long dark hair, worn loose over her shoulders. Just as she seemed to bewitch them, a woman in white robes playing the goddess Athena appeared and stopped her with a curse.

A sudden thunder of drums startled the crowd and Medusa vanished behind the scenery to re-emerge as a monster, her hair a mass of snakes. Then a handsome young actor bounded into the clearing to protect them.

'I, Perseus, know good will always overcome evil!' With a slash of his wooden sword he slew Medusa, holding up her severed head to a rousing cheer from the crowd.

The musicians struck up a traditional dance as the audience applauded but Mary glanced at her husband and saw his troubled look. 'There is a resemblance between this Medusa and the king's new mistress.'

He nodded. 'These mummers' plays are always more than they seem – and the people well know it.'

Brandon returned from London with bad news. 'All they talk about in the taverns is the king's divorce. The people blame Cardinal Wolsey.'

'Has Wolsey not done everything my brother commands him?'

Brandon shook his head. 'They would blame him for the dry summers and freezing winters, if they could. Wolsey has never been short of enemies but I think he has angered Henry once too often – and I sense the hand of Thomas Boleyn behind this.'

'He's back at court?'

'With most of his family.' Brandon scowled. 'It seems they can do no wrong. Henry made Boleyn Earl of Wiltshire and Ormond – and sent him as his envoy to Emperor Charles and the pope, to seek support for his annulment.'

'But they would know Boleyn's daughter stands to profit?'

'Of course. It would be hard to make a poorer choice for such a mission.'

Mary reached out a hand. 'Not so loud, Charles, the servants might hear you.'

'What of it?'

Mary lowered her voice. 'Frances told me Queen Catherine suspects there are spies within her chambers. I think it is best to be careful now.'

'You think your brother would place spies among our servants?' His tone was scornful.

Mary hesitated to answer. 'Who knows my brother's mind?'

'I once thought I did,' he kept his voice low, 'or at least thought nothing he did would surprise me.'

'We live in challenging times. What word is there of Queen Catherine?'

'She is defiant, which angers Henry still further.'

That night the pain in her side kept Mary awake while all the household slept. Brandon had chosen to sleep in his own chambers and she had their bed moved so she could see out of the small window. A full moon, so bright it lit up her room, cast strange shadows into the dark corners.

She turned Brandon's words over in her mind. He'd told her there were three factions now at Henry's court. The greatest was Sir Thomas Boleyn's, as Norfolk had predictably decided to support his niece Anne Boleyn and others had followed, to keep in favour with the king.

Brandon counted himself among Wolsey's supporters, but

now the cardinal had been banished from court his power was waning. Mary shared her husband's loyalty to Thomas Wolsey, even if she didn't always approve of his methods. He had saved them more than once and now it was time to repay their debts.

Mary was one of the most prominent members of the queen's faction. A few brave souls had also spoken out in Catherine's defence, including Archbishop John Fisher, her grandmother's confessor. Most kept their thoughts private, although they muttered their discontent behind her brother's back.

Now Henry openly challenged Queen Catherine's assertion that her marriage to Arthur was never consummated. Mary recalled how, when he married Catherine, Henry had privately admitted his doubts, although it suited him to believe her. She'd asked him then to take her at her word, as to lie about such a thing would be a sin.

Catherine once hinted to her of a great secret she'd not dared to confess, even to her priest. She had been in an impossible position at the time and Mary promised to pray for her soul. Now it seemed the future of the country could depend on her continued denial of the truth.

It was obvious to them all that life could not simply go on as normal while what was now being talked of as 'the king's great matter' remained unresolved. Mary sensed something would happen to tip the balance one way or the other, yet when it did she was still shocked.

'Wolsey is dead?' She stared wide-eyed at Brandon. 'Was he murdered? Executed?' She struggled to think which would be worse.

Brandon's lined face looked grim. 'He was accused of treason against the king.'

'No!' Mary took Brandon's hand in hers. 'Did you ever know a more loyal man than Thomas Wolsey?'

'It was an unjust reward for a lifetime of service. Henry Percy was ordered to bring him back from York to London on a charge of allowing papal interference in matters of state, without the consent of the Crown.'

'But he was acting on Henry's orders—'

'That's the worst of it.' His hand formed a fist. 'They had a spy in his household, his Venetian physician, who testified Wolsey was in secret correspondence with Rome.'

'How did he die?' Mary's voice was little more than a whisper.

'It seems the cardinal fell ill and collapsed on the way to London.' Brandon scowled. 'No one knows the cause but by the Lord's grace he is at least spared whatever punishment Henry had planned for him.'

Mary lit a taper and held it to the wick of the votive candle. A draft of cold air threatened to blow out the flame but it flickered and caught, burning bright in the memory of Thomas Wolsey, Cardinal of the Catholic Church, once Lord Chancellor of England and chief advisor to the king.

Brandon told her when the cardinal was buried in St Mary's Abbey they discovered he wore a cilice of coarse goat hair under his cardinal's robes, a sign of his deep repentance. Even this final, devout secret was mocked in Henry's court by those who should know better.

Mary prayed in her private chapel and wept for the loss of Thomas Wolsey, a friend who tried his best to live within the tenets of his faith. His name would be added to the growing list of those whose souls she prayed for each morning and night. If not for Wolsey, her life might have turned out quite differently.

24

FEBRUARY 1532

A thick carpet of snow covered the frozen Suffolk countryside, the stark whiteness contrasting with the twisting, muddy scars of the roads. The avenue of trees stood bare of leaves, standing guard like skeletal sentinels. Mary looked out on the wintry scene and remembered when she'd first arrived in Westhorpe, on a glorious spring day fourteen years before.

She'd felt her whole life was before her and that she had at last found somewhere to return to, a place to call her home. Now, Mary found herself wondering what the future might hold for them all. She found it hard to believe Queen Catherine was banished from her own court, her ladies sent away, prevented from seeing her daughter or even writing to her.

Lady Anne Boleyn now occupied the queen's chambers at Greenwich Palace, yet made it known she'd refused to become the king's new mistress. It seemed she had learned from what happened to her sister, Mary Boleyn. If Henry wished to have her, the price was to make her his wife and crown her Queen of England.

Mary watched a solitary rider cross their bridge, his horse wary of its footing on the icy road. He wore a heavy fur cape and the collar of his thick fur coat was pulled up as protection against the biting winter wind. As the rider approached the house he stopped and looked up at her window, as if sensing her presence.

Her first thought had been that her husband had returned early from his business in the south. Now she realised it was a stranger and hoped it could be the messenger she'd been waiting for. Calling to her servants, Mary prepared to welcome their visitor.

The man took off his hat to reveal fashionably short hair and bowed to Mary. He looked to be about her own age and dressed in the black robes of a cleric His pale face had a few days growth of dark stubble, suggesting he'd ridden some distance in the freezing weather, but his brown eyes shone with warm intelligence.

'Thomas Abel at your service, Your Grace.' He bowed and handed her a folded parchment, waiting while she read it. The letter of introduction was from Queen Catherine and said the bearer, Thomas Abel, was her personal chaplain, a man to be trusted. Mary recognised her signature and seal.

'You are most welcome, Master Abel. You've come with a message from the queen?'

He glanced at her servant, waiting to take his coat, then turned back to Mary, his voice conspiratorial. 'I wish to see you in private, if I may?'

Mary led him to the room she used as her study, intrigued to know the reason for the chaplain's visit. The fire had been lit by her maid and thick logs crackled as the flames found fresh sap. Thomas Abel warmed his hands until Mary invited him to sit. They waited in silence while her serving girl brought a cup of hot mulled wine, then closed the door.

'How is Queen Catherine?'

Thomas Abel hesitated, taking a sip of the steaming cup of spiced wine while he chose his words before replying. 'The queen has been unwell but shows great fortitude in these difficult times.' He looked directly at Mary. 'I've travelled here to ask if you might assist her, Your Grace.'

'Gladly, Master Abel. In what way?'

'You will forgive me if I speak frankly of your brother, the king?'

Mary nodded, although she worried what he was about to say could be treasonable. Brandon evaded her questions about Henry and rarely shared news from court. He knew it made her upset to think of how Catherine was being mistreated.

Thomas Abel glanced at the closed door. 'I regret that we live in dangerous times, Your Grace.' His face became serious. 'Good men are afraid to speak their minds since the king declared himself the supreme head of the English Church.'

'Everyone talks of it here in Suffolk,' Mary frowned, 'although it means nothing.'

Thomas Abel raised an eyebrow. 'I'm afraid it means a great deal, my lady. The future of the Church is at stake, as well as the future of the Crown. The king has enshrined his new Church in law and has the backing of Parliament.'

'I heard the bishops are against this...'

'Did you also hear what happened to Bishop Fisher?'

Mary felt a sense of misgiving. John Fisher had served as her father's chaplain and her grandmother's confessor. She'd known him all her life. 'Please tell me, Master Abel. I have been in the country too long, it seems.'

'There was an attempt to poison him. By the grace of God, the bishop is a devout man and chose to fast that day. He was unharmed but several members of his household succumbed and two died.'

Mary put her hand to her mouth. 'I had no idea.'

'The bishop's cook was arrested. I shall spare you the details, my lady, but even when he was boiled he refused to reveal who was behind this ... outrage.'

'Boiled?' Mary didn't understand.

'In a cauldron of boiling water.' Thomas Abel frowned. 'A cruel practice, my lady, reserved for convicted poisoners.'

'You are not suggesting my brother had anything to do with this?'

Thomas Abel held up a hand to calm her. 'I simply wish you to appreciate how serious the situation has become, my lady, which brings me to the reason for my visit.' He studied her face, watching her reaction. 'We need you to speak out against Anne Boleyn, before it is too late.'

'Too late?'

'Before a child is conceived, my lady.' He softened his voice. 'Queen Catherine has the support of the people but those who should speak out have been intimidated into silence. For my part, I intend to publish a tract setting out the reasons why King Henry cannot be divorced from the queen, his lawful and loyal wife.'

'You wish me to put my name to this?' She felt a now familiar sense of foreboding. Henry would have Catherine's chaplain executed if he knew his intentions.

'With respect, Your Grace, as the sister of the king you are the one person who could dare to speak out against Lady Anne Boleyn. You could tip the balance of public opinion against her and open the floodgates of support for our rightful queen.'

'I'm sorry, Master Abel, but you've had a wasted journey. I cannot. It would place my husband in an even more impossible position.'

'I understand this is difficult for you, my lady, to cross your brother, but with what happened after the Duke of Suffolk's banishment—'

'What do you mean?'

'I refer to his banishment after he spoke out, accusing Lady Anne Boleyn of ... familiarity with Sir Thomas Wyatt. The king forgave him soon enough but Lady Anne made her own accusation.'

'What did she say?'

'Forgive me, my lady. I thought you would know she accused the duke of incest with his own daughter. No one takes it seriously – except of course your husband.'

After Thomas Abel left, Mary paced her room, trying to control the anger surging through her. She needed to think clearly. Anne Boleyn, once her trusted lady-in-waiting, had insulted her daughters and her husband in the foulest and most public way.

Mary understood why Brandon had said nothing to her about it but she couldn't stand by and let any speculation continue. She had spent too long in the country through her illness. It was her duty to return to London and speak for Queen Catherine, whatever the consequences. The children would have to remain in Suffolk, for their own safety, but her husband would need to be at her side.

Brandon returned to Suffolk Place late at night, in a foul temper, a blue bruise under his eye and his doublet torn. Mary sat up in their grand oak bed, a heavy coverlet over her and a single candle, burning in a silver holder, lighting up her face.

'I had to do it, Charles.'

He sat heavily on the bed and held his head in his hands. Mary expected repercussions after speaking out in defence of

Catherine as she had, but had no idea what form they would take and when.

'Please, tell me what happened.'

'William Pennington is dead.'

Mary gasped in disbelief. 'How?'

'Norfolk's men.' Brandon cursed. 'I think we are done for after this, Mary.'

She reached out a hand and caressed his shoulder. 'Tell me what happened.'

'I'm not sure how it started. William was supposed to meet me at court. It seems he was provoked into an argument and chased from Westminster by twenty of Norfolk's men.' He turned to her with sadness in his eyes. 'William was never a violent man. He ran for the sanctuary of Westminster Abbey but they pursued him there and killed him.'

Mary sat in silence. She'd never imagined such a thing could happen. William Pennington was married to Brandon's cousin Frances, a good woman who was expecting a child in a month or so. Now she'd made her a widow and her child would never know its father.

She remembered their last visit to Westhorpe. Although William was their tenant, he was also a member of the family. He'd been loyal to Brandon and Mary could imagine how he'd tried to defend her criticism of the Boleyns.

'I'm so sorry, Charles.' She put her hand on his arm.

He put his hand over hers. 'I don't blame you, Mary. You were only doing your duty to Catherine. Norfolk gave the orders to his murderous thugs.'

'Thomas Howard always resented us. I remember how his father used to try to provoke you, saying you were descended from Norfolk servants and calling you Henry's stable boy.'

'It's true, but I never gave him the satisfaction of seeing how angry he made me. I had to work with Norfolk at council and court.'

'Yet his son has a vindictive streak. He uses the Boleyn's ambition to suit his own ends.'

'Now the bastard has the king's favour for supporting his own niece as queen – at poor Catherine's expense.'

Mary's hand found the rip in her husband's doublet. She studied the bruise on his face in the flickering candlelight. 'How did this happen, if you weren't there?'

'I had to go after the men who murdered William. At the time, I didn't know he'd been killed, but I knew Norfolk's thugs were after him. The king heard about it and sent Thomas Cromwell to stop me.'

'Thomas Cromwell assaulted you?'

'His men did. They dragged me back to court and threatened to charge me with affray.' He stared into the grate of the empty fireplace as he remembered. 'I suppose they were doing me a favour. I wouldn't have stood a chance against so many – but I would have taken a few with me.'

He sounded defiant and she knew it was true. They'd insulted his honour. He'd said they might be done for now, so there was probably more he'd not told her. She could imagine even Thomas Cromwell had found it hard to stop him reaching Norfolk's henchmen.

'All this was because of me, because I spoke out against the Boleyns.'

'The king is displeased with us, Mary, and there will be a price to pay. For the sake of our family I can never return to court.'

Brandon's bitterness against Norfolk took a new turn when he heard William Pennington's murderers were pardoned by the king. It was said they'd been fined a thousand pounds but he knew Henry well enough to be sure it would never be paid.

'I can't ignore this insult, Mary.' He thumped his fist on the table, startling the serving girl who stood waiting behind him.

'Please, Charles. Anything you do will only make matters worse.' Mary was grateful he'd waited for the children to go out riding as his last outburst had worried them. The girls were old enough to appreciate her explanation but little Henry struggled to understand.

'There are men in London I can call on to defend our honour, for a price.'

'And if they are caught, Norfolk will have you charged with conspiring against the king.'

Brandon shook his head. 'It pains me to know Norfolk thinks he's beaten me.' His eyes blazed with anger.

Mary placed her hand on his. 'You mustn't resort to Norfolk's methods, Charles.' She thought for a moment, aware her husband's career and the future of their family could be at stake. 'Thomas Cromwell was Wolsey's man and seems to be taking his place at my brother's side. He might be persuaded to help us—'

'I think not.' Brandon interrupted. 'You must know I had sharp words for him when he stopped me in Westminster.'

'He did you a great favour. You could be locked up in the Tower of London now, or worse, if Cromwell hadn't intervened.' She took his hand in hers. 'You will write to Cromwell a letter of apology, seeking his support in returning you to the king's favour.'

'No!' Brandon pulled his hand away, then calmed himself and studied her face, as if seeing her for the first time. 'You are right. I have nothing to lose – and who better as an ally than Thomas Cromwell, who seems to have few enough friends yet is as close to the king as anyone.'

'Except, perhaps, for Mistress Anne Boleyn?'

He gave her a wry smile. 'I shall need your help with the wording. It is not going to be an easy letter for me to write.'

Cromwell's reply, when it arrived a month later, astonished them both. Brandon broke the dark wax seal and read it through twice before handing it to Mary. 'We have some work to do.'

Mary took the parchment and studied it. Written in a neat hand the letter was signed with a confident flourish. Thomas Cromwell had exceeded their expectations. He thanked Brandon for his understanding and said the king would visit them to hunt for stags, arriving in two weeks.

'My brother is coming to Westhorpe!' She felt a sudden panic at the thought. 'Do you think he will bring Anne Boleyn? I've heard she always goes hunting with him.'

'Let us hope Cromwell has advised him against it. The king's visit can only mean we are forgiven.' Brandon grinned. 'You were right, Mary. It seems Henry has chosen a good man to replace the late cardinal.'

'We only have two weeks to prepare.' She called to Eleanor. 'Tell your brother and sister to meet us in the hall – and assemble as many of the staff as can be spared. We have important news.'

The two weeks passed in a hectic flurry of preparation. Brandon's rooms were repainted and a magnificent new bed purchased for the king. Mary sold some of her jewels to buy new Arras tapestries and their team of gardeners toiled to make her neglected grounds ready for the tented encampment that always followed the king on progress.

The children became increasingly excited as the time for the royal visit approached. The girls sewed new gowns and even little Henry helped. Nine years old, he shared his father's love of horses and rode out with Brandon and the foresters to scout for stags.

At last the yeoman posted as lookout announced the royal party was approaching. Henry rode at the front with Thomas Cromwell, followed by his mounted royal guard and wagons carrying his luggage and servants. Mary thanked the Lord there was no sign of Lady Anne Boleyn.

The family stood in a row in the July sunshine to welcome the king. Mary thought he looked older as she watched him dismount. He'd put on weight and it was said he suffered with his teeth, as their father had.

Brandon removed his hat, stepped forward and bowed. 'Welcome, Your Grace. It is a great honour you do us.'

Henry beamed and embraced him warmly. 'It is good to see you again, Suffolk. We've missed you at court,' he turned to Mary, 'and you, dearest sister, we are sorry to hear you've been unwell.'

Mary smiled. 'It warms my heart, Your Grace, that you travel to see our modest home. May I present our son, Henry Brandon, Earl of Lincoln?'

Little Henry stepped forward and bowed. 'Your Grace.'

The king studied him for a moment. 'You take after your father, Henry. Would you like to ride with us in the hunt?'

'I would be honoured, Your Grace.'

Mary introduced her daughters who each stepped forward in turn and curtseyed to the king. They had decided Catherine Willoughby should remain out of sight, as her mother had also been vocal in her support for Queen Catherine, and punished by being banned from seeing her.

Henry and Brandon returned from a successful hunt with a handsome stag. Little Henry seemed in awe of the king and was rewarded for his help with a gold coin, an angel, decorated with the figure of St George slaying a fearsome dragon.

The one moment of tension during the king's short visit was when he cursed the lack of progress in persuading the pope to grant a divorce from Catherine. He told them he planned a visit to France to secure the support of King Francis.

Mary saw Brandon's warning glance and remained silent but Henry said she would be required to attend. She caught her breath. She would be second in importance to Anne Boleyn. It would be humiliating to attend her former lady-in-waiting but Henry intended to use her to send a signal to King Francis, the courts of England and France and, most importantly, poor Catherine.

'My physicians advise me against travel, dear brother, although I would ask you to convey my regards to King Francis.'

Henry stared at her for a moment, his eyes as sharp as a hawk, while he decided whether she was testing him. 'That is a great shame, sister. We sail in October, so you will reconsider, if your health improves. In the meantime, you will kindly lend Lady Anne your French jewels.' It was more a command than a request.

Mary recalled that moment, long after her brother's departure. She would have risked her health for another visit to her beloved France, but not with Anne Boleyn. Brandon accepted Henry's invitation, out of gratitude for his forgiveness, although he'd done nothing wrong.

On her knees in her private chapel she prayed for the safety of Catherine's loyal chaplain, who published his views in her support and now languished in the Tower of London. Henry ordered Thomas Cromwell not to rest until every copy was tracked down and burned.

Mary tried to pray for the soul of William Warham, Archbishop of Canterbury, who'd died the previous month. Instead, she found her anger flaring at the thought of Anne Boleyn taking her place at Henry's side in France. She'd had no choice. Her precious French jewels, given to her by King Louis, were loaned and would never be seen again.

25

MAY 1533

Mary gripped the arm of her chair as she fought another wave of pain, her nails biting into the gilded wood. She'd insisted on attending the wedding of her eldest daughter, against the advice of her physicians. Little else would have persuaded Mary to return to Suffolk Place, as she was too weakened by her illness for the journey.

Maria de Salinas, Baroness Willoughby, invited to represent Queen Catherine, seemed to sense something wrong. 'Are you unwell, Your Grace?'

'No,' Mary forced a smile, 'I will be fine.'

She prayed it was true. Her husband spared no expense for their daughter's wedding. More lavish than either of her step-daughter's weddings, the event provided a much-needed opportunity to remind the nobility of England of their wealth and influence. It also allowed Mary to prove the rumours wrong. She was very much alive and well.

In truth, the numbing ache in her side was worse than ever and had moved to her chest. Mary often found herself short of breath and Brandon worried about the toll it took on her.

Increasingly, she would spend all day in her bed, so it took a great effort to make the long journey in her carriage to London.

She'd been too unwell to attend the May Fair in Bury St Edmunds, the first time she'd missed it since arriving at Westhorpe sixteen years ago. Her daughters, escorted by Brandon and Henry, represented the family. Mary's absence would have brought her illness to public attention but for far greater news in London.

In April, a joyous Henry summoned his council to announce he had privately married Anne Boleyn and she carried the heir to England in her belly. Mary cried for Catherine when she heard. As Thomas Abel had feared, it was now too late. The Boleyns and Norfolk had won.

Brandon was tasked with Norfolk to inform Catherine and tell her she could no longer call herself Queen of England. He told Mary she took the news badly and it grieved him to be chosen as the bearer of it. She locked herself in her chamber and nothing he said would persuade her to come out.

His only consolation was that he'd delivered the news with more sensitivity to her feelings than Norfolk would have done. Norfolk bragged about how he'd sent his men to retrieve Catherine's jewels for the king, by force if necessary. It seems she was most distressed that her former lady-in-waiting was to have them. Norfolk's men took everything except for the modest gold crucifix she wore on a chain around her neck.

Mary tried to take her mind off the nagging pain by looking around at the waiting guests. Her stepdaughters, Anne and Mary, both baronesses glittering with jewels, were there with their handsome husbands. After eight years of marriage Anne remained childless and her husband, Baron Grey, had taken a mistress, which would explain Anne's coolness towards him.

Her stepdaughter Mary's husband, Baron Monteagle, had

become a favourite of the king and was to be made a Knight of the Bath as reward for carrying the king's sword at Anne Boleyn's coronation. Mary had two children, a boy named William after his father and a daughter they'd named after Frances.

Outwardly they seemed a perfect family but Thomas Stanley's weakness for gambling and ill-advised investments had put their growing family deep into debt. Brandon did his best to help his daughter with loans he could barely afford. Nothing had yet been repaid and Mary doubted it ever would.

Handsome young Henry Grey, known to everyone as Harry, stood waiting near the altar, a shaft of June sunlight through the window glinting on his ceremonial sword. Brandon had kept his promise to not marry her daughters to old men. At sixteen, Henry Grey was only six months older than Frances, with a promising future.

A great-grandson of Elizabeth Woodville, by her first marriage to Sir John Grey, he'd inherited his late father's title as Marquess of Dorset three years before. Despite his youth, he'd shown the courage to risk speaking out in support of Queen Catherine. Henry banished him from court for several months but Mary saw it as proof they'd made the right choice for her eldest daughter.

She was surprised to see Thomas Howard, Duke of Norfolk, sitting grim-faced at the back. Brandon had refused to invite him but it seemed he'd taken her advice to put the past behind them, for the sake of the children. Mary found it easy to believe rumours about how Norfolk mistreated his wife, Lady Elizabeth, who was unsurprisingly absent.

Mary was also pleased to see that Thomas Cromwell, who'd saved her husband's career, had accepted their invitation. Henry had shown good judgement in appointing Wolsey's man. Although Brandon was reluctant to trust him, Cromwell agreed to Mary's request to release Queen Catherine's c.1a, lain, Thomas Abel, from the Tower.

A commotion near the entrance caught Mary's attention and everyone began to stand. Her brother had decided to attend after all. She held her breath as she waited to see if he'd brought his newly pregnant wife. Brandon had doubted it, as Anne Boleyn knew she would be unwelcome.

Henry entered alone and in good spirits, accepting congratulations as he passed through the guests to the seat reserved for him in pride of place. Mary noticed he wore her priceless pearl pendant, the Mirror of Naples, in his hat. Sending the jewel to him as a gift almost led to her downfall, all those years ago in France, but now she was glad she'd done it.

The choir began singing as Henry took his seat, the cue for Brandon and their daughter to make their entrance. Frances looked beautiful in her elegant new gown, with Eleanor and young Henry proudly following behind. For once, Mary had to be sparing with the loan of her jewels, as her brother was not beyond demanding she hand over to him the few she had left.

She felt the years passing too soon as she watched her daughter saying her vows. She recalled the day of Frances' birth, when she'd sought refuge at the manor house of her old friend Nicholas West. She'd been saddened to hear of his death the previous month. Mary had felt too ill to attend his funeral but Brandon paid his respects to the man who had helped them in France.

Mary sighed with relief when at last the wedding ceremony was over. Maria de Salinas supported her arm as they made their way to the wedding banquet. Although Mary wished to conceal her illness, she felt too weakened by the journey to London to walk even such a short distance unaided.

She thanked Lady Maria as she helped her to her place. 'I am grateful for your daughter's company, Maria, she is a great

ﬞticularly now Frances will be leaving for her

de Salinas smiled. 'Catherine tells me in her letters
ᵥe shown her great kindness, Your Grace.'

ʏou must be proud of your daughter, she is a credit to
you.' Mary glanced at the empty chairs to her left. 'It seems the
king decided not to stay.'

'He is never one to miss a banquet.' Maria sounded scornful. 'Perhaps he has more urgent matters to attend to,
Your Grace.'

Mary turned to her. 'Are you still forbidden to visit Queen
Catherine?'

Maria lowered her voice. 'I should have been more discreet
– he has spies and informers everywhere.'

'The king?'

'Thomas Cromwell.'

∾

Mary opened her eyes as Eleanor appeared in the doorway.
Her daughter was growing up fast now her elder sister had left
home, and looked older than her fourteen years. A marriage
contract had been agreed for her marriage to Henry Clifford,
the sixteen-year-old heir to the Earldom of Cumberland.
Eleanor would become a countess but Mary felt a stab of
regret as she knew the last of her daughters would be leaving
home.

'Good morning, Mother.' Eleanor smiled but her eyes
remained serious. 'How are you today?'

'Well enough, Eleanor. I'm feeling a little better.' Mary lied
to her daughter, a small enough sin to keep her happy.

'Would you like me to have a bowl of soup sent up from
the kitchens?'

'Just a cup of spiced wine, if you will. I find it helps to ease this ache.' She held her hand to her chest.

Eleanor sat in the chair at Mary's bedside and took her left hand, showing her how loose her once tight gold rings had become. 'You must eat, Mother, and take exercise, or you will waste away.'

Mary studied her daughter's stern face. Somehow her illness had reversed their roles. 'Some soup, if you insist,' she didn't feel hungry but knew Eleanor needed an answer, 'and a little bread.'

Mary sat up in bed, resting on her soft velvet cushions while she dipped the bread in the warm bowl of soup. It tasted good and she realised her daughter was right. She needed to build up her strength before Brandon returned from London. It had been several days since she'd last ventured down the twisting wooden staircase and she felt too weak to try.

Eleanor's expression reminded her of the strict governess she'd once had in the nursery at Eltham Palace. Mary worried for her youngest daughter. Her outspoken criticism of King Henry would cause her trouble if she shared her views outside Westhorpe.

'I want to explain the actions of the king, to help you understand...'

'I'm not the innocent child you think, Mother. I understand how the king is bewitched by a younger woman.'

Mary smiled at her daughter's forthright views. She had Tudor blood flowing in her veins. 'Your grandfather always told Henry he must have a son to inherit his throne.' She caught her breath as another wave of pain passed through her chest. 'It was not God's will for Queen Catherine to provide him with one. If not Anne Boleyn, another would have come along soon enough.'

'I can never accept Anne Boleyn as our queen.' Eleanor sounded determined.

'Your father had to, Eleanor, and you must do the same if you ever hope to become her lady-in-waiting.'

'In that case, I shall not do so.'

Brandon smelled of horse sweat and woodsmoke and wore his riding clothes. She'd not seen him since her daughter's wedding and reached out her hand. 'I'm so happy you're back.' Her voice sounded weak. 'I've been unwell.'

'You should not have travelled to London, Mary.' He crossed to the window and opened it. The sweet song of a thrush drifted into the room with the warm summer air. He returned to sit in the chair at her bedside and loosened the fastening at the collar of his doublet. 'Your physicians despair of you.'

'I couldn't miss my daughter's wedding – but I'm not sorry to miss the coronation.'

He gave her a wry look. 'There are to be four days of celebration, although some still risk their lives by shouting "Whore!" and spitting as her carriage passes.'

The thought made Mary smile, despite her illness. 'My former lady-in-waiting might have won my brother's heart but not the affection of the people.'

Mary woke from a troubled sleep as Brandon took her thin hand in his. She felt a sudden misgiving as she saw the sadness in his eyes. 'What is it? What's happened?' Her heart raced as she prepared herself for bad news.

He sat looking at her for a moment as if unsure what to say. 'I have to return to London, Mary, there is much to do.'

'You've only just come home...'

'Eleanor and Catherine have promised to care for you until I return.'

He kissed her, then turned to go. 'I love you, Mary Tudor.'

'I need you here, Charles... Please, stay a little longer.'

'I've stayed longer than I should.' He forced a smile. 'I shall return as soon as Catherine's crown is on our new queen's head.' He didn't try to hide his bitterness.

Mary listened to the steady clump of his riding boots on the wooden stairs, then the girls and little Henry saying their farewells. She heard his horse being led to the doorway and tried to climb out of bed to reach her window before he rode off. Summoning all her strength she managed to stand. The clatter of hooves told her it was too late. Mary sat back on her bed and wept as she wondered if she would ever see him again.

She called for her son and heard him complaining as her housekeeper told him he had to see his mother. She remembered how her brother had been the same when their father was ill, always ready with some excuse. Eventually, Henry pushed open her door and stood at the foot of her bed.

'You sent for me, Mother?'

Mary smiled at her son, who made it obvious he'd rather be out hunting than looking after his ailing mother. She'd never felt the same bond as with her first boy, but loved him all the same. It amazed her that he was ten years old now, with the same rugged looks and adventurous spirit as his father.

'There is a small wooden casket by the window. Will you bring it to me, Henry?'

His curiosity overcame his desire to be back outside in the sunshine. He lifted the casket and placed it on the bed in front of her. Mary unfastened the silver latch and opened the lid. The contents were wrapped in colourful remnants of silk. She reached for one and unwrapped it while her son watched.

'This is the official seal of the Queen of France, Henry.' She turned it in her hand to show him the engraved base and was almost overwhelmed by the memories it evoked. 'I would like you to have it.'

'Is it valuable, Mother?'

'It is priceless. You must keep it safe, to remind you your mother was once the Queen of France.'

Brandon woke her with a kiss on the cheek. She opened her eyes and stared at him, unsure for a moment if she was dreaming. 'You've returned...' Her voice was a whisper.

'I cannot stay long, Mary, but I bring good news. Thanks to Cromwell, the king is fully reconciled with you – and I am back in favour at court.'

She studied his face, pleased to see he looked his old self again, the glint of ambition back in his eyes. She noticed a large jewel in the silver-handled dagger at his belt as it flashed in the light.

'A gift from the king?'

He glanced down at the dagger. 'Your brother is grateful for my support. He made me High Constable for the coronation day.'

'That means he sees you as the senior earl.'

'It might – but Norfolk has demanded to be made Earl Marshal in my place.'

Mary sat up. 'That is an outrage. Thomas Howard can never uphold standards and discipline, the man's a rogue.'

'Henry agreed to Norfolk's demand. He thanked me for taking it so well and offered me the royal forests.' He scowled. 'I could have refused but no longer care.'

With sudden insight she realised what a great sacrifice he'd made for his family. He'd been used by her brother, forced to publicly declare his loyalty to the new queen. It must have gone against everything he'd lived for.

'How long can you stay this time?'

'Only one night. I regret that this is such a busy time at court.'

'But now Anne Boleyn is crowned—'

He held up a hand. 'There is even more for me to do.' He sat at the side of her bed. 'I know how unwell you are, Mary.' The sadness returned to his eyes. 'You hide it from me but I've spoken with your physicians. I will return as soon as I can.'

'Then will you spend your one night with me, my lord the Duke of Suffolk?'

'I would be honoured, my Queen of France.'

Mary lay awake in his arms while he drifted off to sleep. She understood the sacrifice he'd made for his family. He would never admit how difficult it had been to accept Anne Boleyn as his queen, but now he would show her absolute loyalty.

She caressed the greying hair on his chest as she remembered how she'd longed for him as a girl. She had a sudden recollection of the time Henry's lance shattered with brutal force on Brandon's chest. He'd admitted to her he had allowed the king his moment of glory. That was over twenty years ago but he was still putting her brother's wishes before everything.

A shaft of bright sunshine woke her and she reached out to find an empty space at her side. Rubbing her eyes, she raised herself on one elbow and saw him pouring water into her bowl from the jug. She watched the muscles of his bare back, with the familiar scars of old accidents, as he splashed his face with the cold water.

He dried his face and hands then turned and saw her as he

pulled on a clean linen shirt, one she'd spent hours sewing for him. 'I must leave now, Mary.'

'When will you return?'

'A week, perhaps two, then I will stay and care for you.'

'Promise?' She heard the pleading in her voice.

He fastened the front of his doublet and strapped on his sword, then leaned over to kiss her. 'You have my word.'

When she opened her eyes again he was gone but she took comfort from the knowledge he would soon return. She missed her husband more than he would ever know.

Mary asked her maidservant to summon Eleanor and tried to sit up as her daughter entered. 'Will you bring...' The pain stopped her continuing.

Eleanor stared at Mary, her eyes wide with concern. 'Do you wish me to send for the priest?'

Mary shook her head. She was not ready for absolution yet. Although she felt too weak to talk she summoned the strength to continue. 'Bring me that little casket by the window, if you will.'

Eleanor carried it to her bedside and opened the lid. 'I've never seen inside, Mother. What do you keep in it?'

'I wish you to have it Eleanor but...' She struggled to remember then it came to her. 'You must hide it somewhere safe until the king has forgotten.'

Eleanor looked confused. 'Forgotten what, Mother? I don't understand.'

Mary closed her eyes for a moment and prayed for strength. By some miracle she managed to forget the pain and explain to her daughter. 'My brother made me promise to hand over my French jewels...' She took a gasping breath. 'He thinks he has them all but is mistaken.'

Eleanor took one of the folded silks from the casket and

unwrapped it. A fine gold necklace with a large pointed diamond and a single red ruby tumbled into her hand. She held the necklace up for Mary to see and it flashed as the diamond caught the light.

'It's beautiful, Mother.'

'King Louis of France gave it to me – on our wedding day.' She reached out a thin hand to touch the precious jewel one last time. 'Keep it safe for me, Eleanor.'

Mary told her maidservant to comb her long hair over her shoulders. 'I must look my best for my husband.' She struggled for breath as she reached for her silver mirror. 'He's coming home. He gave his word.'

Her maid remained silent and a tear ran down her young face as she stroked the comb through Mary's red-gold hair until it shone. She didn't speak as she dressed Mary in her best nightgown of pure white linen decorated with pearls.

Mary lay back on her bed, each breath an effort. She heard the maid close the door and her soft footsteps going down the stairs, then a deeper voice. Her heart raced. Brandon had returned, as he'd promised he would. She listened for the familiar clump of his riding boots.

Her door opened and she tried to sit to show him how much better she was. She failed and let her head fall back to the pillow, closing her eyes as she coped with the pain and prepared for Brandon's kiss as he entered the room.

Instead she felt a finger trace the sign of the cross on her forehead. She opened her eyes and saw the village priest, a prayer book in his hand and a look of great sadness in his usually cheerful eyes. Behind him stood her daughter Eleanor, her hands clasped in prayer. Their ward Catherine wept at her side.

She tried to ask for her husband but the words didn't come.

Mary choked as she struggled to draw breath. Eleanor stepped forward and helped raise her head with the support of a silk pillow. She saw a table had been set up near the foot of her bed. Covered with fresh white linen, it was empty except for a silver crucifix with a white church candle burning on either side.

'Through this Holy Unction, and through the great goodness of his mercy, may God pardon thee whatever sins thou hast committed...'

The prayer sounded unfamiliar to Mary. She closed her eyes and prayed for her husband. He was a man of his word. He would come as soon as he could. She felt the pain ease, for the first time she could remember, and let her mind focus on the priest's soft-spoken prayers.

'O Holy Lord, Father almighty and eternal God, we pray to thee in faith that the holy body of our Lord Jesus Christ, thy son, may profit our sister who has received it as an everlasting remedy for body and soul, who being God, lives and reigns. Amen.'

AUTHOR'S NOTE

Mary Tudor, Dowager Queen of France, died at Westhorpe before eight in the morning on 25 June 1533. She was thirty-seven years old.

Brandon was not expected to attend Mary's funeral, in keeping with the tradition that husbands did not attend the funeral of their wives. This seems strange now but it would have been a major breach of protocol. He did send his guards to represent him, although the funeral was delayed to allow for a delegation from King Francis to arrive.

Mary was laid to rest in the abbey church of Bury St Edmunds. Her alabaster monument was destroyed in the dissolution of the monasteries and her tomb moved to the nearby St Mary's Church, where it is to this day.

In 1784, Mary's coffin was moved to the chancel of St Mary's and placed under a plain slab of Petworth marble, with the new inscription: '*Sacred to the memory of Mary Tudor, third daughter of Henry VII of England, and Queen of France.*'

Her coffin was opened and it was noted that her hair was some two feet long, a 'reddish-gold' colour, and her teeth were even and complete. Locks of her hair were acquired by historian Horace Walpole, Earl of Orford, and Lady Margaret Bentinck, Duchess of Portland.

Charles Brandon decided to marry his attractive fourteen-year-old ward and did so in September 1533. They had two sons, both of whom contracted the 'sweating sickness' and died on the same day in 1551. Brandon died on 22 August 1545, aged sixty-one, and was laid to rest in the floor of the south quire aisle of St George's Chapel, Windsor Castle, at the king's expense, close to the tomb of King Henry VI.

Lady Catherine Willoughby, Duchess of Suffolk, became a close friend of King Henry's sixth wife, Queen Catherine Parr. (It was rumoured in 1546 that Henry might annul his marriage to make the widowed duchess his seventh wife.)

I enjoyed spending a year researching the life of Mary Tudor, untangling the many myths about her, from causing the death of King Louis with her 'passionate exertions' to her dying of 'grief at her brother's divorce.' Most of her story is well documented, including fascinating details in her many surviving letters, which I have relied on throughout.

I would like to thank my wife, Liz, author and Tudor specialist Sarah Bryson, and my editor, Nikki Brice, for their support during the research and writing of this book. I would also like to take this opportunity to thank the many readers around the world who have encouraged me to explore the real stories behind the Tudor dynasty.

Tony Riches
Pembrokeshire
www.tonyriches.com

OWEN - Book One of the Tudor Trilogy

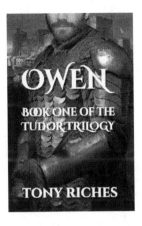

England 1422: Owen Tudor, a Welsh servant, waits in Windsor Castle to meet his new mistress, the beautiful and lonely Queen Catherine of Valois, widow of the warrior king, Henry V. Her infant son is crowned King of England and France, and while the country simmers on the brink of civil war, Owen becomes her protector.

They fall in love, risking Owen's life and Queen Catherine's reputation, but how do they found the dynasty which changes British history – the Tudors?

This is the first historical novel to fully explore the amazing life of Owen Tudor, grandfather of King Henry VII and the great-grandfather of King Henry VIII. Set against a background of the conflict between the Houses of Lancaster and York, which develops into what have become known as the Wars of the Roses, Owen's story deserves to be told.

Available as paperback, audiobook and eBook

JASPER - Book Two of the Tudor Trilogy

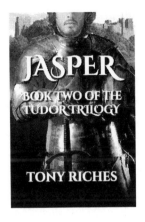

England 1461: The young King Edward of York has taken the country by force from King Henry VI of Lancaster. Sir Jasper Tudor, Earl of Pembroke, flees the massacre of his Welsh army at the Battle of Mortimer's Cross.

When King Henry is imprisoned by Edward in the Tower of London and murdered, Jasper escapes to Brittany with his young nephew, Henry Tudor. With nothing but his wits and charm, Jasper sees his chance to make young Henry Tudor king with a daring and reckless invasion of England.

Set in the often brutal world of fifteenth-century England, Wales, Scotland, France, Burgundy and Brittany, during the Wars of the Roses, this fast-paced story is one of courage and adventure, love and belief in the destiny of the Tudors.

Available as paperback, audiobook and eBook

HENRY - Book Three of the Tudor Trilogy

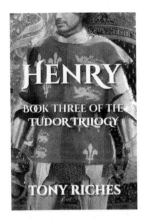

Bosworth 1485: After victory against King Richard III, Henry Tudor becomes King of England. Rebels and pretenders plot to seize his throne. The barons resent his plans to curb their power and he wonders who he can trust. He hopes to unite Lancaster and York through marriage to the beautiful Elizabeth of York.

With help from his mother, Lady Margaret Beaufort, he learns to keep a fragile peace. He chooses a Spanish Princess, Catherine of Aragon, as a wife for his son Prince Arthur.

His daughters will marry the King of Scotland and the son of the Emperor of Rome. It seems his prayers are answered, then disaster strikes and Henry must ensure the future of the Tudors.

Available in paperback, eBook and audiobook

The Secret Diary of Eleanor Cobham

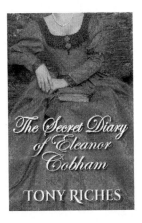

England 1441: Lady Eleanor Cobham, Duchess of Gloucester, hopes to become Queen of England before her interest in astrology and her husband's ambition leads their enemies to accuse her of a plot against the king. Eleanor is found guilty of sorcery and witchcraft. King Henry VI orders Eleanor to be imprisoned for life.

More than a century after her death, carpenters restoring one of the towers of Beaumaris Castle discover a sealed box hidden under the wooden boards. Thinking they have found treasure, they break the ancient box open and find it only contains a book.

Written in a code no one could understand, the mysterious book changed hands many times until it came to me. I discover its code is based on a long-forgotten medieval dialect and I am at last able to decipher the secret diary of Eleanor Cobham.

Available as paperback, audiobook and eBook

WARWICK - The Man Behind the Wars of the Roses

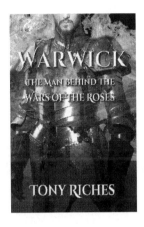

Richard Neville, Earl of Warwick, the 'Kingmaker', is the wealthiest noble in England. He becomes a warrior knight, bravely protecting the north against invasion by the Scots. A key figure in what have become known as the Wars of the Roses, he fought in most of the important battles.

As Captain of Calais, he turns privateer, daring to take on the might of the Spanish fleet and becoming Admiral of England. The friend of kings, he is the sworn enemy of Queen Margaret of Anjou. Then, in an amazing change of heart, why does he risk everything to fight for her cause?

Warwick's story is one of adventure, power and influence at the heart of one of the most dangerous times in the history of England.

Available in paperback and eBook

Made in the USA
San Bernardino, CA
03 August 2018